A playful and provocative Regency trilogy
from

CHRISTINE MERRILL

Ladies in Disgrace

In London's High Society there are
three unconventional women who are not
afraid to break the rules of social etiquette! And
it will take a certain type of rake
to tame these delectably disgraceful ladies…!

LADY FOLBROKE'S DELICIOUS DECEPTION
LADY DRUSILLA'S ROAD TO RUIN
LADY PRISCILLA'S SHAMEFUL SECRET

AUTHOR NOTE

After finishing LADY DRUSILLA'S ROAD TO RUIN, I was curious to see what had happened to her sister, Priscilla, after Dru left home. I could guess what the repercussions would be, after her behaviour in that book, but I knew there would be a man to love her.

And that was how I met Robert, a man who was more comfortable with horses than people. He brought with him a collection of slang terms that I had never heard before. I learned that it was possible to disguise the age of a horse by altering its teeth (bishoping), that a daisy cutter is a stumbling horse, and that a horse with bad lungs is a piper.

But I could find no reason to use a horse ladder anywhere in this story. This is a Regency era practical joke, where the new boy on the farm is sent to get the ladder so the horse can climb up to the hay mow to eat.

Happy reading. And don't let your horse climb any ladders.

LADY PRISCILLA'S SHAMEFUL SECRET

Christine Merrill

First published in Great Britain 2012
by Mills & Boon, an imprint of Harlequin (UK) Limited.
Large Print edition 2012
Harlequin (UK) Limited, Eton House, 18-24 Paradise Road,
Richmond, Surrey TW9 1SR

© Christine Merrill 2012

ISBN: 978 0 263 22526 6

Harlequin (UK) policy is to use papers that are natural, renewable and recyclable products and made from wood grown in sustainable forests. The logging and manufacturing process conform to the legal environmental regulations of the country of origin.

Printed and bound in Great Britain
by CPI Antony Rowe, Chippenham, Wiltshire

Christine Merrill lives on a farm in Wisconsin, USA, with her husband, two sons and too many pets—all of whom would like her to get off the computer so they can check their e-mail. She has worked by turns in theatre costuming, where she was paid to play with period ballgowns, and as a librarian, where she spent the day surrounded by books. Writing historical romance combines her love of good stories and fancy dress with her ability to stare out of the window and make stuff up.

Previous novels by Christine Merrill:

THE INCONVENIENT DUCHESS
AN UNLADYLIKE OFFER
A WICKED LIAISON
MISS WINTHORPE'S ELOPEMENT
THE MISTLETOE WAGER
    (part of *A Yuletide Invitation*)
DANGEROUS LORD, INNOCENT GOVERNESS
PAYING THE VIRGIN'S PRICE*
TAKEN BY THE WICKED RAKE*
MASTER OF PENLOWEN
    (part of *Halloween Temptations*)
LADY FOLBROKE'S DELICIOUS DECEPTION†
LADY DRUSCILLA'S ROAD TO RUIN†
A REGENCY CHRISTMAS CAROL
    (part of *One Snowy Regency Christmas*)

And in Mills & Boon® Historical *Undone!* eBooks:

SEDUCING A STRANGER
TAMING HER GYPSY LOVER*
VIRGIN UNWRAPPED

Regency Silk & Scandal mini-series
†*Ladies in Disgrace* trilogy

To Diana Fox
and the beginning of a beautiful friendship.

Chapter One

Robert Magson, Duke of Reighland, treated each new ballroom like an Indian jungle set with traps not for tigers, but for unwary men. There were so many mamas and daughters in London that he would not have been surprised to see them lurking behind the furniture at White's. And they were all eager to catch his eye, even for just a moment.

It was as though they thought he could decide on a bride based on a single glance in a crowded room. He spent more time buying a horse than that. He would never lay down money without checking teeth, feeling fetlocks and enquiring of the bloodline. Surely the choice of a wife should be made with equal care.

He frowned out into the mob and watched two

or three young ladies curtsy as his gaze roved over them. It was an odd feeling, this sudden deference, as though his slightest glance was the withering glare of the noon sun in a garden full of delicate blossoms. The same girls would not have looked twice at him a year ago. Then his cousin had died. And suddenly he was the catch of the Season.

He frowned harder and watched the crowd contract to give him more space. It was not as if he did not mean to marry one of them. But there were far too many who had hopes in his direction. One could not appear too welcoming, if one wanted even a moment of peace in the evenings.

To be fair, the rout tonight was surprisingly convivial. And he had no reason to suspect his host, the Earl of Folbroke, was plotting against him. The man was too young to have marriageable children and, to the best of Robert's knowledge, had no sisters.

'I hear you are thinking of offering for Benbridge's daughter,' said Folbroke from his place at Robert's side.

It surprised him that that particular bit of news

had travelled so quickly. While he had been paying court to several young ladies in a half-hearted and unenthusiastic way, the matter of Benbridge's daughter had been introduced into conversation only recently. But apparently, it was already *on dit*. 'What might have given you that idea?' he asked blandly. 'I have not even met the girl, yet.'

'According to my wife, Lady Benbridge is telling everyone that your back has been broken by the parson's mousetrap.' The earl smiled. 'As far as the bit that has trapped you? It does not surprise me that you have not met her. None of us has seen her for quite some time. Of course, I would not notice, even if she were here.' Folbroke adjusted his smoked glasses.

It was a continual surprise to Robert that the earl was so casual in calling attention to his blindness. He supposed it prevented people from treating him like an invalid, when there was no reason to. Although he tended to stay at the edge of the room during events such as these, Folbroke looked no more uncomfortable than the other gentlemen that lounged against the walls to avoid the press of bodies at the centre of the floor.

Robert admired his studied casualness and sought to emulate it so that he might appear more comfortable in society than he felt. Four months after becoming Reighland it was still an effort not to turn and search the room for Gregory when someone called him by the title. He offered a silent prayer for the bright and smiling child that had been meant for this honour, just as he longed for the wise counsel of his father. Sometimes it felt that his family had not so much died as abandoned him to make his own way in a confusing world. Now, his frown deepened at the rumours swirling about him. 'Despite what Lady Benbridge might think on the matter, I wish to meet the girl before I offer for her. I might be new to the marriage mart, but not so new that I will take her sight unseen.'

Folbroke smiled in response, as he always did. He was a particularly good-humoured fellow. But Robert suspected that there was something about the situation that the earl found particularly amusing. 'In any case,' he said, 'you must meet Hendricks. He will want to welcome you to the family.' Robert hoped that Folbroke was not laughing at him for he quite liked the man and would hate to find him as false as some of the others who had been eager to offer friendship to his face while laughing behind their hands at his country manners.

'Hendricks,' Folbroke called, 'come here. There is someone you must meet.'

That was it, then, Robert thought, relaxing a little. Hendricks was Folbroke's protégé. Apparently, this event had been meant to arrange a casual introduction to his Grace, the Duke of Reighland. There was no real harm in it, he supposed. He had heard that the Hendricks fellow was damned useful to know. And when it came to navigating the subtleties of London, Robert could use all the help he could get.

A bespectacled man all but materialised out of the crowd, as though the room was a stage and he had been waiting in the wings for an entrance. It was nicely done. Though Robert had been watching closely, he'd never have suspected that Hendricks had been watching for a cue from the earl.

'You wished something, Folbroke?' Hendricks's

voice was raised to be heard over the noise of the crowd, but he still managed to sound quiet and deferential. His choice of words made him seem even more like an Arabian djinn.

'Only to present you to Reighland,' Folbroke shouted back at him. 'Your Grace, John Hendricks is husband to the lovely Drusilla Roleston. Dru is the elder Benbridge daughter and sister to your fair Priscilla.' He stared in the direction of Hendricks, who was dipping his head to hear over the roar of voices. 'John, Reighland is likely to be your brother-in-law. Make nice to him.'

Hendricks's eyebrows raised in surprise before he could master his emotion and turn to Robert with a bow. 'How do you do, your Grace?'

Robert gave him a stiff nod of response. 'Not as well as Folbroke seems to think. She is not my Priscilla, Folbroke. Despite what society claims, my intentions are not set in stone. I have not even met the girl,' he added again, wondering just what was wrong with people in London. They gossiped as though rumour was air and they could not survive without it. 'I do mean to seek an introduction to her. If there is compat-ibility between us...' He gave a half-shrug.

Hendricks nodded. 'If you would permit, your Grace, I would like to introduce my wife to you. She is eager for all things to do with Priss and will be glad to know you.'

'She cannot ask Priscilla herself?'

'Sadly, no.' Hendricks smiled benignly at him. 'Because of me, I'm afraid. The Earl of Benbridge did not think me good enough for his family. To my eternal good fortune, Lady Drusilla did not share his opinion, but now my poor Dru is quite cut off from associating with her sister.'

'And if I might say so, Benbridge is a fool,' Folbroke said calmly. 'You will not find better company in this room than John Hendricks, nor will you find a sharper mind.'

Robert had heard similar sentiments voiced by others. Hendricks was seen as an up and comer in political circles for his pleasant demeanour and his uncanny ability to be always in the right place at the right time. 'Is the attendance of the older sister the reason I do not see the younger here?' Robert asked, slightly annoyed by the fact. On the few times they'd spoken, the Earl of Benbridge had seemed a stiff-backed old fool who was not nearly as smart or important as he seemed to think himself. This was merely another confirmation of it. It was interesting to see that, having to choose between the company of one or the other, Folbroke would rather associate with his inferior than with Benbridge, a man of equal rank. Robert stored the information for future reference.

Hendricks nodded in answer to his question. 'Since we were invited this evening, Priscilla would not be permitted to come. It is damned unreasonable of him. My wife and I cannot forgo society just to prevent embarrassment for a family that will not welcome Dru back, no matter what she does.' He glanced at Robert and pushed his spectacles up his nose. 'If you should happen to marry Priss, you will have our felicitations, of course. But we will make no attempt to ruin the girl's wedding by expecting an invitation and upsetting her father.'

Robert found this even more annoying than the assumptions of his choice of bride. It had never occurred to him to care who was in the pews at

St George's; now he had received his first refusal before the invitations had been engraved. 'This is hardly set in stone,' he repeated. 'I have spoken to Benbridge about it, of course, but I have not even met the girl.' Then a thought struck him. 'But you have, haven't you? How did you find her?'

There was a fleeting expression of caution in Hendricks's eyes, just before he spoke. Then he said heartily, 'She is a great beauty. All blonde curls, blue eyes and dimples. She will make someone a most attractive wife, I am sure. The children will be lovely.'

He'd managed to mention looks three times in as many seconds. Yet Robert was sure that the man did not like her, or her blonde curls. He had chosen the other sister. And it was obvious that he doted on her.

But that did not mean Robert might not like Priscilla, if he ever saw her. A pretty wife was better than an ugly one.

'You will have Benbridge's favour as well,' Hendricks added. 'Priscilla is his favourite.'

'The thought had crossed my mind,' Robert replied. If marriage was to be little better than a connection between powerful families, he could do much worse than an earl's daughter. If he wished to put forth any of his ideas in Parliament, it could not hurt to have an elder statesman at his back. And judging by the value Benbridge set on status and decorum, he must have drilled his daughter in the rules of good behaviour, practically from birth. She would rescue him from his tendency to social *faux pas.*

With the number of men between him and the title, he had never expected to be a duke. But Lady Priscilla had been bred to be a duchess, or at the very least a countess. She would know what was expected of her. And he would not have to give another thought to the running of his households and social life. It would be a great relief.

But it annoyed him that Hendricks could not seem to find any word for the girl other than that she was pretty. It made him wonder if there was some secret. Hereditary madness, perhaps? Given the choice between that or weakness of character Robert almost preferred the second. While he had seen virtuous children with wanton parents, a lack of wit seemed to carry through the generations.

'Priss is the apple of his eye,' Hendricks affirmed, interrupting his musings. 'And here is mine.' The woman who was approaching them seemed sane enough. But she was neither blonde nor blue eyed. Nor did she share anything in common with Benbridge's rather florid complexion. Years of horse breeding told him that such a variety of colouring was unusual in siblings.

'Your wife is Priscilla's stepsister, did you say?' he guessed.

Hendricks gave him an odd look and Folbroke seemed more than usually impervious. 'I said no such thing, your Grace.'

Which meant that too great a knowledge of biology had just led him to question the legitimacy of the former Drusilla Roleston. He doubted that the woman had heard him above the other voices. And her husband was too eager for his patronage to rebuke him.

But it was yet another proof that he needed a keeper to muzzle him in these situations and pave over any mistakes with gracious smiles.

Hendricks appeared to have forgotten the comment already and made the introductions. In response, Robert made a proper bow and responded, 'Lady Drusilla.'

'Please, your Grace,' she said softly. 'You may address me as Mrs Hendricks.' She shot her husband a look that told the world the man had hung the stars and the moon, and there was no greater title in the world than the honour of bearing his last name.

In response, the normally composed Hendricks blushed and grinned.

Even with his time spent travelling amongst the *ton*, Robert knew that it was unusual to see a couple so obviously fond of each other. He was secretly envious. That was what he had expected, before his life had taken its recent and dramatic turn: a woman who would be happy to have him, not just angling after his title. Would that the sister shared this woman's sweet nature. 'Mrs Hendricks, then. I am honoured to make your acquaintance.'

Drusilla turned to him with a hopeful smile. 'John tells me that you have some news of my sister?'

'Only that I might make an offer for her, if she is to my liking.'

He watched as Mrs Hendricks looked back at him with equal curiosity. 'You have met with her, then? Is she well?'

'I have not, as yet, made the lady's acquaintance.' But he must soon, if only to save him from admitting his ignorance, over and over.

'You do not know her, yet you would consider an offer.' The lovely Mrs Hendricks frowned. 'I take it you have been in communication with my father on the subject.'

He gave a little nod of acknowledgement.

'I would hope, sir, that you have the lady's best interests in mind as well. I am sure my father is concerned primarily with your rank and thinks little of my sister's future happiness. My hopes for her are much more humble. I do not wish to see her bartered away from the family to a man who does not care about her.'

Robert glanced between Hendricks and Folbroke, waiting to see if either would prevent the lady from offering him further insult. Folbroke was smiling expectantly at him, as though it was a legitimate question that deserved an answer. Hendricks met his gaze as though he had been thinking much the same thing, despite his dislike for the girl they were discussing and the risk of offending a peer.

Very well, then. He would answer bluntness with bluntness. 'It is true that I know far more of trading horses than I do of marriage, Mrs Hendricks. Until my recent elevation, I had little plan for my life other than the breeding and selling of cattle. But I was known for my sound judgement on the subject. I would have no intention of closing such an important bargain without at least riding the filly in question.'

Folbroke gave a snort of suppressed mirth.

He had done it again. 'That is not to say that I wish to...' He glanced at Mrs Hendricks and then away. For if she understood the thing he had implied, but not meant to say... 'I only want to meet her,' he said at last, exasperated. 'We need to talk...to know each other...socially...before such a decision can be made. But I can assure you that, once the deal is done, I treat anything and anyone under my care with the respect and affection it deserves.'

Hendricks looked more doubtful, as though

calculating just how much respect his sister-in-law was entitled to.

And the former Lady Drusilla continued to stare at him, as though trying to gauge the value of a man who might compare marriage to horse trading and admit to an interest in riding her beloved sister. 'A fair enough answer, I suppose. Knowing my father as I do, I could hardly have expected him to choose a husband for Priss based on some pre-existing bond of affection. I must trust that my husband and Lord Folbroke would not be introducing me to you if they did not think you worthy of my sister.' She gave a small sigh as though the small matter of a dukedom meant nothing to her and Robert stifled his own inadequacy. Then, she softened. 'Please, when you see Priss, inform her that I asked after her good health. And ensure her that, should she need me for any reason, she must feel free to call upon me, despite what Father might say.' There was something in the final sentence that made him think that if the mysterious Priscilla experienced unhappiness, it had best not be at his expense, or the formidable Mrs Hendricks would take swift retribution.

'Very well, then, madam. I will be happy to relay your message.' And he would do it soon, he was sure. The vague interest he'd had in the girl had been piqued to actual curiosity with this interchange. Even if he did not wish to wed her, he very much wanted to meet her and see what all the fuss was about.

Chapter Two

'You will be pleased to know that I have chosen you a husband.' The Earl of Benbridge barely looked up from his newspaper as he casually made the announcement that might permanently alter Priscilla's life.

Did he expect her to be pleased? She frowned down at her plate. She was not. Not in the least. It felt as if her insides were being squeezed with a metal clamp. Her heart ceased to beat and her breathing ground to a halt. Her stomach clenched until the little breakfast she had taken churned weakly inside it. 'Is it someone of my acquaintance?' She kept her tone uninterested. It was always easier to start an argument with Father than to win it.

'Do you know him? Since you rarely leave

the house, how likely do you think it is that you have seen him?'

'I go when I have been invited,' she said, as patiently as she could. 'And to the events that you allow me to attend.' That further limited her choices. 'If you refuse to let me be seen in the company of Drusilla, you can hardly blame me for staying home. The hostesses know that if they lose her favour, they lose the Countess of Folbroke, and possibly Anneslea as well. My sister has become quite the social butterfly since her marriage.'

'Her marriage to a nothing,' her father announced. 'And without my blessing.'

'Do not be jealous of your sister, Priscilla. It does you no credit.' Father's new wife, Veronica, seemed to think it was her place to act as a sage adviser to her stepdaughter on all womanly graces. After their brief time together, Priss found the idea that Ronnie had a store of accrued wisdom faintly ridiculous.

In any case, her statements about Dru were not so much a sign of jealousy as a simple statement of fact. Since the marriage to Hendricks, her father had forced the *ton* to choose a side.

And after only a little thought, they had chosen Dru's. Priss's own scandalous behaviour, last summer, had put the last nail in the coffin of her social life and the trickle of remaining invitations had dried up almost completely. 'I am not jealous, Ronnie. I am happy that Dru has finally got the Season she deserves, even if it has come too late to get her a rich and powerful husband.'

'Bah.' It was the noise that her father often made, when confronted with the stupidity of his actions. If he had given her a Season, Dru would now be married to the man of *his* choosing. Then he would be satisfied. And poor Dru would have managed to be content, instead of as gloriously happy as rumours made her out to be.

Benbridge brightened as he dismissed all thoughts of the absent Drusilla and focused his attention on Priss. 'We will show her the error of her ways, girl. In a month or two you shall be married at St. George's and all the town shall wish for an invitation. You may pick and choose who you like and devil take the rest.'

At one time the thought of delivering slights and nods and setting pace for the fashionable world might have interested her. Now that she had been on the receiving end of it, she'd lost her taste for gossip. At the moment, there was only one person in this imaginary wedding that she really cared about. But she was almost afraid to ask about him.

'I am more interested in the groom than the guest list. Who have you chosen for me?'

'Reighland. That freshly acquired title has made him something of a nine-days' wonder. When you capture his attention, it will be a coup.'

She racked her brain, sorting through the guests at the few parties she had attended in recent months. Had she seen him? Had he been there? Had he seen her? She could find no memory of him. 'And why would he have me?'

'I have spoken to him on the subject. I need an ally in the bill that I am presenting. He is a logical choice. But he has been quite standoffish. When he expressed a half-hearted desire to marry, I informed him that I had an eligible daughter. It was the first overture in what I hope will be a long and fruitful alliance.'

When Benbridge said fruitful, he thought of nothing more than bills and laws. There was no mention of the other fruits that might result in marrying his daughter off to a stranger—nor the acts she would have to perform to achieve them. 'How nice for you,' Priscilla said weakly. 'And now, if you will excuse me, I think I shall retire to my room for the morning. I am feeling quite tired.'

'It is nearly noon, Priscilla. Too late to be asleep, and far too early to retire for the day.' Veronica was eyeing her critically.

Priss searched for an excuse that might meet with the woman's approval, yet allow her to be alone with her thoughts. 'I mean to spend an hour in prayer.'

Veronica took another sip of her coffee. 'Very well then. It is not as if your character does not need reforming. But remember, too much piety is unbecoming in a girl. I have no objections, as long as you have recovered from the effects by evening and are attired in your newest gown. We will be attending a ball at Anneslea's and you will be meeting your husband-to-be.'

Tonight, already. That left her only a few hours to find a way out of her father's plans for her. It seemed she would be praying for deliverance.

* * *

A few hours later, Lady Priscilla Roleston surveyed the ballroom and wondered if Veronica might have been right about the dangers of prayer and solitude. She felt for all the world like a girl on her first come out. Her gown was fashionable and she'd been assured that it flattered her. But the neckline, which had been acceptable when she'd ordered it, now felt exposing to the point of immodesty. People would stare.

At one time, she would have welcomed the attention that a daring dress would bring her. Now, she just wanted to be left alone.

But it seemed that was to be a hopeless wish. Her father's mind had been set on the subject of the impending introduction. No amount of feigned megrims or foot dragging had had any effect on him or his new wife.

And that was the best she could manage, really, when thinking of Ronnie. Although the woman had attempted to force Priss into calling her 'Mother' their ages were close enough to make the idea laughable. Even the word 'stepmother' was a struggle. She did not wish a female parent of any variety, though Papa had claimed that it was out of concern for her that he had married again so late in life. She needed a chaperon and wise guidance.

Perhaps he was right. At barely one and twenty, Priss expected her character was fully formed, for better or worse. But if she had wished to use her youth and good looks to capture the attentions of a foolish, old peer, she could not think of a better teacher than the new Lady Benbridge.

Since Priss heartily wished to remain unmarried, Ronnie was proving to be more hindrance than help. She must hope that the Duke of Reighland, whoever he might be, was not as willing to take a pig in a poke as her father expected.

'Straighten your shoulders, Priscilla. We cannot have you slouching tonight. You must put your best foot forwards. And smile.' Veronica prodded her in the back with her fan, trying to force her to straighten.

Priss took care to let no emotion show on her face as they approached the knot of people in the corner of the room. Why should she bother being nice, just to please whomever Father had chosen as the latest candidate for her hand? Considering the men he had threatened her with over the years, she had very good reasons not to encourage an attraction.

But she straightened her shoulders, just a little. The continual effort of hunching, trying to seem a little less than she was, was both taxing and painful.

Veronica surveyed her appearance with a frown. 'I suppose it will have to do. Now come along. We are to be presented to the guest of honour. It is rare for an eligible peer to come to London, almost out of nowhere, right at the height of the Season.'

'Which means he will be surrounded by girls,' she said to Ronnie, trying to dash her hopes. 'There is no reason he should choose me from amongst them. Or be thinking of marriage at all. I am sure he has other things on his mind. Parliament, for example. No amount of good posture and manners on my part will make an impression.'

'Nonsense. Benbridge assures me that he is practically in awe of his own title and enjoys the attention immensely. How can he not? He never in a million years expected to be more than a gentleman farmer. Suddenly, his father, cousin and uncle are all dead in the space of a year. And here he is. It really is the most tragic thing.' But Veronica grinned as she said it, all but salivating at the thought of such an eligible, yet so naïve, a peer.

'Yes,' Priscilla said firmly. 'It is tragic. Devastating, in fact. His cousin was barely three years old. I am sure there will be another year at least for me to meet the man. He cannot intend to marry so quickly when he is still grieving for his family.' But though the new Reighland wore unrelieved black for the boy who had been his predecessor, his mourning did not extend to a complete withdrawal from society if he was attending parties all over London.

'On the contrary. Rumours say that he is on the hunt and means to return to his lands properly wed by the end of the session. He has seen the results of waiting too long to get an heir, with his uncle dying of age while the heir was still so young and vulnerable. The Reighland holdings are too remote to see much society. It makes sense to him to choose a bride while he is at market.'

'Inadequate breeding stock in the north, I suppose,' Priscilla said. There were rumours that the duke had been much better with horses than he had with people, and that his Grace's general gracelessness extended to his doings with the fair sex. But for all of that, he was still a duke and much could be forgiven—especially by one who was eager to marry.

He seemed just the sort of man her father would choose for her. One with little else to recommend him other than rank. As she glanced at him from across the room, she had to admit that there was nothing about him that she imagined would make for an easy husband. He did not need the title to intimidate her. He was an exceptionally large man with broad shoulders, bulging muscles and large hands. His thick black hair hung low over his face, which had matching heavy brows. The slight shadow on his jaw meant his valet would have to keep a razor sharp and ready more than once a day. If he would at least smile, she might have thought him jolly, but his looks were as dark as his coat.

The simpering virgins that surrounded him were dwarfed in comparison. But it was a mob and, thank the gods, she would be lost in it. Perhaps her father was wrong about the understanding they had. Priss could be just another face in the crowd. The introduction could pass out of his memory as quickly as it had entered and she could return home to her room.

'Make some effort to distinguish yourself…' Veronica prodded her again '…or I shall speak for you.'

That would be even more embarrassing than being forced upon the man by her father. 'Very well, then,' Priss said, with a grim smile. If Benbridge and Ronnie were so eager for her to make this a memorable evening, she would give them what they wanted in spades. It would be so unforgettable that they would have no choice but to remove her from town to avoid further embarrassment.

And so she was brought before the estimable Duke of Reighland, who was even larger up close than he had seemed from a distance. She was glad that this would be her only meeting with him, for prolonged contact would be quite terrifying. She kept her head bowed as she heard Ronnie speaking to the host and hostess, who then turned to their guest and offered to present Lady Benbridge and Lady Priscilla.

Reighland's voice boomed down at the top of her head. 'How do you do?'

She heard Veronica's melodious, 'Very well, thank you, your Grace.'

Priscilla made her deepest, most perfect curtsy, offered her hand and then, looking up into the face of the man, smiled and whickered like a horse.

There was a stunned silence. But she did not need words to know what Veronica was thinking. The horror emanating from her was so close to palpable that Priss was surprised she had not already turned and shouted for Father to summon the carriage. They would make a hasty retreat and she could expect the lecture to continue nonstop until such time as they had a mind to remove her from the house.

No one moved. It was as though they could not dare breathe. And now that she had created the situation, she was unsure how to get out of it. Judging by his looks, she had expected immediate outrage and an angry outburst from the duke. He might even be moved to shout at her and storm from the room.

It would not matter. She had been shouted at by experts, now that her poor sister was no longer in the house to take the brunt of Father's temper. What could this stranger possibly say that would hurt her?

But Reighland was staring at her with no change of expression and an unusual degree of focus. She felt the slightest upward tug on the hand he held to move her out of her curtsy to stand properly before him. She did not need Veronica's advice to straighten her spine for she needed every last vertebra to hold her own against the tower of manhood in front of her.

At last he spoke. 'Lady Priscilla, may I have the next waltz?'

If he wished to upbraid her for her manners, he could do it in company and not by hauling her around the dance floor and trapping her in his arms for the scolding. 'I am sorry, but I believe I am promised.'

'How unfortunate for the gentleman. When he sees that you are dancing with me, I am sure he will understand.' He cocked an ear towards the musicians. 'It seems they are beginning. We had best go to the floor. If you will excuse us, Lady Benbridge?'

And so she was headed for the dance floor with the Duke of Reighland. She had little choice in the matter, unless she wanted to have a tug of war over her own evening glove. His grip on her arm was gentle, but immovable.

And now they were dancing. He was neither good nor bad at the simple step. She did not fear that he would tread upon her toes. But neither did she feel any pleasure in the way he danced. He approached the waltz with a passionless and mechanical precision, as though it were something to be conquered more than enjoyed.

'Are you having a pleasant evening?' he asked.

'Until recently,' she said.

'Strange,' he said, staring past her. 'I'd have said just the opposite, if you had asked me. It has suddenly become most diverting compared to other recent entertainments.'

'I would not know,' she said, 'for I have not attended any.'

'I understand that,' he said. 'It is because of

your sister's recent good fortune. I met her last evening at the Folbroke rout.'

Now she had to struggle to remain blasé. *He had seen Silly.* She must remember to think of Silly as Dru, just as Drusilla's friends did. Dru had many of those now and not just a little sister to tease her with nicknames. It had been months since the last time they had been in the same room together. But then they had not spoken and stayed on opposite ends of a ballroom that might as well have been an ocean. Priss had been forced by Veronica to cut her own sister dead.

If Ronnie got wind of it, she would snap this tenuous thread of communication, even if the man offering it was a duke. Priss replied to Reighland's news with a single, 'Oh.' It hardly summed up the extent of her feelings. She wanted to pull him to the side of the floor and interrogate him until she had gleaned every last detail of his exchange with Dru and could recall them as clearly as if she had been there herself.

But the dance could not go on for ever and she did not want to give the man reason to speak. She would have to do without.

He had noticed her silence. 'It surprises me to find you so uninterested. Mrs Hendricks was most eager for any news of you. Do you find yourself jealous on her account?'

'Certainly not. It is about time that Drusilla had the chance to be happy.' She looked longingly back at the wallflowers, wishing she was amongst them. Perhaps one of them had been at the Folbrokes' party and could give her the information she craved. 'It seems I am out of practice in social settings.' She glared up at him. 'I do not remember the conversation being quite so rude, when last I waltzed.' He would let her go now. That had been a direct insult and he could hardly ignore it.

But her barbed words bounced off his thick skin as though they meant nothing. 'You must make an effort to get out more,' he replied. 'It was at my request that you were invited here. I wished to meet you. I will see to it that you receive further such invitations.' He said it without a smile. Did the man have no emotions at all?

'If you wish,' she added for him.

'Of course I wish. That is why I will do it.'

'You misunderstand me, your Grace. What I

meant was that you should have finished your last sentence with the phrase "if you wish." Then it would mean that you would see to it I received further invitations and could accept them if I desired. It would imply that I had a choice.'

He ignored her lack of enthusiasm. 'If I give you a choice, I can well guess what your answer would be, although I am at a loss as to the reason for it. You seem to have taken an instant dislike of me, though you have known me for all of five minutes. I suspect that you would have formed the same opinion of me without even leaving your house, if I had given you the chance. But that would not do at all. It is time that you are brought out into the light so that a man can get a proper look at you.'

'Why would you need a proper look at me?'

'I mean to marry,' he said, as though it were not obvious. 'And you are a front runner. But no matter what your father might think, I cannot be expected to make a decision based on his word alone.'

'He could have shown you a miniature and you could have made a judgement from that,' she said. It was clear that her opinion did not matter. Of course, she supposed, since the man was a duke, her acceptance was assumed. Why would she refuse?

Other than that he had the manners of a stable hand.

'It would not have been the same,' he assured her. 'You are quite lovely and I am sure no picture would do you justice.'

'I am not so different from many others,' she insisted. 'If you wish for a pretty bride, you would be better served to make the rounds at Almack's. Everyone who is anyone is there.'

'In knee breeches,' he added. 'There is a limit to what I will go through, simply for the sake of marrying.'

'They are proper attire for evening,' she said bluntly.

'They are uncomfortable,' he said with equal bluntness. 'And they do not suit me. I will wear them at court, of course. I mean no disrespect to the Regent. But beyond that, trousers will have to do.'

'So you are willing to limit your choice of bride, based on your unwillingness to dress for evening?'

'Just as you are limiting your choice of husbands by not attending Almack's,' he said.

Touché. She could not explain her way out of that without admitting that she could no longer get vouchers. 'Perhaps I do not wish to marry,' she hazarded.

'Then you should go for the dancing,' he suggested. 'You are very good at it.'

'Thank you,' she said glumly.

'If we marry, I will not worry about having to hire a dancing master for you.'

She stumbled. *He knew.* Not all, perhaps. But enough. She pulled her hand from his, prepared to quit the floor.

He grabbed it back again and kept her in place. 'You will not get away from me so easily. Wait until the end of the music. Anything else will make you appear skittish.' He looked into her eyes. 'I do not tolerate skittishness.'

'And I do not care what you do or do not like,' she said.

'Then we are not likely to get on well.' He gave a thoughtful nod as though he were marking a check on the negative side of some invisible list of wifely qualities. 'Other young ladies are much more agreeable,' he said. 'One might even say that they fawned.'

'I expect so. You are a duke, after all. A marriageable miss cannot aspire higher than that.'

'Then why do you not express similar behaviours?'

'Is there anything about the title that imbues it with an amiable nature, a pleasant companion, a loving mate, or...' she struggled to find a delicate way to express her misgivings '...any kind of compatibility between us? You are young, of course.'

'Twenty-six,' he supplied.

'That might be an advantage in your favour. Barring accident, I would not have to be worried about widowhood. But I have met many men to whom I would much rather be a widow than a wife.'

His rather forbidding face split in a smile that was as surprising as it was brilliant. Straight white teeth, full lips, which had seemed narrow as he'd frowned at her. And there was a spark in his eye. For a moment, she almost found him attractive.

Then she remembered that he was her father's choice, not hers.

'I intend to live to a ripe old age,' he affirmed. 'Do you ride?'

'I beg your pardon?'

'I said, do you ride? Horses,' he added, as though there could be any other sort of riding.

'No,' she said hurriedly, hoping that this was the correct answer to put him off. 'I am deathly afraid of horses.' In truth, she quite liked them— probably better than she liked his Grace. But one could not be expected to marry a man based on the contents of his stables.

His smile had turned to thoughtful disappointment. 'That is a pity. You do a creditable imitation of one, I notice. Although it does not suit you. This Season, I have met several young ladies from whom a snort and a neigh would not have surprised me in the least.'

The joke was not subtle. She almost upbraided him for his cruelty before he added, 'That did not bother me much, however. Looks are not everything in a woman. And I quite like horses. I breed them, you know. I have rather a lot of land devoted to the business of it. In the country, of course.'

'Then it is as I said. We would not suit at all. I cannot abide the country.' Another lie.

'You would not be there all the time, you know. Much as I do not like to be away during the prime foaling time, now that I am Duke, I will be forced to attend parliament, and all the balls, galas and entertainments that accompany the Season. I suspect you could have your fill of town were you married to me.'

And then retire for the rest of the year to a country estate, far away from the prying eyes of the *ton*. She imagined acres of soft rolling green dotted with grazing mares and their little ones nudging at them. It was tempting, when he put it that way. 'As you complained earlier, I rarely attend the events of the Season now that I am here. It is just as likely that I would be forced to socialise when I did not wish and then be forced into a solitude I did not enjoy.'

He gave her a sidelong glance. 'It sounds rather like you have taken it into your head not to be happy with anything I might offer you.'

She returned the glance. 'Is it so obvious?'

'Quite. Since you are prone to such candour, will you tell me the reason for it? If I have given you offence, as I frequently do, it would be useful to know how. I would welcome a critique of my approach, so that I do not repeat the mistake with the next young lady.'

Her lips quirked as she tried to suppress a smile. 'There. Just now. You should have said, "If I have given offence, I humbly apologise".'

'Without knowing why?'

'Definitely. That is the way to a lady's heart.'

'And if I were to begin with this apology, you would feel differently towards me?'

'No.'

He drew back a moment, as though running through the conversation in his head. 'Then I shan't bother.' He stood in silence next to her, as though plotting his next move.

Why did he not just go away? She had been the one to give offence. And he was the one with all the power and new enough so that he hardly knew how to wield it. Did he not realise that his rank would allow him to take umbrage at the most trivial things, storm off or deny patronage? By now, he should have reported to her father that there was no way he could be leg shackled to such a thoroughly disagreeable chit and that would be that.

It would be a Pyrrhic victory, of course. There would be punishment and frigid silences awaiting her at home. But it would be one step closer to spinsterhood and the forced rustication that she craved.

Instead he seemed stubbornly attached to her. 'Now, let me see. You do not like riding, or balls, or the city, or the country. What does that leave us? Books?'

'I am not a great reader.'

'Shopping?'

'I have no wish to outfit myself in such a way that I am merely an ornament to my husband.'

'But you are most charmingly arrayed and, as previously noted, quite pretty.'

'I do not like flattery either.' But if she were totally honest with him, she would admit that she quite admired persistence.

'I suppose pleasant conversation cannot be a favourite of yours, or we would be having one now.' He gave her another sidelong glance. 'Clearly, you enjoy arguing. And there we will find our common ground. I can argue all night, if necessary.'

'To no avail. I will never agree with you, on any point.'

'If I sought your agreement, then that would be a problem.'

'That is precisely the problem I have with you,' she snapped back, growing tired of the banter. 'No one seeks my agreement. I am to be presented with a *fait accompli* and expected to go meekly along with it, for the sake of family connections and political benefit.'

'Aha.' He was looking at her closely now. 'You are trying to avoid a favourable match because it has been presented by your father. You have someone else in mind, then? Someone not quite so rich? Or without a title?'

'Do not flatter yourself to think that I love another,' she replied. 'Perhaps I simply do not want you.'

'But that is not true either. You hardly know me. But you have formed an opinion on the Duke of Reighland, have you not? Your answer to him is a resounding no.'

'You are he.'

'Not until recently,' he informed her. 'But I am quite aware of the pressure to marry according to one's station, at the expense of one's wishes. That is the purpose of this interview and several others I have organised recently.'

She smiled in relief, sure that if he had spoken to any other girl in London, it would cement his poor opinion of her.

He smiled back and once again she was surprised at the blinding whiteness of it. 'I must inform you that you have passed with flying colours. I look forward to calling on you, at your home, and on speaking to your father about a further acquaintance.' And with that the dance was over and he was escorting her, in stunned silence, back to her stepmother.

He liked her.

Even now, thinking of that rude whinny, he could feel his lips starting to twitch. He carefully suppressed the emotion. It was far easier to deal with people if they suspected that 'Reighland' was hovering on the edge of displeasure. They jumped to attention, in a vain attempt to keep the impossible man happy and not be the one upon whom the impending storm would break.

If he had been amiable, or, worse yet, laughed in their faces at their ridiculous behaviour towards him and offered friendship, it might be possible to dismiss him, title and all, as the unworthy upstart he sometimes felt he was. They would remember that he was the same lad they teased unmercifully at school. Robert Magson, the bear with no teeth. Once they had realised he would not fight back, it had been declared great fun to bait him. The torment had not stopped until he had gained his majority and retired to the country estate.

Now, those same men and their wives feared him, because they feared the title. If they realised that Reighland was just a thin veil over his old self, they would know how much power they still held. And it would all begin again.

So he glared and felt the crowd tremble at the possibility of his disapproval. It was better that they were kept off balance and at a distance, as they had been since his arrival in London. It meant he had made no friends, but neither had he any real enemies.

And until recently, tonight had been going according to course. Though she might sneer at his manners tomorrow, tonight the hostess was fawning over him, desperate to keep his favour. Several young ladies had been nudged into his path by their mamas, rather like birds forced from the nest into the mouth of a waiting cat. And just like those birds, they had been, to the last, wide-eyed, gawky and rather stupid. He had done the nice, of course, danced with them and fetched several glasses of lemonade, which allowed him to avoid adding his own dull wits to theirs.

Then he had spotted his supposed intended, just as he had hoped to. Hendricks had been right, the girl was a prime article. Pretty enough to put the others in the shade.

Or shadow. For there could not exactly be shade, could there, if the sun had set?

He brooded on that for a moment, then returned to the matter at hand.

The beautiful Lady Priscilla had seen through him in an instant. Apparently, she was not impressed by the farmer with the strawberry-leaf coronet.

In response, he'd been instantly attracted to her. But it was obvious that the sentiment would not be easily returned. Perhaps that was why he found her so fascinating. Of the three or four likely candidates he had found for his duchess, she might not be the prettiest in London. Close, perhaps. He almost preferred the dark good looks of Charlotte Deveril, despite that girl's lack of a titled father.

Lady Priscilla was an earl's daughter, with connections equal to two of the other girls he favoured. And her reputation…

There were rumours. When he'd questioned friends, no one had had the nerve to speak directly of the flaw. But he was sure it existed, if her own brother-in-law could not manage unequivocal approval of her. Even without the presence of Mrs Hendricks, he'd had to give a more-than-gentle hint to tonight's hostess that he wished the presence of both Benbridge and his family. He had been informed that the new Lady Benbridge would be welcome, of course. But there had been something in the tone of the discussion that implied everyone would just as soon forget that there was a Lady Priscilla.

Perhaps it was that they knew she would mis-behave in his presence. She did not offer shy and hopeful glances through her eyelashes. She did not flatter. She did not hang upon his every word, no matter how fatuous. She would not pretend one thing to his face, only to talk be-hind his back.

What she felt for him was plain and undis-guised dislike. And it was directed to the duke and not the man inside. She refused to agree with him, in even the slightest details of his speech. She wanted no part of him and did not bother to hide it.

Therefore, she was the only one worth hav-ing. Whatever she might be, she did not bore him. And if he could win such a proud crea-ture for himself he would know that the past was finally dead. Once Priscilla was married, whatever small scandal lay in her past would be forgotten. His wife would be beautiful, well bred and the envy of the *ton*. He would give her free rein in wardrobe and entertaining. Their house would be a show place and the feigned respect of his peers would become real.

But it was still a surprise to find that the most

perfect woman in London was dead set against marrying above her station. Perhaps, a year ago, when he was a not particularly humble horse trader, she'd have courted him, just to spite her father. Or perhaps not. It would take time to find the full reason for her contrary behaviour, but he was willing to be patient.

Her distaste of riding was another problem. What was he to do with a woman who did not like horses? Granted, he had escorted two of his final four candidates down Rotten Row just this week. In the saddle, they were mediocre at best, sitting their beasts like toads on a jossing block. It had pained him to watch.

At least, when he could persuade the Benbridge girl to take to a mount, she would have no bad habits that needed to be broken. He could teach her not to fear and eventually she would enjoy it. He imagined her fighting every step of the way. The thought excited him, for sometimes it was the most spirited mare that made for the best ride.

Then he reminded himself, yet again, that women were not horses. Life would be easier if they were. He could not exactly break her spirit with a rough bit and a whip. But it would be better to have to argue and cajole for every compromise than to have a woman with no spirit to break.

The combination of riding and spirited women made him smile into his glass and take a long savouring drink. He had not expected to feel the low heat he was feeling for the woman he had met tonight. He had imagined the getting of an heir to be a momentary pleasure, surrounded by a lifetime of awkwardness and frigid courtesy. At best they would develop a fondness for each other. But suppose there could be passion as well?

Then it would be better if it were mutual desire, he reminded himself. He already knew the foolish course he was likely to take. He would do well to remember, before it was too late, that a passionate dislike from his spouse might make him long for the frosty indifference he was avoiding now.

And here was her father, eager to know how the dance had gone, but too subtle to ask directly. If Robert did not acknowledge him, the man would be hanging about all night, waiting for an opportunity to speak. 'Benbridge,' he said. 'A word, please.'

'Of course, your Grace.' The old earl looked at him speculatively and it reminded him, as always, of a stallion he'd had that would give the impression of docility, only to bite suddenly at the hand that held the apple. Reighland held precedence and they both knew it. But Benbridge thought in his heart that he was the superior and would show him that, if he could find a way.

'I have had the opportunity to speak with your daughter, and have found her to be…'

Fractious, ungrateful, uninterested and bad tempered.

'…quite charming. She is most lovely as well. May I have your permission to pay further visits upon her, with the object of a possible match?'

'Certainly, your Grace.' Benbridge gave only a slight lowering of the head, as though the honour were equal.

'The girl would have to be interested as well,' Robert reminded him. 'I would not wish to press my suit upon her, if she were otherwise engaged.' Despite her objections, it would make the most sense if she was pining for another.

'She is not so promised,' Benbridge said firmly. 'Even if she had plans in that direction, I would forbid all but the most appropriate match for her. After the misfortune of her sister…' There was a slight narrowing of the eyes and an even slighter twitch of the cheek to show what he thought of his other daughter's marriage. 'Priscilla will not reject you, your Grace. She would not dare.'

For a moment, Robert felt quite sorry for the girl. He wanted to pursue her, but his slightest interest was seen by her father as tantamount to an accepted offer. No wonder she refused to show him partiality.

'I must see her again, so that we might decide if we suit each other.' The earl might not care, but Robert would much prefer a wife who could at least tolerate him.

'Of course,' the earl replied, with just the slightest touch of obsequiousness. Then he stared across the room at his daughter, as though deciding on the best way to bully her into good behaviour to secure the proposal.

Silently, Robert damned him for his overconfidence. At the very least he would meet with the girl again and press the advantages of marrying a man who was not only rich and titled, but well on his way to being fond of her—and warn her of the danger of disobeying such an unaffectionate father.

Chapter Three

'Priscilla, you have a visitor.'

No, she hadn't. For whom that she actually wished to see would be likely to make a call? Her old friends had cast her off quick enough, after her fall from grace. The sister she longed to see had been banned from the house. And she had gone out of her way to do nothing on the previous evening to warrant a call.

But rather than scolding her for her rudeness during the ride home, both her father and Veronica had seemed inordinately pleased with the turn events had taken. It was as though they'd shared some bit of information between them that she was not privy to.

Please do not let it be the duke. Because what would she do with the man, should he persist? 'Tell whoever it is that I am indisposed.'

Her bedroom door opened and Veronica poked in her head. 'I certainly will not. Reighland is in the sitting room, and you are going to see him.' She crossed the room, seized Priss by the arm and pulled her to her feet, brushing the wrinkles from her gown and smoothing a hand over her hair to rearrange the flattened curls.

'I am not prepared. I do not wish to see him.' *And I do not wish to marry him.* She doubted pleading with Ronnie would help, but neither would it hurt.

'You are unprepared because you spend your days hiding in bed with your Minerva novels, feigning illness to avoid company. Now come downstairs.'

'Send him away.'

'I certainly will not.' Ronnie was pushing her out into the hall and put a firm hand in her back to hurry her along. 'If you mean to put him off, you must do it yourself. And if you do, you will suffer the consequences for it. Your father will not be pleased.' She said it in a dark tone to remind her that there were worse things awaiting her than social ostracism, should she fail.

Priss gave her a mutinous look. 'Do not be so

melodramatic. Father will do nothing worse to me than shout and sulk, as he has done the whole of my life. Perhaps he will banish me from the house, as he did Dru. Although how that is a punishment, I do not know. It is clear to all of London that she is the better for it.'

'It is not your father who should worry you, dear,' Ronnie replied, voice cold and venomous. 'You should know, after spending several months under the same roof with me, I will be far less forgiving. If you will not go to the duke, I will bring him to you and lock the bedroom door behind him until the matter is settled.'

The image of being so trapped with such a forbidding man made Priss a little sick, and she thanked the fates that she had not been caught *en déshabillé* today. While her father might view this as an alliance with a powerful man, she had no doubt that Ronnie would engineer her total disgrace with any man available, simply to have her out of the house. The woman was all but thrusting her through the door of the salon where her guest awaited.

But she showed no sign of following. Priss grabbed her arm, trying to pull her into the room as well. 'You are going to sit with us, of course,' she said hopefully. 'For surely a chaperon—'

'He is a duke,' the other woman whispered. 'He does not require a chaperon.'

'It is not for him,' Priss snapped back, embarrassed that the duke could likely overhear this interchange, for he was scant feet across the room. Could they not at least pretend that she had some honour left?

'You were happy enough to escape the care of your sister, while she was still here. It makes no sense, a year later, that you are having a fit of the vapours over a few minutes alone with a man.' Her stepmother pushed harder. 'He is a duke. He wishes to speak to you alone. Benbridge said he was most specific on that point. I do not mean to be the one to argue.'

'My father is allowing this?' Priss felt another small bit of her world crumbling. She had received continual signs from Ronnie that her presence was an inconvenience. But usually Papa was more subtle with his displeasure.

'Your father thinks that Reighland is an excellent catch. He is amenable to certain laxities if it smoothes the way for an offer.'

'But what if Reighland is not as honourable as he seems? What if he takes advantage?' Priss whispered back, directly into Veronica's ear.

The other woman's eyes narrowed and she pulled her head away. 'Do not play the sweet-and-innocent miss with me, Priscilla. If he takes advantage, then you are to do as he says and come to me afterwards. We will tell your father of it and the duke will be forced to offer with no more nonsense. But whatever you do, do not ruin the opportunity, for I doubt you will have a better one.'

Priss's heart sank. It was plain what her father expected of her. Society expected it as well. But knowing what she did, she could not imagine how she would manage it. If Reighland offered today, she would have to say no. The skies might open and hell might rain down on her if she disobeyed, but then perhaps Papa would see she was in earnest and she would have some peace. She disentangled herself from Ronnie and glanced into the mirror on the hall wall, touching her hair and straightening her skirts. Then she turned and went into the salon, where Reighland awaited her.

The footman announced her and she waved him away with a flick of her hand, trying not to flinch as she heard the door closing behind her. She focused all her attention on the man in front of her, muttering, 'Your Grace', and dropping a curtsy letting her eyes travel up from the floor until they met his face.

And it was such a long way for her gaze to travel. He was well over six feet. She noticed the sprinkling of dark hair on the backs of his hands and up his wrists, disappearing into his shirt cuffs. It made her wonder what the rest of him would be like, without his clothes.

She quickly stifled the thought, for it only made her more frightened. There was a harmony to him, as though nature had sought to make an animal both intimidating and powerful. In the bedroom he would be just as large as he had been in the ballroom.

'Please, Lady Priscilla, if we are to be friends, let us not stand on ceremony. You must call me Robert.' His voice matched the rest of him. Deep, growling, with just a taste of a rasp that made the hairs on her neck stand to attention.

He was examining her now, top to bottom,

as she had him. There was no hint of lust in it, which was just as well. If she'd thought that that was the first thing on his mind, she'd probably have run from the room in terror. This was more clinical, as though he was wondering about sound teeth, good wind and strong limbs.

But the desire that she use his first name was a very bad sign.

'Has your father explained the purpose for my visit?'

'No, your Grace,' she said, avoiding the offered intimacy. 'But I am not so dim that I cannot guess it.'

'And what say you to it?'

She searched her mind for a response that did not use the word that came most easily to mind: *trapped.* 'I thought I made it clear to you yesterday evening.'

He gave her the same blank look as he had on the previous evening. 'You merely said you would not be agreeing with me. I do not see that as an impediment to matrimony.' No talk of wooing at all. The man did like to cut to the chase.

He thought for a moment. 'You would have to agree at the altar, of course. But after that…'

Was he joking? It almost seemed that he might be. But his expression was so closed that it was impossible to tell. 'Are you sure you are quite sane?' she asked. For madness was the only other explanation.

'Is it necessary to be so?' he asked innocently. 'I was given to understand that my title was hereditary. From what I have seen of others in the peerage, you are the only one concerned with my sanity. If you mean to ask next if I am stupid, I will admit that I am not as quick as some. But in my brief stay in London, I have found many who were greater dullards.'

He was joking, then. But did he expect her to laugh? He seemed most sober. Perhaps he was seeking a mate who would be amused by him. More likely, she would be the butt of the joke, once he knew her better. His dry comments would seem innocent enough when he spoke them in public, but she would know the true meaning and would be left burning with shame.

And she could not abide a lifetime of that. 'May I be frank with you, your Grace?'

'It shall be an exciting change from the hesitant sentiments you have thus far expressed.'

'My rejection is not against you, personally,' she lied. 'It is only that I do not wish to submit easily to marrying any titled man that my father might choose.'

He gave her a sad smile. 'Then I fear you will submit with difficulty. With force, if necessary.'

Was this meant to be a threat? She would receive no help from Veronica, should he choose to make good on it. Priss felt another rising tide of panic. 'Do you mean to force me, then?'

'I shall not have to. Your father seems quite sure of your co-operation, no matter what you might say. You know better than I what he is capable of.'

Maybe it had been a warning, then. But her obvious difficulties had not bothered him enough to give him a distaste for a union with the family. 'And you would accept a wife who was so unwilling.'

'Benbridge will see you bound to someone, this Season. If you hold any choice in contempt, then you could do worse than to take me, should you be obligated to marry.'

Papa could not drag her screaming to the altar, but he was crafty, and Ronnie even more so. They had ways that she could not comprehend. The duke was right. There could well be worse choices. Her dislike of this particular man was not as instantaneous as she'd expected. But the size of him was simply too intimidating, and time was not likely to change it. 'You are no better than he is, if you care so little about how I come to you.'

'But I am hoping that you might come to think of me as the lesser of two, or more, evils,' he said, still without smiling. 'The devil you know, rather than the devil you don't. Personally, once I am set upon a course, I do not intend to take no for an answer. And I am set on having you.'

She stared back, planning her next move. If he would not let her cry off, then she would have to work harder to give him a distaste of her. She smiled back at him, with a suddenness and brilliance he would know was false. 'I am happy to be given the opportunity for such an advantageous match.'

He snorted. 'Are you, really? You did not look it a moment ago.' He was examining her again.

'But I believe the last half of the statement. This will be an advantageous match. From your side, at least'

She bit back a furious retort. He was correct, after all. It was simply rude of him to mention the fact.

'I am recently come to the title, of course,' he said, with humbleness that was as false as her smile. 'I did not expect it. The old duke's heir died within the same year as his father, my father already having passed...'

'It matters not to me how you came to be a duke,' she said, still half-hoping her bluntness would put him off. 'It only matters that you are one at the time of offering. Beyond that, I have little interest in you.' She tried to look eager at the notion of such a prestigious match. Perhaps he would not want a title hunter.

He was staring at her again, thoughtfully. 'Considering your pedigree, it should be advantageous to the man involved as well. You are young, beautiful and well born. Why are you not married already, I wonder? For how could any man resist such a sweet and amenable nature?'

'Perhaps I was waiting for you, your Grace.'

She dropped her smile, making no effort to hide her contempt.

'Or perhaps the rumours I hear are true and you have dishonoured yourself.'

'Who…?' The word had escaped before she could marshal a denial. But she had experienced a moment's uncontrollable fear that, somewhere Dru had been that she had not, the ugly truth of it all had escaped and that now her happily married sister was laughing at her expense.

'Who told me? Why, you did, just now.' He was smiling in triumph. 'It is commonly known that the younger daughter of the Earl of Benbridge no longer goes about in society because of the presence of the elder. But I assumed there would be more to it than that. And I was correct.'

Success at last, though it came with a sick feeling in her stomach and the wish that it had come any way but this. She had finally managed to ruin everything. Father would be furious if this opportunity slipped through her fingers. It would serve him right, for pushing this upon her. 'You have guessed correctly, your Grace. And now I assume that this interview is at an end.' She gestured towards the door.

'On the contrary,' he replied. 'You have much more to tell me before I depart from here. Does the sad state of your reputation have anything to do with your family's willingness that we might meet alone?'

'There is no reason that we should not,' she replied. 'He expects that you will offer for me, not rape me on the divan in the lounge.'

If her frankness startled him, it did not show. 'And what if I did?'

'Then I would cry to my father and he would demand that you marry me.'

'As you might at any rate,' he pointed out. 'The door is closed and we are alone. Should you wish to tell tales about my behaviour, I would have no evidence to refute them.'

'Perhaps I would if I wished to trap you into marriage,' she snapped. 'It is you who have come to me and not the other way round. I never gave you any reason to think I wished a union. If your intentions are not in that direction, then, as I said before, you had best leave.'

He ignored the door and looked her up and down again, walking slowly around her, so as to view her from all angles. Then he spoke. 'Truth now. I will not tell your father, if that is what you fear. You have my word. Is there another, perhaps someone inferior to me, that you might prefer?'

'Would it matter?' she asked in exasperation. 'Between the two of you, you and my father seem to have settled the matter.'

'It might,' Reighland said, after a moment. 'And you did not answer my question.'

'If we are taking my opinions into account at this late date, then I shall tell you again: there is no other. All the same, I prefer to remain unmarried. Even if I sought marriage, it would not be with you. We do not suit. I thought I made that clear to you, when we danced.'

'I see.' He was staring at her again, appraising. 'You do not wish to leave the loving bosom of your family.'

She almost laughed at the absurdity of it. 'Of course I do. There is a dower house on the property in Cornwall that stands empty. And land further north where I might stay with my mother's sister. Perhaps I could go to Scotland. Any of those would do for a genteel spinsterhood. That is all I seek for myself.'

'Then I am sorry to disappoint you. As I said before, your father has no intention of allowing that. You will be married. If not to me, then to some other. Since you have no concrete objections, other than an illogical dislike of me, I will speak to your father. We will formalise this arrangement by the end of the month.'

Arrangement. Was that all it was to him? She had known when it came time to marry that there would be no love match. But she had not thought it would be quite so passionless as this. And so she blurted, before he could leave, 'If you mean to go ahead with this, then you had best know the whole truth, so that you do not reproach me with it on our wedding night. I am no longer innocent.' She would pay the price for her honesty, she was sure. The duke would storm out and tell her father. Then she would get a long lecture from Benbridge and his new wife about her stupidity in disobeying their orders and casting aside the only match they had been able to make for her.

But at least it would be over.

The Duke of Reighland was still standing there, giving her the same curious, up-and-down examination that he had been. Then he asked, 'Are you pregnant?'

'Certainly not!' Her cheeks heated and her palm itched to slap him for being so bold as to ask. Then a thought struck her. 'If I was, then why would I bother to tell you?'

'Why would you have told me anything?' he asked back, just as sensibly. 'If you wished to marry me, you would have kept quiet on the first point. But if you truly wished to frighten me away, you'd have lied about the second. The two statements, taken together, only make sense to me if they are true. They seem to imply that you are a most candid young lady. The truth is an admirable quality and quite rare in London. It must be cherished when it is found. I have learned all I wish to know. I will have you.' He stepped closer to her and she felt a sudden panicked scrambling desire to move away, back across the room before he would touch her.

But he did nothing more than bow before her, taking her cold hand in his and offering a kiss that was the barest touch of his lips against the skin. 'Now, with your permission, I will depart.' He rose and smiled. 'And with or without your permission, I will visit you again. While I am decided, I think we have more to discuss before an announcement can be made.'

She sat down on the couch behind her, numb with shock. He left the room and she could hear him speaking to her stepmother in the hall, arranging for another visit.

He was decided.

What had she said to him that had made the decision? She had done everything in her power to put him off. The truth, there at the end, should have been enough to send him running from the room. She was not good enough for him. Any rumours he might have heard of her elopement were true. She was ruined.

Yet he meant to come again. To persuade her. She felt a shudder rising from deep within her and tried to tell herself that it was revulsion. That was not true. But neither was it desire. She did not find him attractive. He was too large, too imposing and in all ways too blunt. She was not exactly frightened of him. That would be like fearing a mountain, or perhaps a cliff that one had no intention of standing on. It was more like awe, really.

She was not used to being in awe of anyone. The glamour of a title had been tarnished to her years ago.

And as for men?

She removed a handkerchief from her sleeve and delicately mopped her brow. Those secrets had been stripped away as well. Men were not nearly as pleasant as they appeared. She would be quite content to do without them, if only it would be permitted.

Veronica's voice, as she saw the duke to the door, was light, flirtatious and sycophantic. Whatever Priss might feel on the subject, her prospective husband was a favourite of the household and she was unlikely to escape him.

She thought of the size of him and the way he would come to her, naked, hairy as a bear, crushing her body with his weight, sweating and grunting over her as he pushed and thrust.

There was a soft rip and she noticed that she had torn the lace on the corner of the handkerchief she'd forgotten she was holding. She would need to mend it before an explanation was required of her. There had been a time when she might have lost a hundred such linens and experienced no punishment. But that was when Dru had still been in the house and there had been no Veronica, eager to find fault with her.

The duke was barely gone from the room when the doors to the salon burst open and her stepmother entered. 'Well, then?'

'He has offered,' Priss affirmed glumly.

Veronica clapped her hands together in triumph. 'Lucky for us and far better than you deserve. I will put the announcement in *The Times* immediately.'

'He does not wish to announce it yet,' she said.

'Then we will allow him to make that decision.'

'I have not said yes.'

Veronica was across the room in a moment, her hands in Priss's hair to pull her gaze up to meet her. 'Perhaps your father might permit your wilfulness, but we have seen where that led. When the time is right, you will say yes, like any sensible girl, because, my lady, in a few months there will be no space for you in this house. I will need your room for a nursery.'

'There are a dozen rooms that will suit just as

well,' Priss said, glaring back at her and feeling the claws tightening against her scalp.

'But I favour the light in yours,' Veronica said with a small tight smile. 'You will be out of this house and you will be thankful that we are sending you to such a fortunate marriage and not out into the street as you deserve. But you will not be allowed to remain here, courting further disgrace. I will not let a girl who does not have the sense to keep her legs closed associate with children of mine.' She released Priss's head with a jerk that cracked her neck.

And then Veronica was smiling again. 'Come, my dear. We will go to Bond Street and buy you a trousseau.'

Chapter Four

John Hendricks owned an unassuming house in an equally humble neighbourhood. Robert scolded himself for the assessment, remembering that he'd have thought no such thing before the title had foisted on him the various entailed properties in all their grandeur. There was nothing really wrong with this place, although he wondered what Lady Drusilla made of it, after living as Benbridge's daughter.

He knocked upon the door; when it opened, he announced himself and pushed his way past the housekeeper, tossing his gloves into his hat and giving her his most aloof ducal glare. Then he demanded to be shown to the receiving room, or whatever place was deemed best for a meeting with Mr Hendricks.

He watched the servant melt before him with a subservient curtsy. 'I will get him immediately, your Grace.'

Of course she would. It was late for an uninvited call, of course. Not the thing to arrive at a man's house without some kind of warning. But now that he was 'his Grace' instead of plain old Mr Magson, the rules no longer applied.

Sometimes, he rather missed the rules. Dammit, he liked Hendricks. At least a lot more than he liked being Reighland and throwing his weight around. But today there would be no more pussyfooting about the truth. He wanted answers and he wanted them now, before his own native foolishness overcame good sense and he continued to press his suit on a girl who was showing every sign of being completely inappropriate. Even in his worst and least confident days, he'd had more sense than to chase after the leavings of other men when seeking a wife.

'Your Grace?' Hendricks stood in the doorway of his own home, offering an unironic bow as though it were he who had entered unexpectedly. 'How might I be of assistance?'

'You can leave off bowing at me, for one thing,'

Robert muttered, unable to control the impulse. 'You might well want to bounce me out into the street when you hear why I have come. The respectful greeting will only make that more difficult.'

'Perhaps,' said Hendricks, with the faintest lift of an eyebrow. 'But we will not know until you have made your request.'

'Tell me about Benbridge's younger daughter. And not the nonsense you were spouting at the party. I want the truth this time.'

'It really is not my place—' Hendricks began.

'Yours as much as anyone else's. I will have the story in the end. She's already told me the more interesting half of it. The girl is no longer a maid.'

Hendricks sucked his breath in between his teeth in a sudden hiss, but said nothing.

'If the circumstances mitigate the truth, I should like to know it now. Who? When? Why? And who else knows of it? I heard rumours of an elopement with a dancing master. But I refuse to base my decisions based on tittle-tattle from gossiping old ladies. Any accurate information you can provide about Lady Priscilla will be welcome.'

Hendricks rose and went to the door of the sitting room, glancing into the hall to be sure that they were alone, before shutting it. 'I would rather my wife not hear what we are discussing. It is a sensitive subject in the family as you can imagine. Dru was charged with watching the girl and feels quite responsible for anything that might have happened. And I do not know the most intimate details, of course. It was several days before we caught up with the couple. The situation might not be as dire as you make it out.'

'I make nothing of it,' Robert said. 'It is Priscilla who seems sure of events. She should know them, if no one else does.'

Hendricks swallowed. 'And I can trust that, since I am speaking to the Duke of Reighland, the story will travel no further than this room.' The statement was obvious and unnecessary. Apparently, Hendricks did not trust him to keep the secret, without reminding him that he was a gentleman. It rankled.

He swallowed his pride, reminding himself that the man before him was near to Benbridge's family, no matter what the old earl might think of him. Then he responded, 'You have my word. I mean the girl no harm. But neither am I some poor gull in a country market, willing to buy a horse with bishoped teeth and piping lungs. An alliance between Benbridge and myself would be useful. But there is the succession to think of.'

'You think you might still consider her a suitable choice, after knowing the truth?' Hendricks pushed his glasses up the bridge of his nose as though seeking a better look at him.

'I am here, aren't I? Most men would be gone already.' Men smarter than himself, perhaps. But he had taken a liking to her and there was no reasoning with his first impression. He was still half-hoping that Hendricks would tell him he had misheard the girl. Or that he was the victim of some horribly unfunny joke. 'I have no real proof that Lady Priscilla will have me. Although she would be a fool to turn down the offer, she is resisting.'

'Priss is not known for her foresight,' Hendricks said drily.

'Obviously.'

'But if you mean to pursue her, then you shall

have all I know of it.' Hendricks moved into the room, gesturing to a chair and offering port, before taking a seat himself. It was a decent wine and a comfortable chair. Robert appreciated the gesture, which seemed sincere, and not an effort to get on his right side for some gain later. If Hendricks was the climber he appeared to be, he was subtle and not some common sycophant.

Hendricks began. 'Late last summer, I met Lady Drusilla Roleston in a mail coach on the way to Gretna Green. She was seeking word of her sister, who had eloped with a dancing master named Gervaise. I offered my assistance. We caught the couple before they crossed the border and I dispensed with the fellow.'

'Permanently?'

Hendricks laughed. 'Hardly. He ran off with little encouragement, when he saw that he was more likely to come away with a beating than any money. Without guarantee of settlement, he had no real desire to take the girl for a wife.'

'So there was no real affection between them?'

'I cannot speak for man or girl. I can only report what I observed. Although Priss made a fuss at the time, she was over it by the next morning.

It did not appear to me that either of them was broken hearted at the parting. I brought the sisters back to London safely and made my offer for Drusilla. Benbridge showed no desire to hear it. But Dru was willing, even though it meant an estrangement from her family.'

'How many days was Lady Priscilla unchaperoned?'

'At least three.'

Which probably meant that the elder sister was just as compromised as the younger had been. And willing to have Hendricks to spite her father. There was a story there, he was certain. But it was no real concern of his, since it did not figure in his bid for the other girl. 'Three days is more than enough time for mischief to be done.'

Hendricks shrugged. 'If a man is determined, three minutes in a drawing room is enough, even under the eyes of a chaperon.'

Robert gave the man a stern look. 'Not what I wished to hear from a man who had ample opportunity to be alone with my intended on the way back to London.'

'But true, none the less,' Hendricks admitted. 'Although it was unorthodox for me to be travelling with either of them, my affections were quite firmly fixed on the other sister by the time we turned back towards the city.'

'And when Priscilla returned, was it to the censure of the *ton*?'

'There were rumours, perhaps. But nothing more than that. Without Gervaise, there were no facts to back them with. It was not the disaster it might have been, had she been both imprudent and unlucky. If she is avoiding society, it is more from her own sensitivity than fear of embarrassment.'

Robert nodded in agreement. 'Disgrace can be swept under the rug, if one meets it with a bold face.' While Priscilla did not seem to be the sort to melt in the heat of society's stare, he had hardly known her long enough to make a judgement.

'Benbridge has done more to hurt the girl than she did with her own behaviour,' Hendricks added. 'The foolish feud he seeks with me makes it appear that Priscilla has some biological need to avoid society. But it has been nearly eight months since my marriage to Dru. From what I can tell, Priss looks just the same as she did on the day that I met her.'

No unwanted pregnancy, then. There had been time enough to see the results of that. 'Since that time, how has she behaved? Have you had wind of any new scandal?'

'I think it is likely that Priscilla learned a hard lesson and did not need to learn it twice. As far as I am aware, there have been no further incidents. She does not appear to be embracing rebellion. Benbridge hardly lets the girl out of his sight. Her social life was much constrained, once her sister was not there to serve as escort.'

'And now there is the new Lady Benbridge.' Robert dropped the name and waited for the reaction.

There was the faintest pursing of Hendricks' lips, as though he had no desire to think ill of a woman who was now his wife's stepmother. 'Perhaps I speak from affection. But Dru was a much steadier influence and more likely to act in the best interests of her sister, although Priss did not always see it as such.'

'Not as likely to hitch Priscilla to some ill-mannered stranger, just because he is a duke?'

Hendricks looked him up and down, then, as though appraising him. And for a moment, Robert was sure that, no matter how much the man might make of a connection himself, he would choose family over rank. 'I would think it little business of mine what the manners of the man were when he spoke to others, as long as they were good enough to suit his wife. And I would add that I wished to see Priscilla married to a man who, regardless of title, had at least a modicum of affection for her. She is far more likely to be loyal to someone who cares for her, than one who wishes to marry her father.'

'And you are wondering if I am such a man?'

'Perhaps I think it is time that someone wondered it. My wife is right. For all her faults, Priss deserves some happiness. She is unlikely to gain it if her father is left to choose a husband for her. If you wish the truth, then I will tell it to you: it matters not how you behave, or what Priscilla thinks of the matter. When Benbridge sees you, he will look no further than the title. After the coup of catching an earl, Lady Benbridge sees Priss as being little more than an inconvenience and will have her out of the house one way or another. If, after what you have learned today, you are not interested in pursuing this matter, then a rapid and strategic retreat is in order. Lady Benbridge will not be pleased that Priss has told you of her past to scare you off. She will trick you into dishonouring the girl, if she can make the match in no other way.'

'I suspected as much. It was only confirmation I sought when coming here.' Robert rose, setting his wine glass aside, and Hendricks followed him to his feet. 'Should you see her, you may tell your wife's sister that, at this time, I have no intention of retreat. I have learned nothing that has changed my intention to make a match with Lady Priscilla. But I do not intend to force an offer on a woman who does not want me. Further study of the situation is in order. And then we shall see what we shall see.'

Chapter Five

'Priscilla, whatever am I to do with you?' Veronica was standing in the doorway to her bedroom again, shaking her head in disapproval. 'You knew to expect a caller, yet you have done nothing to ready yourself. You cannot greet a duke in such a shabby dress.'

Priss had assumed that, when given the time to reflect on what she had told him, he would see his error in courting her and sever the connection. But it appeared that he was more persistent than sensible. 'I had quite forgotten,' she lied. 'Tell him to return another day. Perhaps tomorrow I shall have enough time to prepare.' She was being childish, to the point where she bored and annoyed even herself. But when man and family would not listen to a plain refusal, she was forced to use any trick she could muster.

'I most certainly will not send him away.' Veronica came to the side of the bed and hauled her upright, spilling a half-finished game of Patience off the unmade bed. 'If you refuse to dress, then he will see you as you are now. Perhaps it will embarrass you sufficiently that we will not have this problem when he comes again tomorrow.'

They were planning for tomorrow already? Then she had just as well let him see her in a sad state today. Until she could manage to make him see that she was not appropriate, he would stay camped out in the salon and she would have no peace at all. 'Very well, then, I am justly punished for my lack of preparation. Let us go downstairs so that I may humiliate myself.'

Veronica frowned at her, as though recognising that she had been caught in her own trap. But she released Priss's arm and allowed her to proceed under her own power to the main floor. When the footman opened the door to the salon, her unwanted suitor half-turned to see her entrance, clearly interested but using his status to remind everyone that he expected to see those around him scurry to attention and not the other way round.

It annoyed her no end. She took her time with the short walk to his side, turning the last few steps into a dawdle as the doors closed behind her, leaving them alone. 'Your Grace?' She made a proper curtsy, feeling much as she had on the previous day, only perhaps a little more desperate. This meeting should not be happening. Her revelation should have put an offer well out of reach.

Which might mean he had other things than marriage on his mind. It might amuse him to keep the daughter of an earl as a mistress and would certainly tell the *ton* just how high above them he considered himself. If he made an inappropriate advance, she could do little to counter it. Her only chaperon was hiding on the other side of the house so that she would be unable to stop an indiscretion until it was far too late.

She watched him uneasily, waiting for him to speak.

'I have a gift for you.' The duke seemed almost childishly pleased with himself as he pulled a long thin box from under his arm and held it out to her.

She took it cautiously and lifted the lid just a crack before letting it fall closed again as her worst fears were realised. 'I cannot accept these,' she said flatly.

'Why ever not?'

'They are too intimate.'

'They are gloves.'

'Yes. I know.' Long, spotless and white. She was sure, if she touched them, they would be of the finest and most perfect kidskin and a rival to anything she might have bought for herself. She placed her hand on top of the box lid so that she could not be tempted to open it again and pushed it back towards him. 'A lady would never accept a gift of clothing and a gentleman would never offer.'

His brow furrowed, as though struggling with an unfamiliar concept. 'They are hardly indecent.'

'That is not the point. They indicate an interest in my person.'

'Of course they do,' he said, still surprised. 'Because I am interested in your person. It would make no sense to marry a woman who did not interest me in that way.'

So he was still talking about a wedding. That was some consolation, since it proved he would not spring across the room and fall upon her like a ravening beast. If she had actually wanted to marry him, she'd have been in alt. But clearly he did not understand what he must do, when making a proper offer to a lady. 'If you really wished to marry me, you'd have brought another sort of gift entirely. A book, perhaps. Or flowers.'

'Flowers will die,' he said firmly. 'That cannot send the sort of message I would wish. And as for books? It is not that I never read, but I doubt that the things I favour would hold any interest to you. What would you have said if I'd brought you a stack of stock journals, tied up with a pretty ribbon?'

'I'd have thought you mad.'

'There. You agree with me.' He pointed to the gloves. 'Those are pretty, practical and will last you longer than the average bouquet. And do not argue modesty, for they cover an extremity I can see quite plainly now.'

Which left her wishing she had changed to a

more appropriate gown with full-length sleeves. He was staring at her hands, her wrists and the length of her arms in a way that felt strangely as if he was staring inappropriately at some other more personal part of her body.

She hurriedly opened the box, removed one of the gloves and slipped it on, so that he would cease ogling her.

It was a very nice glove. Though his manners were abominable, she could not fault the man's taste. The leather caressed her hands and hugged tight to her arm like a second skin. The top was finished in a carefully punched scallop, so delicate that it almost seemed like lace. Hardly thinking of what it must look like, she put on the other glove as well, then held her hands out in front of her to admire them.

'Here. Let me do up the buttons for you.' He took one of her hands and turned it over, doing up the line of mother-of-pearl buttons at the wrist.

She felt the little hitch in her breath as his large hands worked cautiously over the tiny buttons and brushed against the sensitive skin at her pulse. Then it was gone and he was holding her hands just by the fingertips, so that she could feel the heat and pressure through the thin leather that covered them.

'They are lovely on you,' he said, with little passion. 'And though I can imagine a bracelet of diamonds resting there, it is hardly necessary to improve the beauty of your wrists.'

That was more the sort of flattery she'd expected from a potential suitor. It annoyed her that she felt moved by it. And the gloves were not helping, for they made her feel both cherished and caressed. She hurried to undo the buttons and take them off again. 'They are still inappropriate. But I thank you for them.' Now that she had seen them on her hands, she did not really want to give them up. She cursed herself for the weakness, but put the gloves back in the box to set aside for later.

'You're welcome,' he responded. 'And why did you run away with your dancing master?'

'I beg your pardon, your Grace?' She dropped the box in her haste to be rid of the gloves, then looked quickly around the room, fearing that someone might have heard.

He must have seen her guilty flinch, but made

no comment on it. 'It is a simple enough question, I am sure. And one that only you know the answer to. I will repeat it more loudly, if you wish.'

'No.' It was quite possible that Veronica was listening at the door. Of all the topics of conversation she did not wish to open with her stepmother, it was the one that would lead to another rant on the foolishness of her elopement. 'You do not need to repeat yourself. I heard your question quite clearly.'

'Then I expect an answer. You must have had a reason. Or is this merely the sort of whim that you are prone to?'

'I ran because I wished to escape a tyrant.' If he'd meant to warn her of her father on the last visit, he must understand what she meant by this statement.

'You wished to trade one for another, more like,' the duke said, watching her reaction closely. 'Did you have reason to think that the man would be a kind and generous husband? If he was crafty enough to have taken you away, he had designs on your fortune.'

'Gervaise lacked any craft, I assure you. It was

I who engineered the elopement. And I had no intention of marrying him. Not really. I expected to be caught before we could wed and dragged back in disgrace, which is exactly what happened. Then I would be sent with my sister to rusticate in the country.'

'You said you do not like the country.'

'Not particularly. But the city was intolerable, as long as my father was in it.'

'And you thought, if you had shamed yourself sufficiently...'

'That I could avoid a situation just like this one, where I was forced to marry a man I hardly knew.'

'You wished to avoid me.'

Because it must be about the man and his enormous self-importance. She rolled her eyes. 'I suppose now you will tell me that you are hurt. But you asked for the truth and I gave it to you.'

'Then I will give you truth as well. That seems like a surprisingly stupid and convoluted plan. Much could go wrong.'

'Much did. I was caught, as I expected to be.' And Gervaise had decided that there was no reason to wait for Scotland to assert his conjugal rights. She pushed that particular unpleasantness from her mind. 'But I did not take my sister to the country. She'd met Mr Hendricks, in the few days I'd been away.' She looked into his eyes, wondering how much he understood of her sister's life before her marriage. 'It was far worse for Drusilla here than it ever was for me. It pained me to see her constantly belittled and punished for my mistakes. And I made many, I assure you. I was a wilful child and I could not manage to control my own temper, when listening to his unreasonableness. But she bore the brunt of his anger. Her marriage got her out of this house, which was the thing I'd hoped for all along.'

'You thought, by eloping, that you would help her?'

'I thought that it might be good for both of us. I assumed that she could be chaperon to my disgrace and that we would be sent off together.' She gave a helpless shrug. 'Instead, she was happily married and I have been all but incarcerated, to prevent it happening again.'

'I see,' he said.

'I doubt you do. You are a man and can never

really understand what it means to be so totally under the thumb of another human being. You have freedoms that I cannot even imagine.'

He laughed. It was an empty, bitter sound for a man so normally free of emotion. 'The freedom to walk in a dead man's shoes, you mean.'

'The shoes of a duke,' she said. 'They are hardly a hardship.'

He gave her a disgusted look. 'I came to that position because two men I loved and respected died before their time. And a baby as well. Perhaps, in your family, heartlessness and calculation are the orders of the day, but I would happily trade the title to give any one of them life. And to have my old life back as well.'

Of all the things she'd thought to feel for the man, she had not expected sympathy, or the sudden rush of kinship. She reached out and clasped his hand and felt him start in surprise. There was a moment's awkwardness as they both adjusted to the unexpected contact. Then she said, 'I am sorry for your loss. You are right. I am being selfish again. It must have been quite difficult for you.'

'You as well,' he agreed. 'Having met your

father, I doubt he grieved overlong for the man who held the title before him. Now he is willing to barter you for the small advance that a connection to me might bring.'

He sighed and looked at her. 'Of course, I am not much better. I was willing to take you nearly sight unseen, if it meant the best thing for my own name.'

'Thank you for admitting it,' she said, surprised yet again by his inappropriate candour.

'But now that I've met you, it is something quite different,' he added. 'I wish to know you better and it has nothing to do with your father's name or title.'

She had been waiting a lifetime to hear someone say something just like this. Why, now, must it be this particular man? The undercurrent of fear she felt when she looked at him was still greater than any tender feelings. 'That is very flattering,' she said cautiously.

'But…' he said, placing a finger upon her lips to seal them against further words. 'I already know you so well that I can predict your next words will be an attempt to put me off. So let us stop before we get to the equivocations that

I am sure will follow. Will you admit that you barely know me?' When she made an effort to speak, he added, 'A nod will be sufficient for an answer.'

She nodded.

'And will you agree that sometimes it is possible to change your initial, and might I add totally illogical negative opinion about a person, after further acquaintance?' He saw the militant glare she gave him and clarified, 'You do not need to think of any particular person. I just wish you to admit to the possibility.'

She gave another helpless nod.

He removed his finger from her mouth. 'Then will you allow me a week, or perhaps two, to dance with you, to visit with you, to spend time in your company. If I cannot persuade you in that time, I will admit defeat.'

And in that time, Veronica and Benbridge would grow more and more certain. The inevitable failure would not sit well with them and she would pay the price for it, she was sure. 'But my father—'

'Will not be part of our discussion,' he said firmly. 'In the time we are together, I will keep you safe from the intentions of others, while seeing to it that you are more regularly welcomed in society. If we must part, I will make sure there are no repercussions from your family.' He was glaring again, looking large and dark as a bear. She did not want to think what it would feel like to have that anger directed at her.

But she rather enjoyed the idea that he wished to use it in defence of her. 'What do you expect in exchange?' she asked suspiciously, for she ought to know by now that no gift was ever offered without a cost to be paid later.

'I expect a fair hearing,' he said. 'And that you wear the gift I have offered you when we dance tonight.'

'Tonight?' She shook her head. 'Where is this dancing to take place? I have no outstanding invitations.'

He gave her a grim little smile. 'You will. See to it that you answer in the affirmative. And now, if you will excuse me?' He offered her a low bow and reached for her hand, raising her fingers to his lips. She steadied herself against the kiss she was sure was coming, then relaxed in surprise as she felt the passage of nothing more than a warm breath from the kiss that he had directed to the air just above her knuckles. 'Until tonight?'

It was a question. 'Tonight,' she agreed. She was unsure of what might happen that would make any difference in her feelings, but she was curious enough to want to see it.

Chapter Six

Veronica proclaimed her well turned out for the evening; after admiring herself in the mirror, Priss could almost manage to agree with her. This Season, everything felt wrong. Tonight's gown, a white silk embroidered with dainty sprays of white-and-pink flowers, was complemented by a single strand of pearls and a few pink rose petals in her hair. The effect was lovely and suitable for a girl of her age. In the hazy glow of candlelight she would give an appearance of innocence, but in her heart it felt like some bad joke.

It still stung that she had not managed to procure vouchers for Almack's this Season. Her friends were dancing there tonight. The crowd here was older, married and rather staid. She would have thought it to be just the sort of party that would have Dru in her stead. It made her wonder if there was a better event occurring somewhere nearby.

She chided herself for that brief bitterness and set it aside. This was quite enough for her, she was certain. The champagne was cold, the ballroom glittering and the music lively. And she had to admit, she was enjoying her new gloves. They matched the dress, of course. To others they might appear quite ordinary. But when worn, the soft and supple leather was like a caress from a lover's hands. They felt as she did: normal on the outside, but hiding a sinful nature.

The company did not matter so much, any more. Once the rumour got about that Reighland was interested in her, there would be few men willing to compete with him.

She should be happy, she knew. While he was not to her taste, it could have been much, much worse. He was not old, nor was he particularly unkind. Blunt, perhaps. But she had made several fatal *faux pas* in response and he had adjusted to each of them with barely a rise of his heavy black brows.

'Lady Priscilla.' Once again, the hairs on her neck stood up, as though the sound of his voice was a command to them.

She turned. She dipped her head and curtsied. 'Your Grace. I did not expect to see you there.'

'I can't imagine why not. You know it was I who saw you were invited. Asked the Hendricks to stand down for an evening, so that I might see you in candlelight.'

'I meant standing so close behind me.' And just as she'd been thinking of him. She felt a dull flush of embarrassment creeping behind her ears and stared at the floor. 'Thank you, your Grace. It was most kind of you to procure this invitation.'

He must have heard the reluctance in her voice, for he responded, 'But it was most mannerless of me to mention the fact. Sorry.'

'Apologies are not needed.' Where was her tongue? She should give him the sharp side of it, as she had before. Last year, the *ton* would have laughed along with her, thinking her impertinence to be charming. When had everything changed?

There was another awkward pause and he

took a swallow of wine from the glass he held. 'If I am not in your black books, then you had best learn to look up at me when we talk. While the top of your head is very pretty, I would just as soon see your lovely face. If you can manage it, smile as well. It will be a longer evening than it already is if you mean to spend it frowning at my feet while I insult you.'

To look up would remind her of his size, and of so many other things that she preferred not to think about. But he was right. Opportunities to get out of the house were rare enough and would be rarer still should she behave strangely. She forced her chin up to meet his gaze, summoned what grace she could from deep inside herself and let it flow out in a smile that she knew to be both charming and attractive.

But no longer effortless.

It was returned, from her companion, with little more than a solemn nod. 'Very good. I was told that you were beautiful. But the word hardly does you justice.' At one time, she'd have thought it flattery and responded with a flutter of her fan. But from this man, it was such a plain statement of fact that to react to it would be like blushing at a mention of the weather.

He set his glass aside and offered a hand to lead her to the bottom of the set. 'A dance, then? I imagine we can pull together in harness, for a few simple steps at least. Of course, you will find that I am no dancing master...'

And there was the mention of her elopement again. Was it possible that he meant it as an idle comment? Or was it meant as a joke? Could he not see that her past was no laughing matter?

He either did not notice her awkwardness, or pretended not to, leading her through a few turns and placing a hand upon her back. But the jibe stuck with her as they moved clumsily together. What had Gervaise said, in those stolen moments when he had taught her to waltz? That the movements of the dance were but an echo of the act of love. And remembering how that had gone...

The man beside her, huge and oafish, was all but dragging her through the dance, his big hands on her waist as they turned together. She tried not to imagine him as a lover. On her, over her, in her, labouring over the act as he was over the movements. And the room spun in a way that had nothing to do with the pattern of the dance, tipping uneasily, as though it could throw her off. Suddenly, she was sure that if she stayed here one moment longer, she would be known as the odd girl who became sick in the middle of a crowded ballroom.

She pulled out of his grasp, touching her hand to her face, and glanced up into his shocked eyes, whispering frantically, 'Air.' Then she pulled away from him and ran for the terrace doors, not caring the embarrassment it would bring and the latest *on dit* that would be floating through the *ton* tomorrow. Lady Priscilla Roleston had left the Duke of Reighland standing open mouthed on the dance floor.

Damn.

He had been so eager to see her tonight, surprised to feel such pleasant anticipation at a second chance to speak to her in a single day. He had watched as she entered the room, then reminded himself that this was not meant to be a love match and that he did not exactly wish for one. The Duke of Reighland could not afford the highs and lows of hope and despair that mere mortals experienced. It was difficult to keep track of the doings in the House and at Court, and with his many tenants and properties, without wandering after some girl like a mooncalf.

There might be passion, of course. She was a damn fine-looking girl, just as he'd been told. And she was wearing the gloves he'd bought her on her slender pink arms. He could imagine himself, peeling them off again, kissing every inch of exposed skin. But that feeling could not possibly last. She was at least interesting to talk to, although she had some very odd ideas.

She did not ride, he told himself firmly, trying to quell the eagerness. He could change that in time, he hoped. But if her aversion to horses proved deeper than her aversion to him, he would have to accept failure and withdraw his offer.

But after what he had just done, she would have to hate horses near to death to equal what she must feel for him. Why had he been foolish enough to bring up the matter of the dancing master yet again? He had meant it as a joke.

It was a year in the past and truly insignificant to him.

But for her it was a fresh hurt and each outing in society a foray into enemy territory. She would have to grow used to the comments, if she was ever to overcome them, just as he had. To let the taunts roll off her back, to make a joke of herself when no other way would work, and to grow tall, to grow strong…

And that advice would be quite useless. Ladies did not solve their problems on the fields of Eton, but then neither had he. He'd run for the country the first chance he'd had. If he had been a disappointment to his father, that good man had never said so, but he had been a scholar and had encouraged circumspection over foolish displays of bravado.

There would be no running from trouble now and no father to advise him. He and Priss would both have to stick it out and ignore the sidelong glances and harsh words. If the aloof Benbridge was any indication, she must have been bred to believe that others did not matter. Why could she not behave so now?

He went to the refreshment table to fetch her

a lemonade. Then he thought the better of it and stepped behind a potted palm to dump half the cup away and top it off with brandy from his flask.

Next he went to the verandah, where she waited, staring morosely off into the darkness.

He pressed the cup into her hands. 'Drink.'

She took the first sip and choked. 'Whatever did you do to this? It is foul.'

'That is at least half spirits. You seemed in need of more fortification than lemonade would give.'

She took a deep breath and drank half of it down in a gulp. 'Do you mean to take advantage of me, then? For I believe we've established that alcohol will not be necessary.' She gave a harsh laugh. 'Between my loose morals, my stupidity and my father's desire that I entrap you, you might do just as you wished with me and I would welcome the indignity.'

Had other men tried? he wondered. Or had her father encouraged it? She seemed bitter and fragile, and very much alone. He chose his next words carefully. 'Do I mean to take advantage of you? You are a tempting morsel, I must admit. If the opportunity presents itself I would not turn it down. But it will not be tonight. Let us sit for a moment, then we will return to the ballroom, the best of friends.'

'Why do you bother,' she asked, 'if you think so little of me?'

'I do not think less of you. But I fear you think less of yourself. I spoke poorly, just now. But it frustrates me that you worry so about what others say, now that it is too late to change things. You are who you are. Others may take that, or leave it alone.'

'That is an utterly male way to think,' she said, as though it were some kind of fault. 'And a rich and titled male at that. They are the only sort that could walk away from past mistakes and let the world be damned for caring.'

'Perhaps,' he admitted, wishing it were true. 'I have a vague knowledge of the rules of female society. But I cannot say I care much about them. Am I being far too obtuse if I suggest that you limit your concern to the opinions of those people that truly matter?' *As though she would ever count him in that category.*

He took a breath and reminded himself that,

since his accession to the title, he had no reason to worry. 'My opinion should matter, for instance. I think well of you. The others are unimportant.'

'And that is exactly what I do not understand,' she said, staring up at him. 'I need to know... why.'

'Why?' he asked.

'Why you are doing this?' She shook her head in confusion. 'The dancing and flirting, the attention to my needs. Why are you *courting* me?' Her voice dropped on the last word, as though it was something shocking or scandalous.

'Am I courting you?' he asked, with mock innocence.

'It appears that you are.'

'So my behaviour cannot be construed as kindness or friendship.'

She gave him a tired look. 'The last I checked, it is London at the height of the Season. You are an eligible duke. There is little kindness or friendship to go around.'

'Perhaps I am attracted to your refreshingly honest nature.'

'Or my father's title. I understand the reasons

for your offer. They are purely political and none of my concern.'

He thought for a moment. 'No. I do not think that is it. As you have pointed out to me, I would hardly need to waste my time on you to curry favour with him. I have but to vote as he does and that should be enough. It is he who is attempting to curry favour with me.'

'True,' she said, making a sour face as she sipped at the cup he had given her.

'And I am willing to allow it, as long as it does not impinge on my own goals or desires.'

'Which makes you sound little better than my father. It gives me no reason to think that my life will be any better than it has been. It does not explain to me why, after all I have told you, that your goals or desires include me, particularly.'

'I should think that would be obvious. You are attractive and good company.'

'I am not trying to be,' she admitted.

'And that is why I enjoy being with you.' He glanced back towards the ballroom. 'The other girls I have met in recent months try far too hard. It is clear that they give no thought at all to whether we might suit in any way other than that I am Reighland. They are willing to bend themselves into knots if it will get my attention.' He looked down at her again. 'You, at least, have spine enough to speak the truth. Further investigation is necessary.'

'So in trying to put you off, I have done the thing most likely to draw you in.'

'Exactly.'

'And I suppose I cannot suddenly turn agreeable.'

'I would think it a double blind,' he said. 'And I would continue to press my suit. Or I would assume that my charm had finally won you over and it would increase my ardour.'

She could not help herself and laughed at the idea that he might possess anything like winning charm.

He stared past her, out into the garden, and smiled in relief. 'You ask why I court you, Lady Priscilla. Then I will tell you. There are damn few people here with the courage to laugh in my presence. Even fewer who would dare to respond when I was joking at my own expense. In you? I see something. You will pretend it is not there. But you show hints of a most admirable courage. It may disappoint me that you cannot display it in your own defence, but I admire it all the same.'

'Thank you.' Her response was the barest of whispers.

'It is a lovely night, is it not?' He fell back on banal small talk to fill the awkward silence.

'Yes,' she agreed.

'Stars,' he said, making a vague gesture toward the sky.

'Yes.'

'A fresh breeze.'

She inhaled and nodded.

'And a beautiful woman.'

She faltered. Then managed another, 'Thank you.' Her voice was a little stronger, but she continued to look straight forwards, out into the darkness.

'A kiss would not be inappropriate,' he suggested. 'Between a couple on the verge of a commitment.'

'Are we on such a precipice?' she asked.

'We could be,' he admitted. He waited for the usual arguments. She did not wish to be married to anyone, least of all to him. But if they did marry, there was little point in pretending that this was anything other than inevitable. The Duke of Reighland wished it and her father had agreed. It would be done. Why must he dress it up as something that it was not: a normal court-ship with moonlight, and soft sighing breezes?

If she did, he would answer that some part of him longed desperately for that pretence. He might have been an ordinary suitor, full of sweet words and flattery. He would have lured her here to steal what he was about to take by right. And she would be feeling the anticipatory fluttering inside, the excitement of a single, stolen kiss. There would be no dashed expectations, no fear, no disillusion. Just the sure belief that every moment would be as sweet as this one.

Next to him, she closed her eyes and turned towards him, waiting woodenly for the kiss that would break the spell and return them both to the truth.

He reached for her and ran the pad of his thumb over her mouth, wishing that it might be as soft as she was. He had never felt anything so delicate in his life. He brushed as lightly as he could against the firmly set lower lip, feeling it part from its mate ever so slightly. He caught his breath as he felt the tiny, almost accidental kiss on the tip of his finger. He slid it lower to rest against the line of her jaw. And then, at last, he leaned forwards and let his lips touch hers, soft, warm, just wet enough to show the life in them. Through his own barely open lips, he could taste the brandy he had given her and feel the gentlest touch of her tongue against his.

Time passed. He measured it by each breath they shared. But he dared not move. He rested against her mouth, not as an invader, but as though he were a sleeping part of her own body. It made him think of lying by her side, late at night, drifting into dream with the firm press of her against him, anchoring him like a ship that had come to harbour.

And then he drew away, slowly as he had come, closing his lips and pushing off from hers with the faintest increase of pressure, before his hand dropped away.

She opened her eyes, blinking once, as if she was trying to clear her mind of what had happened.

Somewhere in him, he felt sadness that she

would be eager to forget something so utterly perfect as that moment had been.

He had kissed before.

And this was different.

It lacked the sense that all of his other kisses had, of being an immediate prelude to something else. While that type of kiss was certainly exciting, it came with the knowledge that he must keep a bit of himself apart, revelling in the physical release while leaving his heart untouched. But with Priscilla, for the first time, he had opened himself totally to another person and revealed a vulnerability that no peer could admit to having.

And she was smiling at him, as though nothing had happened. How dare she dismiss him in this way?

He readied a retort.

Then he looked into her eyes and saw that she was as shaken as he by what had happened. She might not admit it, but he had won her with a single kiss. All the rest would be formality and pretence.

He returned a smile as false as the one she gave him, for it would anger her if he revealed the triumph he felt. 'Shall we return to the ball-room, Lady Priscilla? If you allow me, I will escort you to supper. I understand that the food here is mediocre and my conversation is rumoured to be quite dull. It will be just the thing to settle your nerves.'

Chapter Seven

That night Priss awoke in a cold sweat. She had been dreaming about the night in the inn, when everything had gone wrong. She had to get hold of herself. It was clear that these little spells of unease were growing worse and not better with the possibility of a large and virile fiancé.

She owed Reighland more of an explanation than she was giving him, that was for certain. He had done nothing to deserve her distaste of him. Since he showed no sign of ceasing his pursuit of her, she might end by fainting dead away in front of the altar if she did not tell him the truth and put an end to this.

Until his arrival, she'd at least managed to banish any demons from the daylight. But in sleep her mind always seemed to turn a situation that had been merely unpleasant into an actual nightmare. It annoyed her. It was unfair to Gervaise to twist things around to make some sort of villain out of him, when it had been she who had orchestrated the events of their elopement. She was willing to pay the price for her recklessness with well-deserved social ostracism.

But Gervaise had been no better or worse than she'd expected and she would do well to reiterate the actual events to herself to banish any nonsense.

On the first night they'd stopped, after leaving London for Gretna Green, he had taken only one room for them. She had nervously suggested that two might be better. But he had said, quite bluntly, 'You were the one who wished to run away and be married. You must have known what that would mean. Scotland is only a day or two off. In my mind, we are practically married now.'

Practically married was quite different than legally married. Still, if she wished to have any say in the matter of her own future, she must learn to stand by her decisions, even if she had begun to suspect that they were wrong. If she wanted to be stopped before the border, it would be better that they dawdled. She would be ruined no matter what went on in the bed tonight. She might as well satisfy her curiosity as to what actual ruination entailed.

'Very well, then,' she said. 'One room. And we shall share the bed.' She thought it would make him smile. He had been quite free with his humour when they'd been still in London. But now he was smiling to please himself, making no effort to put her at her ease.

Once the door was closed, he wasted little time. He kissed her. It was not like the gentle little busses he had given, when they'd stolen time together in the ballroom. He simply put his tongue on her lips and pushed it into her mouth.

She withdrew. 'What are you doing?'

'That, Priss, is how married people kiss. I thought that you knew that, at least.'

'Oh.' She stood still and let him do it again. He was moving around in her mouth and she assumed that she was supposed to do something similar. She tried. He seemed to like it, though she could not quite seem to understand what the bother was. It was nice, she supposed. But not much more than that.

And then, with no further preamble, he had thrust a hand down her bodice and squeezed her breast. She was used to the sly touches he managed sometimes, when they danced. There had been the gentlest brushes of his hands over her bodice, under the guise of adjusting her posture when teaching a new step. Then there had been hurried and false apologies, accompanied by the blinding smile, to make sure she noticed what he had done.

Those touches had left her trembling, almost too weak in the knees to go on with her lesson. She had been sure, no matter what was likely to happen on this trip, that there would be more exciting moments such as that.

But now he was kneading her, as though she were an insensate lump of dough, and grunting with pleasure.

'Gervaise,' she said, 'more gently, please...' Or at least she tried to say. For he could not seem to let her have the use of her own tongue to speak. When he did stop the kiss long enough for her to object, he hardly looked her in the eye.

'Too rough? It's because the gown is in the way. So let's see them, then. Off with it.' He seemed most annoyed that she fumbled with the closures, for she was not accustomed to dressing without the help of a maid. At last, tired of waiting, he spun her around and did the job himself with such speed that she feared he would split a seam.

But he lied. He was no more gentle with the gown hanging about her waist than he was before. Now, he could use his teeth on her. A few minutes after that, he had pushed up her skirts and dropped the front of his breeches…

She had lain in bed afterwards, with him snoring beside her, wondering about what had just happened was worthy of song or poetry. It had been short and painful; it had hardly seemed that she was involved in it at all.

She could not even tell herself that it was the pain of the first time. When Gervaise awoke, it was much the same. It had gone on in that way for three days at each stop they'd made, until she'd managed to lock the door of the room before he could enter. He'd complained bitterly about the unfairness of it. But she'd shouted back at him that he had no right to upbraid her, that he was lucky to have had as much as he had and that, no matter what had happened, she would not marry him now if he was the last man on earth.

She had wished then that she could go back to Drusilla and demand an explanation, or at least some reassurance that it would get better with time. But when she had run away, Silly had known even less about the physical aspects of love than she did and would do no more than give her a scold and drag her back to London.

Instead, the Drusilla who'd found her had been starry eyed with love. She had seen the kisses that her older sister had shared with Mr Hendricks and known that there was poetry in love somewhere. But apparently it had not been meant for her.

Now everyone assumed that she was to belong to the Duke of Reighland. She had never met a soul more devoid of music in her life.

Until tonight's kiss, at least. He had been understanding about her flight from the dance floor. The stolen moments in the garden had been the sweetest that she had ever spent. Even now, the gentleness of the single kiss managed to quiet her heart, which was still beating hard from the exertions of the dream.

Without being able to help herself, she was drawn to Reighland. There were a hundred ways it would not work, of course. He was too close to her father. He was too powerful. He might seem gentle, but so had Gervaise, at first. Things would change the moment they were truly alone.

She rolled and punched at the pillow, trying to find some cool place where she could lay her head and rest. The Duke of Reighland might not love her, though he at least appeared to be fond of her.

But that would not overcome the very obvious fact that she did not think, no matter how gently he treated her, that she could face performing the marital act again. If it had been bad with Gervaise, then what would it be like with this hulking stranger? Tenderness would not make him any smaller. And if he chose to be a vigorous lover?

Her palms curled in on themselves and she squeezed until she felt the pain of her nails, imagining herself clutching the bed sheet as he pummelled her, wishing the image were in any way erotic, so that she might trick herself into believing she wanted this. No matter what he would do, it would hurt her. And he would want it again and again, for the rest of her life.

Until such time as he grew bored with her, anyway. Then he would take away the pain and the pleasure as well. He would take away his gentle understanding, his dry jokes and his sweet kisses, and spend them on some other woman.

She stared at the ceiling and willed herself to sleep. Her last thought before the dreams returned was that the end of any physical pain Reighland might cause would be unequal to the agony of loss that might follow.

Chapter Eight

This could be yours.

It was impossible not to think it at least once upon seeing such a house. Once she'd admitted to it, she could rest easy and think no more about it for the rest of the evening.

Priscilla surveyed the foyer of Reighland's London home, the paintings on the walls, the thickness of the hall carpet and the perfection of the ballroom, with a critical eye, exercising her covetousness like an atrophied muscle. It all could be hers, if she married him. But she did not really wish to marry any man simply to gain control of his house. If she had learned nothing in the last months of seclusion, it was her ability to do without.

He had probably hoped to inspire just such a

reaction by inviting her here. She had suspicions that this rather grand event had been organised so that she would visit his home and admire his wealth. He'd made no mention of a rout when they had been alone at the ball three days ago. But the invitation had arrived the next morning with the first post. She expected he had kept some poor servants up half the night gathering guest lists and scratching out addresses to meet his impulsive demand. In response, it appeared that half of London had cleared its schedule and called for a carriage.

But now Reighland was pushing his way through the crowd towards them, holding out a welcoming hand. 'Benbridge, Lady Benbridge, welcome. And Lady Priscilla, of course.' He was favouring her with a rare smile, which did nothing to diminish his intimidating nature.

'Your Grace.' She made a polite curtsy, then let her mind wander from the exchange of greetings, talk of the weather and of politics.

Reighland broke off suddenly, as though sensing her lack of enthusiasm. 'But my talking nonsense with your father can hardly be of interest to you, Priss.'

The slight to Papa made her flinch, as did the use of her nickname. She had given him no permission to use it, but she could not very well object to it in front of Ronnie. It was clear that the rest of her party would accept any familiarities foisted upon her with enthusiasm. 'It is all right, your Grace. Pray, do not let me interrupt your conversation.'

'No, it is not. I would never forgive myself if your first visit to my home was less than enjoyable. If you will excuse me, Benbridge, I will escort your daughter around the room. I am sure that I have some delicacy here that will tempt her.'

'She would be honoured,' Veronica said firmly, before Priss could think of a plausible objection. 'And we would be happy to relinquish her. Come, Benbridge. We must not monopolise our host.'

Father allowed himself to be led off with only a token objection, proof that he was as complicit in the illusion as Veronica. Once again, she was alone with Reighland—or as alone as one might be in a packed ballroom. But considering her precarious position in society, that sometimes felt quite alone indeed. Now Reighland was smiling down at her like a child presented with a new toy.

She returned a jaundiced stare. 'So, what are these temptations you speak of? Or was it merely a ruse to spare yourself my father's company?'

He dipped his head, as though it was possible to talk intimately with a voice that boomed as his did. 'If I made up lies to spare myself the company of everyone I find tiresome, I suspect that I would speak no truth for the rest of the evening. Come, I have prepared a treat for you.'

'Not another lemonade with brandy, I hope,' she said.

'Not unless you wish it,' he said. 'Hopefully, now that I am proving myself to be no threat to you, we will not have to resort to such fortifications.'

She glanced at the refreshment table, which was as perfectly done as the rest of the room. 'I am not interested in prawns or sweetmeats, either. Perhaps, if you had somewhere quiet that I might sit…' she gave him a firm look '…in privacy. I fear I have a bit of a megrim.'

'Really?' He gave her an equally firm look. 'Is

that the best you can do to put me off? Threats of a headache will not work with me, I assure you. If you will look around, you might discover the entertainment I have provided.'

She could not think what he meant. The music was lovely, but no different than many other parties. The women were the same tiresome crowd that she saw wherever she went. And no gentleman would dare encroach on her space if she was to be perpetually set upon by Reighland.

Then the crowd parted and she saw what he must mean. Her brother-in-law was chatting amiably with a man on the other side of the room. She tried to appear unmoved while searching the room for any sign of her sister. But even a sight of Mr Hendricks was a treat so rare that she could barely contain her surprise.

Reighland, ever observant man that he was, noticed the change in her and said, taking a sip of his drink, 'John Hendricks is in attendance tonight, if you desire to speak with him. I understand you have a family connection.'

'He is family,' she admitted, 'but I am discouraged from talking to him.'

'How unfortunate,' Reighland said, giving her

a curious look. 'I had hoped that you would have a chance to converse. He seemed eager to speak with you. But if you are not so disposed...'

'No,' she said hurriedly. 'I have no difficulty with him. But Father did not approve of Dru's marriage. He will be livid when he realises that they are in attendance.' She felt the skin tense at the back of her neck, as though her body was bracing for a confrontation.

'I expect he will,' Reighland said nonchalantly. 'If his opinion mattered to me, I would have given him the guest list to approve. I arranged this for your benefit. Does it please you?'

Please her? Her heart was galloping. How did he know, on such a limited acquaintance, that this visit was more precious than jewels? She stared hungrily across the room at Mr Hendricks. If she could manage it, she would have time enough to apologise to him for the first and only impression she'd been able to give. He must think her a wilful, selfish fool after the way she'd behaved on the road to Scotland.

If she could gain his attention for a few moments, before Father and Veronica realised what she was about and forced her to leave, there might be some little, precious time. 'It pleases me very much,' she said, trying not to show the extent of her elation as her mind raced to think of all the things she wished to say and to ask.

'Your sister would be here as well, but she was indisposed.'

Indisposed to see her, perhaps? Or her father. Priss's spirits fell a little. Perhaps she could get Hendricks to reveal the truth and take some message back to Silly. But the fact that she could talk to him at all would be a special treat. 'I understand.'

'There will be other opportunities to see her,' Reighland added, as though it were the most natural thing in the world to force her father to associate with the working class. 'Do not fear Benbridge's reaction. He would not dare confront me in my own home on my associations. Even if he did, I doubt it would matter. I am quite enjoying Hendricks's company. He is a dashed clever fellow and I prefer a quick wit to an old title. I fear, if you take me, you shall have to put up with my quirks on that.'

'I will?' As though it would matter to her. 'If you were expecting a scold from me, your Grace,

I will disappoint you as well. I would most like to see more of Mr Hendricks.' Without meaning to, she smiled at him as though he were a favoured suitor who had rewarded her with such flattery as to be worthy of distinction.

Surprisingly, when confronted with the full force of her carefully nurtured beauty, the duke blushed. It made her colour as well. In her months of reclusion, she had forgotten how to flirt. In days past, she would have cooled his heat with a snap of her fan, perhaps catching the eye of some other swain with a fickle comment. Then she'd have led the pair of them a merry dance for the rest of the evening, playing one against the other.

Instead, she stood before a pink-faced Reighland with a silly smile on her face and they stared at each other as though there was no one else in the room. She dropped her eyes and fumbled with her reticule. He searched the room, catching Mr Hendricks's eye and signalling him to come. 'And here he is.' He looked relieved as he made the introduction. 'John, so good to see you again. Of course you know my guest of honour?'

'I do indeed, your Grace.' Mr Hendricks bowed and gave a subtle half-turn of his body that closed their little conversational circle off from the rest of the room. 'Lady Priscilla?'

She reached out and clasped his hand, feeling him start against the sudden contact. 'It is so good to see you, Mr Hendricks. So very, very good. Tell me, my sister, is she well?'

'Unfortunately, no. She is ill this evening.' He did not glance at Benbridge, or show any disapproval of her that might demonstrate it was a lie, but then he was the most subtle of creatures. He would not have admitted to anything so rude as a harsh truth.

Reighland turned suddenly and then looked back at them with a warning smile. 'Perhaps the two of you would like to continue this conversation in the card room or in some out-of-the-way spot. I see another guest who deserves my attention.' Then he turned and said with false jollity, 'Benbridge! A moment of your time.'

Dear, sweet Robert had foreseen the problem with her father and was giving her time before action could be taken that would part her from her prize. She seized Hendricks by the arm and did her best to propel him in the opposite direction. 'A turn about the room, Mr Hendricks? I feel a sudden need for fresh air.'

'I suspect you do,' said Hendricks, regaining his calm. 'And how is your father, Lady Priscilla?'

'Much the same, sir.'

'How unfortunate for you.'

'But tell me of Silly. Drusilla, I mean,' she said, abandoning the childish nickname for her sister. 'It is nothing serious that keeps her at home, I hope.'

'A passing indisposition, I am sure.'

'Be honest with me, Mr Hendricks. Father's presence here was not the thing that upset her, was it? Or mine?' She added the last a bit more quietly, afraid of the answer.

Hendricks laid his hand on hers, in an awkward show of sympathy. 'Not at all, Lady Priscilla. She is truly ill. And very disappointed to be at home tonight. She misses you terribly.'

'And I her. Your words are a balm to me, Mr Hendricks. The house is quite empty without her.' She looked away hurriedly and fluttered her fan. 'Not that I do not wish her to be happy, sir.

And she is happy with you, I am sure. She looks much better than she did at home. Softer, somehow. She smiles more. I have seen her about town, even though Veronica does not allow me to speak to her.'

'Ahh, yes. The new Countess of Benbridge,' Mr Hendricks said with a knowing smile. 'What is she like? We have not been permitted an introduction, you know.'

Priss burned with shame at being on the wrong side of this foolish argument. 'You are not missing much, sir. She is well suited to my father, I think. Grasping, ambitious and full of her own importance. And very eager to secure her place in the household, before Father comes to his senses. You can tell my sister it is probable we will have a brother before the year is out.'

'My felicitations to her,' he said. 'And to you as well.'

'Me?'

'On your impending nuptials. The *ton* can talk of nothing else.'

'If you are speaking of Reighland, it is not set in stone, just yet,' she said. 'I barely know his Grace.'

Hendricks laughed. 'He said much the same of you, only a few days ago. He is a very cautious man.'

'He does not seem so to me,' she said, risking a moment of honesty. 'He is pursuing me most shamelessly.'

'That is because he is smitten with you,' Hendricks said.

Smitten. Of all the possible reactions from a suitor chosen by her father, she had not expected that one. 'You must be mistaken.'

'On the contrary. He has spoken to me about you. I am afraid you have made a conquest.'

He had spoken to Reighland. Dear God, what secrets had they shared with each other? Between her admission to the duke, and Hendricks's knowledge of the past, she wanted to sink through the floor. 'It was never my intention to snare him. But he is most persistent.'

'And you have been honest with him,' Hendricks said, admitting his knowledge without saying another word. 'That was kind of you, I think.'

'He deserves the truth, if nothing else.'

'He is surprisingly tender-hearted, despite his rank and appearance.'

Was Hendricks warning her not to break poor Reighland's heart? The idea was so outrageous it made her laugh. 'I will do my best to let him down gently, then. I do not think we will suit.'

'You do not?' Hendricks seemed genuinely surprised. 'I am sure your father would say otherwise. Personally, I could not imagine a better catch for you.'

'But from what you know of me, given a little time, you could imagine a better catch for him, I am sure.'

'I would never—'

She cut off his objection. 'Without the family connection, you would not be so kind, sir. There are many other girls, some of them here tonight, who are my equals or superiors in birth and more proper and agreeable as well. It would content me to see him married to any of them and for Father to cease his scheming and let me retire to country spinsterhood.'

'You would not have to do that, even if the duke does not take you. There are other men, I am sure...'

'And I do not want any of them,' she said with a sigh. 'You know me. Better than you would like to, I'm sure. I am willing to admit that I am not fit to be the wife of a worthy man. There is sufficient money for me to cede the field and live quietly alone. Is it really such an unrealistic demand?'

Mr Hendricks looked worried and adjusted his spectacles, as though it might help him to see what she was seeing. 'It is a very sensible idea. And I would encourage it, if it were not my wife's sister suggesting it.' He patted her hand again. 'Dru would rather see you settled nearby. Away from your father's influence, but close enough so that you might visit.'

'Dru has always wanted more for me than I deserved,' she said simply. 'Tell her not to worry. Whatever happens, I am sure I shall be fine. If I can manage to get Father to send me away as I wish, then I shall certainly write to her often. But for now, I do not think we should risk my father's displeasure any more than is necessary. I would hate to think that Benbridge tried to make difficulties for the two of you, because of my carelessness.'

Hendricks gave her a curious look, followed by a nod of approval. 'You must not worry on our account, Lady Priscilla. My position in society is secure, even if your father attempts to discredit it. But I thank you for your concern and will relay the message to your sister. We shall meet again soon, I am sure, and you will be able to tell her yourself. And here is Reighland again.' They had completed a circuit of the room and he was offering her arm to the duke as though she were some precious item that he had been allowed to borrow for only the briefest time.

'No, really…I would prefer…'

Hendricks shook his head. 'I think the duke wishes to speak to you again. And should your father wish to speak to you, it might be better that he have a few moments to collect his temper.'

'That is probably true,' she said with a sigh. Truly, it was not so bad to be with Reighland. He had shown unusual foresight in arranging this party for her. The least she could do was be grateful.

Robert congratulated himself on a job well done. He had arranged this meeting on little more than a hunch. But the smile Priscilla had given him when she'd spied Hendricks was of such brilliance that he could not believe there was no meaning in it. Now she was standing before him, a veritable blushing flower of devotion, looking up at him with those enormous blue eyes and saying, 'I wish there were some way to show you how much such a kindness meant to me.'

'Do you, now?' Surely, it could not be this easy.

When he had thought to marry, he had imagined it to be an arduous process of coaxing some passionless virgin out of her clothes and into his bed. But here was a girl who was not only lovely, but who had some basic understanding of what her beauty did to a man. And tonight she was smiling at him as she never had before. It seemed they had reached an understanding.

He meant to marry her, of course. What harm could there be in allowing her to express her gratitude? 'I have not shown you the house yet,' he said, doing his best to add a hidden meaning to the words. 'Would you do me the honour?' He gestured towards the door.

She gave one doubtful look in that direction, as though to acknowledge how improper it would be to go off alone in the middle of the party. But after that token of modest resistance, she gave a single, graceful nod of acquiescence.

A brief tour of his home would not hurt to sway her further in his favour. It was magnificent, with wide marble stairs running up the middle in an elegant curve and a series of hallways leading off to various receiving rooms, studies and salons. It had impressed him when he had first seen it. He'd stood in the gilt-ceilinged foyer, momentarily stunned that it was now his. While Benbridge's town house was grand, Reighland's London residence was spectacular.

How could any woman resist it?

Of course, he could barely remember to speak about it as they walked, so much was he enjoying the company he was with. He did not even notice how far they had come from the people gathered in the ballroom until he realised that he could hear the echo of his footsteps on the polished wood of the floor over the distant sound of voices.

They need go no further than this for what he had in mind. It was perfect, really. They were all alone. Her skin, which was near to flawless in the best of light, glowed like a pearl in the illumination of the single candle that had been left to make for easy passage of servants while discouraging strangers from straying.

He had never been the sort of man to be easily moved by a pretty face. Well, perhaps never was too strong a word. He had watched such girls be won by young men who were wittier, handsome and more at ease in their own skins. And he had decided that his own inevitable disappointment was not worth the brief pleasure the pursuit might bring.

But things had changed, now that he'd met Priss.

She glanced over her shoulder and the same light that had touched her skin made her curls glow gold. 'Where are you taking me?'

'I am trying to get you alone, of course,' he said, surprised that she needed to ask. 'You are almost twenty-one, are you not? By now I should think that other gentlemen have tried such tricks on you. If they have not, then London lads must be surprisingly stupid.'

She gave a weak laugh. 'Last year, perhaps. I have learned to be more circumspect with my reputation. We had best be returning, before we are missed.'

'In a little while,' he agreed. 'But first, I wish to receive the thanks that you were offering in the ballroom.'

He tugged on her arm, pulling her through a doorway and into a darkened parlour, shutting the door behind them.

'I meant for a verbal thank you, only,' she said, with a breathless giggle.

'Or a polite note?' He was close enough so that he could smell the wine and strawberries on her breath and feel her curls tickling his chin. His body quickened in response.

'I did not mean any more than that,' she said again, placing her hands against his chest to add distance between them. But she did not push him away. Instead, she rested them there as though trying to choose between a shove or a caress.

He stayed still. If he waited, time and moonlight would tip the balance in his favour. 'And if I wanted more?'

'Then I fear you shall be disappointed.'

'A kiss?'

'I would prefer not.' It was a prim little statement, totally at odds with the soft mouth that uttered it.

'You allowed one on the verandah, when last we met,' he coaxed.

'I do not think you mean to kiss me quite in the same way,' she said, 'if you need to lure me so far from the others.'

'I think you are probably right,' he agreed, dipping his head to nuzzle her ear.

'And I think that is probably unwise,' she said again. But she was leaning in to him as she said it, putting up the sort of token resistance that any lady would. *You do not have to be shy with me,* he thought. *Not now. Not ever.*

'Oh, yes. I should think it very unwise.' He traced the line of her jaw with his tongue and felt her tense, then relax with a sigh.

He tipped his head to the side, hesitating for a moment before his lips touched hers. This must be perfect, if nothing else in his life was. And it would be harder than he had thought, simply because he was.

Hard.

She was a sweet thing, sweeter than he had ever expected to have for himself. All the sweeter for the tartness on her tongue when she talked to him. She smelled like French lilacs after a spring rain, rich and yet subtle and full of memory. He wanted to crush her body against his face, take her into his mouth, roll in her.

There would be time for that. All the time in the world. So he counted out three of his own heartbeats before moving again, touching gently, lip to lip.

Another three beats and he ran the tip of his tongue along the seam of her lips, following the downward curve of her frown.

Not yet, then.

There was a dimple on her cheek and he focused his attention on it, brushing it with his mouth until it relaxed as she smiled.

Better.

He slipped to her ear again, breathing against it, sucking the lobe into his mouth and aching as he thought of the lips to her sex. She gasped.

Was she sensitive there, or was she reading his mind? He tugged at it with his teeth and heard another gasp. Her mouth was open, then. He could take it, if he wanted.

And he did want.

Too soon, he reminded himself.

He kissed her throat, trailing down the cord in it until he had reached her shoulder blade, dipping his tongue into the hollows along the way. Then he drew back, for it would be too tempting to go lower, deeper, to lick his way down the rest of her body.

She was panting now, panting for his kiss. He pressed open mouth to open mouth breathing with her, stroking her hair with his hand. Her tongue fluttered at his lower lip. He touched it with his own.

She touched back. She licked gently at his teeth and he felt a moment's triumph. She was trying to arouse him. As if that was necessary. He caught the tip between his teeth and drew her tongue into his mouth, urging her to learn him.

Then he returned the favour. Her mouth felt ripe, kissable, and he nipped harder to brand it with his attentions. Anyone who looked at her would know what she had done and who she had been with.

She did not fight against it. Instead, she moaned and pressed her body closer to his, as though eager to be claimed by him.

The nearness of her filled him with a reckless pleasure he had longed for when Reighland was a thing on some distant horizon and no part of his life. If this goddess would have him at all, it would be for himself and not the title she disdained. When he was with her, he would be nothing more than a man and she nothing less than a woman. They would spend nights, wrapped in each other, laughing and loving. It would take the cold sting out of the days of endless duty. She would be a blessing on his life.

And he would give himself to her, give her pleasure. Give her children or jewels. Or both. He would give her anything she wanted, if only she would give of herself.

She was a fragile little thing, like a tiny bird in his hands. He must remember to be gentle. He brought one hand up to cup her breast and used the other to bend her back in his arms, half a dip, half a swoon. Then he kissed her senseless, pressing her hips to his with the firm hand that held her low along her back.

This was right. They joined where they were meant to, hip to hip, hard to soft. They could not do more. Not here.

But why not? It was his house, she would be his bride.

'Unhand me this moment, you beast,' she whispered, turning her head and pressing a hand against his throat.

He laughed. 'A beast, am I? I swear I was tame as a lamb, before kissing you. But now I will show you just how wild you have made me.'

His knees bent, taking her with him to the floor.

'No,' she said, a little desperately. But even as she refused him, a part of her seemed to revel in his attention. She was leaning backwards, away from him, as though trying to escape. But her hands were twined in the lapels of his coat drawing him down with her. 'No,' she whispered again, but she spread her legs as he lay on top of her.

'You need not worry,' he said, lowering his mouth to her breasts. 'We will be married soon enough. No one will know if you give in to me now.' He was inching her skirt upwards now, one hand on the flap of his trousers.

'No.' She struggled weakly under him. 'No. Please. Do not.'

He paused, fingers splayed on her bare hip. 'Do not pretend to hate me, Priss. I saw the way you toyed with me in the ballroom. It does not do to play the outraged virgin when you kiss like a courtesan.' He grinned at her so that she would know he was only teasing. 'I am so hard for you I can barely think. Now spread your legs for me and lie still for just a moment.'

Suddenly she was fighting for all she was worth, scratching at his face. He dodged the clawed hand just in time before her nails could lay a bloody trail on his cheek and covered her mouth with his hand to stop the scream that would bring the house down upon them. 'What the devil? Priss. Calm down.' He eased his body off hers, pulling his hand cautiously away so that it could grip her arm. She gasped, staring wild eyed at him as though she did not know him. For a moment, there was no sign of the willing woman he had kissed just moments ago. Then she took in a great breath and calm began to return.

'Talk to me, Priss,' he urged, wishing he could hold her close until the fear had fully passed. Instead he withdrew his hands from her shoulders, giving her space. 'Tell me what is the matter.'

'There is nothing the matter,' she said, pushing her skirt back down her legs. 'As long as you do not do what you were attempting, I will be fine. I cannot bear to be touched in that way.'

He rocked back on his heels, confused. 'And I can think of little else when I'm with you. We have a problem, do we not?'

She laughed bitterly. 'You say 'We' in such an easy, natural way, as though this means anything at all to you.' She wrapped her arms tight around her own body as though his touch had chilled her to the bone; the distance it created between them made him ache. 'I have not agreed to marry you, no matter what my father might have told you. Yet you think I will give myself cheaply on the parlour floor, just because I was foolish enough to do it for another.'

'I never thought that,' he argued. 'I do not want anything less for you than to be my duchess.'

'And I cannot be that for you. No matter how much I—' Her lips sealed suddenly, tight, and she watched him, frightened and stricken.

'What, Priss? Finish what you were about to say.' She had been going to say she wanted it. He was sure.

'It is nothing.'

'I do not care. Tell me any way.' For just a moment, her expression had changed, softening and sorrowful. Then she had looked away from him so that he might think her hard and unwilling. But the brief hesitation gave him reason to hope.

She took a breath and framed her words carefully, so that they might seem impersonal. 'No matter how much I enjoy your company, and how much I appreciate what you are trying to do in separating me from my father and reacquainting me with the rest of my family, I cannot lie with you. I cannot even bear to think of the act. What kind of a wife would I be, to you or any man, if I cannot do that thing?'

'It is not me particularly that frightens you, then. Any man would have the same response?'

She gave a hesitant shake of her head.

'You are afraid of me.' He was shocked. Confused. And perhaps just the slightest bit angry. How could she be afraid of him? When had he ever done anything to deserve that? In his heart, he knew, of course. He was no longer the careless boy he had been. He had been kind to her and very careful, but she sensed the brutality in him and feared it.

But why had she kept it from him? 'When did you mean to tell me of this?' he asked sternly. 'You denied me from the first moment we met. I thought you were only being coy with me. What reason would you have, otherwise? I swear I have done no wrong to you.'

'I had hoped that you would lose interest if I gave you no encouragement,' she said.

'If you did not mean to encourage me, then why did you allow me to bring you here?'

'You were being so kind to me,' she said, clearly confused herself. 'And tonight I thought perhaps when the time came, my fondness for you would make it possible to bear the pain of the violation.'

'Pain?' He released her arms, suddenly unsure.

He could not have been hurting her. When had he been less than gentle? 'It is only the first time that is painful, Priscilla. And much as I might regret it, that moment for you has passed.'

'But it was the second time and the third as well,' she insisted.

He had not wanted to think of her fall as being less than a momentary and regrettable lapse. Clearly, it had been more than that, yet she had not enjoyed it. Jealousy and sympathy warred within him. 'Did you tell your lover of the trouble?' Concern for her won out and he leaned forwards, wanting to comfort her, but seeing her shrink from his touch.

'I tried. But he said that I should lie still, spread my legs and be quiet.'

Robert swore, forgetting the company he was in and the fact that she already feared him. He took a deep breath and sought to mend the mistake. 'I apologise for my actions and my words. I behaved no better to you, using almost the same words to gain your compliance. When I meet the fellow who hurt you, I will kill him. He has taught you to think all men are animals. And I am behaving no better than one.'

'No, please.' She forgot herself and gripped his arm. 'Do not think to hurt Gervaise. He is not worth that.'

'And you are,' Robert said, enjoying the thrill it gave him to feel her leaning upon him.

'But it was all my fault,' she said, closing her eyes. He could see the sleepless shadows under them and put a tentative hand on her waist so that she might draw closer and rest her head on his shoulder. 'And again, tonight. If I had shown sense and refused to come away with you...'

She looked ready to cry. Without thinking of how it might frighten her, he pulled her close in a hug, doing his best to keep the gesture innocent. 'It is not your fault. None of this was. While I might say your charms are irresistible, you notice that I was able to master myself when you refused me. Only a clumsy and unskilled lover would have continued, knowing the lady was in pain. I promise you, with another man, it will be different. With me, for example.' He tried to keep the offer casual, lest she think he expected an immediate recommencing of activity.

For a moment, she almost seemed persuaded, relaxing in his arms and letting him support her.

Then she shook her head and pulled away from him. 'It will be worse.'

'I beg your pardon.' It was a most unwelcome sentiment from a woman he cared about. And unjust as well. There had been no previous complaints about his lovemaking. But it did not seem proper to tell her so. 'Explain yourself immediately.'

'Perhaps it is because I come to you with too much knowledge,' she muttered, turning pink and clearly embarrassed to even explain the problem. 'And perhaps you are right and the fault was Gervaise's. But the thing is…' She glanced down, and hurriedly away. 'Gervaise is shorter than you. And slimmer.' She paused significantly. 'And quite probably smaller in other ways as well. If that did not work, then how…?'

He rocked back on his heels again and laughed so long and so hard that he had to reach into his pocket for a handkerchief to wipe his eyes.

The door to the room opened suddenly and John Hendricks was staring down at them in disapproval. 'What the devil are you on about, Reighland? Priscilla, come away from him immediately.'

She gave a little yelp of embarrassment and moved to rise. But before she could Robert dropped a hand heavily upon her shoulder. 'Do not move a muscle, Priss.' He gave Hendricks his iciest, most Reighland-like stare. 'As you can see, nothing untoward is occurring. We are sitting here, having a harmless conversation.' It was a bald-faced lie. He was sitting like a tailor upon the floor, with a fading erection, and his lady love was leaning back against a wall. Though her skirts were properly arranged to hide her legs, she appeared to have escaped a vigorous tumbling by the narrowest margin. If Hendricks had arrived a few moments earlier…

But he hadn't. Robert held his gaze, unwilling to admit wrongdoing.

Hendricks gave him a narrow-eyed glare. 'Then you must continue the conversation in the main room, for the sake of the lady's reputation.'

'The lady's reputation is perfectly safe with me,' Robert said, smiling. 'It is not as if you will need to force me to marry her, should someone hear of this. I will do so gladly, the minute she will have me. But there are some matters that we must settle, in private, before I return her to the party. If you would allow us a few more moments alone, I would be most grateful.' Then he looked up at her brother-in-law, with as much contrition and sincerity as he could manage.

After taking a split second to decide, Hendricks said, 'Only a few minutes, mind. I will be loitering at the end of the hall to ensure that you are not disturbed. But I will stay close enough that I might come if I am called.' This was directed to Priscilla, who, thank the gods, made no effort to refute his story.

'Sit on the furniture and not the floor,' Hendricks added. 'There is little point in having the stuff if you don't mean to use it. I will give you five minutes. Then it is back to the dance floor for the pair of you. Have a care, Reighland. Dru will have my head if any harm comes to her sister.'

'Thank you.'

The door closed behind him.

Robert stared at her in silence for a few moments, giving Hendricks the time to retreat. Then he reached out and took her hand with a smile and helped her to a divan, taking the seat beside her. 'Your assessment of my…umm…attributes is flattering, Lady Priscilla. But while a young lady who is still quite innocent might see certain things as a detriment, most others I have been with considered them an asset.'

For all her supposed wickedness, the idea that women might find pleasure with a large member seemed to surprise her and her eyes went wide. 'If other women like that, then that is the sort you must choose, I fear. I do not think I am the best wife for you.'

'On the contrary. I think that it is more a matter of changing your mind on certain subjects than it is about adjusting my choice. I have no intention of giving you up over...an accident in biology. If you would be willing to meet with me again in private, I think, at the very least, I will be able to free you of what is likely to be a debilitating fear of the unknown.'

'Are you seriously suggesting that we...?'

'Postpone the remainder of this conversation until tomorrow,' he finished. 'Tonight, we will enjoy the food and the dancing and each other's company. You will not worry your beautiful head about what happened in the past. It is a lovely evening. It would be a shame to waste it in fear or recrimination.'

'But tomorrow?' The poor girl was still looking at him as though she expected, at any moment, he might unbutton and display his wedding tackle.

He sighed, wondering if his manners were really as rakish as all that. He had been hasty in his approach. But by his soul, he'd never expected her to be shy on this of all subjects. 'Tomorrow, you will come to my rooms and we will talk,' he said at last. 'Whatever happens, there will be no pain. No fear. I promise. Perhaps we will only use the time to discuss your future, with or without me.'

'All right,' she said, very quietly. 'We will do as you suggest.'

'Very good.' He stood then and reached out a hand to her, almost lifting her back on to her feet with his strength. Then, very gently, he wiped a stray lock of hair from her face and said, 'This is what comes from stealing kisses in dark corners. I have quite disarranged your curls. No matter. We will make it worth the trouble.' Then, very sweetly, he kissed her upon her closed lips.

He made sure the gesture was perfection in its innocence. She did not pull away, though she coloured for him again. But this time it was the barest hint of pink in the dim light, as though she had been pleasantly surprised. He walked her from the room and handed her to Hendricks, that he might be the one to escort her to the lady's retiring room to recompose herself.

When he saw her later, it was to take her arm and escort her into dinner. Later in the evening, when Charlotte Davering attempted to cut her dead, he was there with a glass of champagne, offering an easy misdirection so that the slight failed miserably. He danced every waltz with her, holding her at a respectful distance, all the while making clear that he had a claim upon her.

And when it was time to part, he raised her hand to his lips and whispered, 'Until tomorrow?'

If it had been a command, she would have run. She would have refused and that would have been the end of it. But he'd made sure it was a question imbued with all the hope growing in his heart.

Only after he heard the breathless 'Yes' did he allow himself so much as a kiss on her gloved knuckles.

Chapter Nine

Priss walked through the marble archway of Reighland's foyer, a mixture of trepidation and relief. Father had been furious to discover Mr Hendricks at the previous evening's party, nearly angry enough to embarrass himself by snubbing the duke. But Priss had underestimated the hold that Ronnie had over him and that woman's eagerness to get an unwanted stepdaughter out from under their roof. Benbridge's feathers had been smoothed, the evening had continued without incident and Mr Hendricks had made a strategic retreat, quitting the party after he'd rescued her from the embarrassing incident on the salon floor.

It had not been his place to protect her honour. She had a father and stepmother who should have been seeing to that. But that same step-mother greeted the idea of today's unchaperoned trip to Reighland's with an emotion near to glee, eager to offer what was left of her honour up so that the peer could do what he liked with it.

Reighland had promised not to hurt her, she reminded herself firmly. But she had little doubt that today's meeting would end with her on her back, as Reighland attempted to demonstrate that the marital act could be performed success-fully. She meant to allow it, if only to show him the error of his ways.

It was a shame, really. Under other circum-stances she might have enjoyed his company. His manners were rather odd, as were his looks. But he had a gentle soul, for all that. And he had been kind to her. His kisses so far had been both pleasant and disturbing. When she thought of them, as she had for most of the night, her emo-tions became a tangle of fear and pleasure, leav-ing her without sleep but also without nightmare. She was tired now. Tired of his courting and Ronnie's continual curiosity about it. And tired as well of the anticipation of impending disaster.

At least, after today, it would be over.

The house was even more spectacular than it had been by candlelight, though she did her best not to notice. She walked at a stately pace, looking neither here nor there at the height of the ceilings, the richness of the hangings or the art upon the walls. The lack of chaperon would be reason for the servants to gossip, without her gawking at the house as though trying to set the right price on her attentions.

She allowed herself to be shown to the same salon that she had visited the previous night. Reighland awaited her there. The servant announced her and withdrew. They were alone again.

Silence fell and she tried not to look down at the carpet to find the exact spot where they had struggled. She was a lady, after all. It was not the sort of thing that deserved acknowledgement. Though she had to admit, in daylight it was a fine rug.

Reighland was looking his usual somber self in a black coat and a pensive expression. If he was pleased to see her again, he managed to conceal it well enough. Though there was nothing lecherous or avaricious about his behaviour, she could not manage to bring herself to smile for him.

He bowed. 'Are you feeling well this morning, Lady Priscilla?'

'After my behaviour last night?' she said, embarrassed to be reminded of it.

He gave her a non-committal shrug. 'Any young lady would be given to such a display, considering the circumstances.'

'At least you did not have to force brandy upon me to calm my nerves.'

'I would do it again, if required,' he said. 'But today I am hoping that tea will suffice. The things are laid before us. Will you pour, please?' Reighland took a seat on the sofa and looked up at her.

She frowned. It was quite rude of him. He should have made sure she was seated and sent for a servant to handle the tea things. But she was so tense that she doubted she'd have taken a seat if he offered. At least preparing their cups would give her something to do with her hands other than wringing them nervously and awaiting the inevitable.

She ignored the place at his side and took a

chair opposite, taking up the pot and pouring out his tea on the little table between them.

'Keeping your distance?' he asked and she saw the edge of his lips twitching in a smile.

'After last night, I think it is wise, don't you? Do you take sugar, your Grace?'

'If I were truly interested in tea, then, yes, I take sugar in it.'

She handed him the cup and looked directly into his eyes. 'And just what is it that you are interested in, your Grace?' *Come now, Reighland. Put your cards upon the table. You are making me so nervous that I can barely stand it.*

He took the cup she was offering, then set it down on the table. 'Firstly, I wish to apologise for my behaviour. I will not say it was uncalled for. If ever a mouth was made to be kissed, I am sure it is yours. But I proceeded with undue haste.'

'Your apology is accepted, of course,' she said without looking at him. 'As I said last night, it is I who should apologise to you. I was the one who went off with you, down a darkened corridor. After I'd told you of my past, what else were you to think of me?'

'You are entirely too hard on yourself,' he said, picking up the cup and taking a sip, before setting it back down again. 'Let us call it a simple misunderstanding, between friends, and leave it at that.' He patted the upholstery at his side. 'There is room enough for you here.'

She ignored it. 'I would not wish to crowd you.'

'It is what I wish,' he said, patting the seat again firmly so she would know that it was a command. 'As I explained last night, it is time that you lost your fear of me. It is groundless, I assure you.'

She sighed and rose, crossed to his side and sat. But it seemed that the nearer she was to him, the smaller she felt. She shrank against the opposite arm, putting as much distance between them on the divan as she could.

He gave her a critical look. 'Why are you so reluctant to sit beside me?'

'I merely preferred the other seat,' she said.

'And now you are lying to me. After I told you that your honesty was your most appealing characteristic, I am most disappointed in you.'

'I do not like to be touched,' she reminded him.

'As you said last night. But I am not touching you now,' he pointed out as gently as possible. 'Your continued resistance does not bode well for us. If we are to be married, I mean to touch you.'

'And I am not one of your horses, willing to submit tamely to your demands,' she snapped back.

'If you were, I'd have thrown a saddle on you by now,' he agreed. 'I am being as patient as I can manage. It is not as if I mean to practise the marital act upon you, along with my tea.'

If that was not his intention, than why was she here at all? 'You are always most adamant that we meet alone,' she reminded him. 'And everyone seems so convinced that I will disgrace myself again to cement the bargain. I am sure, even now, Veronica is hoping that you are doing just that.'

'Then damn Lady Benbridge, and her husband as well, for making this more difficult than it needs to be,' he barked with surprising vehemence. Then he looked back to her and gentled his tone. 'I have not yet taken advantage of the solitude, have I?'

'No, you have not taken advantage. In daytime, at least.' Each agreement with him felt like a lost battle. But this one at least made her smile.

A thought suddenly occurred to him. 'Perhaps it is time I started.' Before she could question him, he reached to the floor and scooped her two feet up and into his lap.

'What are you doing?' The sudden action made her tea cup rattle and she spilled a bit on the saucer. But the length of her legs maintained the distance between them and he stayed where he was, making no effort to close the gap.

'Nothing that need worry you,' he said. 'You will notice that while I am touching you, it is an extremity that keeps the maximum distance between us.'

'Stop it this instant.' She struggled, but he kept a firm grasp on her ankles.

'You do not know what I am attempting, yet.'

'But I am sure that I will not like it.'

'You are quite sure of what you like and dislike, aren't you?' he said. 'You understand that horses are not born knowing they will be ridden.'

'Yes,' she said. 'But as I informed you before, I am not a horse.'

'True. But you must understand that I would not ride a horse before I knew every inch of the animal. And that would be a sound way to treat a wife as well. You notice I am not pawing at your bodice, or forcing kisses upon you. I am only touching your feet.' He gave a tug on her ankle. 'You do not have to lock your legs together at the knee. I have no intention of reaching up your gown.'

She was working to control her unsteady breathing and gave a twitch of her skirt to make sure that her legs and ankles were properly covered. 'They are still a part of my body. And if they are so remote from the areas that interest you, I do not understand why you would bother with them.'

'They interest me because they are a part of you.' He reached out and pulled her slippers off, one by one, and tossed them over the back of the couch. She did her best to ignore the sudden shock of her feet coming in closer contact with a much more intimate portion of his anatomy. Then she stilled herself, knowing that continued struggling was likely to result in just the sort of inflammation of feeling that frightened her.

'In my experience,' he went on, as though there was nothing out of the ordinary with her taking tea with her feet in a gentleman's lap, 'feet can be quite sensitive. A light massaging might be pleasant in ways that you have not yet experienced. And you need not worry,' he added. 'I mean to limit my contact with you to areas below the ankle.' Then he stroked her insteps and laid his palm flat against the soles, measuring their length against his hand.

'You are quite mad,' she said with a nervous clearing of the throat and took a sip of tea.

'Possibly,' he muttered and traced the curves of her feet with a few firm passes of his fingers. 'But I am doing you no harm, am I?'

'That is not the problem,' she said. It wasn't painful. He was right in that, at least. But it certainly was not relaxing. Her voice sounded strange and tight, and her stays felt the same way. Though she knew the need for it, she could not seem to keep her legs still. She tried to draw her feet up under her skirt, but he kept a firm grasp on them until she relaxed again with a sigh.

'That is better,' he said softly. 'I ask no more

than that you let me give you pleasure.' He ran the tip of a finger back and forth from heel to toe.

She wished he had chosen any other turn of phrase, for it made her think of the sorts of feelings that she had experienced late at night, when she was quite alone and had discovered the exquisite sensitivity of her own body. The places she felt his touch now were far away from the soles of her feet. She concentrated on the feel of the cup in her hand, smooth, hard and growing cold. It was much safer to think of that than the soft, hot, wet feelings in the rest of her body.

'Priscilla,' Reighland said her name sharply, as though trying to wake her from a doze. 'Attend me when I am talking to you.'

She opened her eyes, surprised to find that she had closed them. His touch was growing more insistent and it made her forget where she was as her mind drifted to dark, intimate places. She pressed her lower lip with her teeth to bring back some semblance of reason. 'Yes, Reighland?'

'I asked you, if you had nothing to lose by it, would you do me the honour of relaxing in my presence? Could you take pleasure in my company?'

'Yes.' It was a sigh, as though the word had been torn from her, and she was not sure if she'd meant it as answer to his question, or as a response to the movement of his hand upon her arch.

'Very good,' he responded. 'You will forgive me for saying it, but you are behaving like a skittish mare. You must learn to accept my touch, for I will not walk you down the aisle, only to find at the end of the night that you cannot bear to lie with me. I have the succession to think of. It would be beyond foolish to bind myself to a woman who could not abide my company, no matter how well placed her father is.'

A moment ago he had been promising to do nothing. Now he was talking of marriage and succession, and all the while his hands stroked her feet, leaving her hopelessly confused. 'Either you mean to have me, or you don't,' she said, shifting uneasily on the cushions. 'Decide and be done with it.'

He laughed quietly. 'You have too much experience and still no knowledge of the subject.

But then, you had an extremely inept teacher. Let me put it plainly. If we are to be married, then I will have you, either before or after the ceremony. More likely it will be both. But what happens between us will happen because you wish it to be so. And it will not happen today.'

'Then stop talking about it,' she said, sagging back against the arm of the divan.

Reighland laughed as his hands circled her feet again, the thumbs rubbing firmly up and down the insteps, as though he was marking the time, waiting for some sort of answer from her. But she could think of nothing more to add, so she remained silent. If he was silent as well, then she needn't think of ways to parry his arguments. She let her head roll back against the cushions and closed her eyes again, wishing she was back in her room and these gentle touches were part of some pleasant dream. One where nothing more need come of it than to enjoy the moment, with no response on her part required. She felt the relaxation travelling up her body until it was a struggle to keep her knees tightly together.

But struggle she did, for that would be far too much like an invitation. The firm stroking felt too good and the heat was pooling in strange places throughout her body. That was what he had wanted, she was sure. He wanted her to respond.

At last she gave into it, arching her back to feel her breasts pressing against the front of her dress. He tugged at her toes, until the special place between her legs was wet and tingling. He pressed her feet down into his lap to show that he was affected as well. And the knowledge that she was cradled against his aroused body sent her tea cup clattering to the rug. 'Reighland,' she said with a gasp, sure that he would break his word, but not nearly as frightened as she had been. 'You are the very devil.'

'You think that, do you?' He pinched her little toe and she gasped again. 'You must be a wicked little sinner, then, to be so easily tempted by me.'

Then she began to feel the subtle tugging on her stockings. He was trying to pull them down her legs. In a moment, those supposedly innocent hands would begin to creep upwards to scrabble at her garters. Then there would be the sudden push that parted her knees, and the thrusting fingers that sought to soothe the way for invasion. She started upright and ready to fight against him.

The tugging stopped and she relaxed enough to realise that his hands still rested on her heels. 'Did I not tell you that it was not to be the way you fear?'

She opened her eyes, wondering if she'd spoken her thoughts aloud, still unsure of what she was to say.

'I can tell you are worried,' he said patiently, still not moving. 'I read your mind in the tension of your body, the look on your face.'

'I am sorry,' she said. 'I cannot help what I feel.'

'It must be very difficult for you,' he agreed, 'to feel so frightened.

'Not really,' she said. 'As long as I avoid such intimacies as this, it is not an issue.'

'But that would mean you would never be touched,' he said softly. 'And never loved. It will be safe, of course. But very lonely.'

God, yes. She was so lonely. When she lay down at night, she had taken to pleasuring herself to ease the aching fear.

She could feel one of her stockings beginning

to sag, as it slipped from beneath her garter. She tensed, waiting. But she felt nothing but the slow drag of the silk down the length of her leg, like a long soft kiss. Then, he began to gather it, drawing it down and off her foot.

When nothing more happened, she released a little of her fear in a sudden shudder of pleasure. He paused again and the tension in her body built. 'But if you do not mean…then…why?'

'Why this?' He pulled the stocking the rest of the way off, rolled it and tucked it into his pocket. 'To prove that I can, I suppose. And to prove to you that the world will not end if I touch your body. No harm has come to you, has it?'

She thought. 'Well, no.'

'You are experiencing no discomfort?' His fingers were now running along the bare flesh of her foot. And without meaning to, she wiggled her toes. It tickled.

He sensed her response and changed the pressure, tracing light patterns with his fingers on the sole of her foot.

She took a deep breath and dug her fingers into the upholstery to keep from touching herself. 'No, I am not experiencing discomfort.'

He began to tug on her other stocking. 'Then I shall take the other from you as well. And put them in the dresser of your room.'

She straightened and pulled away. The suddenness of her movement achieved his ends more completely than he could have, for the stocking came free and pooled in his hands. 'How dare you. You are certainly not invited to come to my room.'

He gave the final tug that freed it from her body and stuffed it in his pocket with its mate. 'Pardon me, Lady Priscilla. I meant the room which shall be yours, when I make you my duchess. You will find it is large and most generously appointed. If there is anything you wish, other than a place for your stockings, please let me know. I will be happy to provide it.'

It had been a foolish overreaction on her part, and she was almost tempted to apologise. But then she remembered that she was sitting with her feet in the lap of the Duke of Reighland as he talked of innocence and stripped the clothing from her body.

And now his fingers could touch her bare toes, separating them and stroking the tender flesh between. The slow thrusts made her forget her fear and press back against his hands and his body. Her womb clenched and, as though he could feel the change in her, the movement of his fingers increased.

'This is nonsense,' she said, as though she could dismiss the feeling.

'But you like it, do you not?' He was raising the foot very slowly and she could feel the breeze on her legs as her skirt slipped up her calf. But as she stared up at him, he made no effort to look beneath it, keeping his eyes focused on hers. And then he touched his tongue to one of her toes and bit down gently upon it.

The resulting climax took her unawares, making her whole body shake. The sensitive bud between her legs exploded with sensation. Her toes clamped together around the thickness of the thumb cradled between them. She imagined him resting snugly in her body and rode the waves of pleasure the image created.

The tremors subsided, leaving her embarrassed but sated. And she realised what she had been doing: rubbing the other foot shamelessly against his lap, trying to arouse him to break his promise.

But he was looking down at her with an expression that could best be described as bemused. 'You may act as though you know it all, my dear. But I could teach you that you are sorely mistaken.'

'That will not be necessary.' Although perhaps, if they were anything like what she had just experienced, a few lessons from him would not go amiss.

'You are sure? Because I am eager to oblige you.'

She lifted her free foot out of his lap and set it firmly on the floor. 'No, thank you.'

'Very well, then. I suppose you should be going soon or people will hear of the visit and wonder what we have been up to. But if you will allow me a farewell kiss...' His fingers circled her ankle and he lifted it to his lips, fixing them upon the little knob of bone there.

And a shock of feeling seemed to rush up her body from that point. She felt lips and tongue, and—oh, God—his teeth, rasping against it. Her nipples tightened and there was another wash of delight that left her limp and gasping on the sofa, hands clasping furiously against the cushions. Dear Lord help her, it had been twice in as many minutes. If the duke chose to press his advantage over her and take the sort of liberties she'd expected, she would be powerless to resist.

She bent her knees quickly, yanking her foot from his grasp and putting it on the floor with its mate, giving a quick snap at her skirts so they fell back into place to cover her legs. 'Give my stockings back. Immediately.'

'No.' He was smiling at her again, as though he knew exactly what had occurred. 'As I told you before, they will wait in my house until you are ready to retrieve them.'

She tucked her feet back under her skirts. 'I cannot go about without them. Someone might see.'

'Put your shoes on and be quiet about it. If you do not act as though anything is out of the ordinary, no one will notice.' He stared down at the floor. 'Although I would hardly blame a man for looking. You have a well-turned pair of ankles, I must say.'

'It is rude of you to comment on the fact.'

Now he grinned. 'Hardly the rudest thing I have done in my life. I fear you will have to bear with much, when we are married. At school, it seemed I was always saying the wrong thing at the wrong time. The other boys encouraged it and made me the butt of every joke. Of course, it was more amusing to them than it was to me.' He winced in recollection. 'Many a schoolmaster tried to cane manners into me, but as you can see, it did little good.'

He said it lightly enough, but there was something hidden, a shadow behind that carefully guarded smile that made her wonder if Mr Hendricks was right about Reighland's tender side. 'Were you punished for fighting with them?'

'Lord, no.' He looked at her earnestly. 'I was broken of that bad habit long before I was sent off to school. I was always large for my age, you see. And clumsy. I tended to squash butterflies rather than catch them.' He shifted nervously. 'And there was one unfortunate incident with a little friend. All boys play rough. And I did not mean to hurt him. But it took six weeks in bed to mend his broken arm.' He said it hurriedly, as though it was a difficult moment that needed to be got through. 'I was quite young,' he added. 'You needn't fear me. I have learned to be very careful with living things. You must have noticed that I dance like a daisy-cutting horse that cannot pick up its hooves. When we wed, you will lose more than the usual amount of crockery to my accidents. But it will be no worse than that.' He was staring at her, his expression curiously vulnerable, and she could almost see the boy who had cried over his injured playmate. But then she saw the toe of one of her stockings was peeping out of his pocket.

'You have been most gentle with me,' she assured him. 'I know I have nothing to fear.' Even if she did, she would do her best to master it, for his sake.

'That is good to know,' he said, clearly relieved. 'I am sure that most of London still thinks of me as the hulking idiot whom they used to tease.'

'They would not dare to embarrass you now,' she reminded him softly.

'Because I can mask my bad manners with rank. And that does seem to be the only thing that matters to some people, does it not?' He glanced up and past her, at the door to the hall. And she wondered was he thinking of her father?

'Yes,' she said simply. 'It is.'

'But I have learned to bear it with good grace,' he said with a smile. 'Words and gossip do not hurt. And duelling and brawling over every slight would be far too dangerous for those around me.'

'Really,' she said, unsure of what to make of this latest insight into his character.

'You will take me in hand, once we are married, and smooth my rough character.' There was nothing at all guarded in the cheerful optimism she saw in him at the thought of marriage to her. Of all people. And to her surprise, she had to bite her tongue to keep from offering to take him in hand, right here in the parlour. After the pains she had taken to explain her problems, she was liable to undo it all with reckless words and a moment's overconfidence in his gentle nature.

But Reighland did not seem to notice her distress. He stood up and walked to the back of the sofa, where he had thrown her slippers. He retrieved them and came back to her, kneeling at her feet and reaching for them.

To see him there, beneath her, gave a curious tug at her insides, as though the sight of him willingly humbled should mean anything at all to her. She gingerly put a toe out from beneath the hem of her skirt.

In response, he lifted her foot again, cradling it as he slipped the shoe back on. Then he repeated it with the other. When it was through, he did not immediately get to his feet, but waited there, as though expecting some response from her.

'Thank you,' she said, biting back the urge to dismiss him like a servant. Today, his displays of devotion were making her feel more guilty than frightened. It seemed the less he asked of her, the more she felt obligated to give him.

'Will you be attending the Tremaines' ball tomorrow evening?' he asked politely.

'I think that is between you and my father. I have no say in my social schedule. But if you require my presence, I will not be permitted to refuse.'

If he was as fond of the truth as he claimed,

the statement should not have bothered him. But his expression darkened and, for a moment, she expected an angry retort. Then he mastered himself, rose from the floor and took his place beside her on the sofa. 'I would prefer a wife willing to admit that she welcomed my company.'

It was petty of her to refuse him that, when it was clear to them both how she felt about him. But he had tricked her into having those feelings. It was hardly fair. 'You wished me to smooth your manners? Then you should cease upbraiding me for presenting the facts as I see them. If you and Father wish me to go to the Tremaines', then I will do as I am told. Why must you have more from me, when you are getting your way in this?'

He snorted in disgust. 'I understand why you let someone else make your decisions. You have done poorly in the past and do not wish the responsibility. But at least you might think of me as a man who means to choose for himself what is right, without the guidance of society or politics. If I decide to have you, it will be because I think we suit and not for other reasons, do you understand?'

'Not really,' she said. He was the duke again, not some soft-hearted little boy who needed her love.

'You will have to take me at my word, then. Until I can convince you, of course. And I mean to be quite persuasive.'

She swallowed nervously, trying to imagine what he might do that was any more persuasive than what he had already done.

He stood and offered her a hand, helping her to her feet. But her legs were still weak from pleasure and she tipped alarmingly in his direction.

Without a word, his arm came out to steady her, wrapping around her waist to pull her close.

She could not find it in herself to resist, but instead let her body melt easily into his. He was big and warm and solid against her, comforting and arousing all at once. She did not want to lose this feeling, to go home where everyone was cold and censorious. She wanted to stay here and be held.

But to do that would mean… 'Reighland?' she said softly.

'Yes?'

'I enjoy your company.'

'Until tomorrow night?' he asked, as though nothing unusual had just happened. But he was smiling.

She pulled away from him, straightened her gown and glanced at herself in the mirror, trying to pretend that nothing had changed for her, either. Despite the turmoil that raged within her, not a hair was out of place. And although she had never intended to be happy, her reflection told another tale. She was smiling as well. 'Until tomorrow night,' she agreed.

Chapter Ten

Monsieur G. has returned to London after a prolonged absence. He will likely have a certain lady hopping to his tune, though lately she has been leading the Duke of R. on a merry dance.

Robert fingered the bit of newsprint in his hand, then threw it into the fire. He'd seen the comment already, in the morning paper, and hardly needed a second copy, delivered anonymously by post. The purpose behind it was quite clear: someone wished to expose Priscilla to ridicule and to anger him sufficiently to part from her.

That they'd made doubly sure that he could not miss the scrap of gossip angered him almost more than the thing itself. It was not enough that they bandied his name about in the news. But

it seemed they felt the need to explain the significance of it, as though he could not read for
himself. They were making him feel slow and
stupid, just as they always had.

But who were they? He reminded himself
firmly that if he could not manage to put a name
to the persons bothering him, then their opinion
hardly mattered. Receiving the little notice was
embarrassing, he could hardly say otherwise.
But he must remember it would be far worse for
Priscilla. And there was probably nothing to it.
The fact that this Gervaise fellow was once more
in a city of over a million meant nothing to him,
nor should it mean anything to her.

Other than bad memories, of course. He understood the power that those might have. But
his were little more than childhood nonsense and
hers were quite different. Priss had been near
to panic the first time they'd danced and again
when he'd tried to make love to her. Robert was
still not sure if any man her father had chosen
would have received a similar reaction, or if her
fear of him was out of the ordinary.

But he was quite sure that she was not attempting to frighten him away so that she could run

back into the arms of her first lover. She'd given him no reason to think that she remembered Gervaise with anything less than contempt. If there was anything to this ugly little bit of news, she would certainly tell him. She had been honest enough about the subject before. It was that very honesty that had drawn him to her in the first place. And if she still wanted to lose him, there could be no quicker way than to admit that she preferred another.

He would ask her when he saw her tonight and see what she had to say on the subject. Then he'd ask her if she still 'enjoyed his company'. From any other woman he'd have thought it faint praise. But Priscilla had purred it at him, as if it had some other meaning entirely. Though he'd have preferred her to call him by his Christian name after what had gone on in the salon, she pronounced his title in a way that made him think Reighland was a very lucky fellow indeed to have won such a lady.

Robert grinned into the fire and poked the last of the paper to ashes. She was not ready to say that she loved him. But when she did, it would be the truth. And having heard her version of the elopement, he would waste no more thought on anonymous gossip. But one thing was certain: if he caught Monsieur G. in London and lost his temper, the *ton* would see how fast Gervaise could dance on two broken legs.

'There is a package for you with the post,' said her father, dropping a brown-paper bundle beside Priss's breakfast plate on the way to his own chair.

She carefully slid the packet over the corner of exposed newspaper peeking from beneath her napkin. Ronnie had waved the paper in front of her with an angry rattle of pages, then ripped out the offending page and passed it to her, before her father might see it.

Monsieur G. As if he was entitled to such a continental title. When they had been alone together, he had lost all trace of a French accent. But that had been but one small point amongst many greater disillusionments and hardly worth mentioning. Whatever his nationality, why was he back in London? And why had anyone noticed the fact?

Most importantly, what did it mean to her? She

had no desire to see him again. But the knowledge that Reighland might notice the comment and connect it to her was suddenly too much to be borne. She had warned him that she was not an acceptable choice. But now that she was beginning to suspect that, just perhaps, she might have been wrong, Gervaise was back and the old scandal would be raised again.

She quietly slipped the paper off the table, into her lap and under her napkin, rolling it into a ball and tucking it into the pocket of her gown.

'Well, what is it, then?'

'Nothing, Papa,' she said hurriedly.

'How can you be sure until you have opened it?'

The package. She had been so distracted that she'd already forgotten it. Whatever it was, the contents were a surprise for she had expected no deliveries. It was not her birthday, nor any other holiday or anniversary that she could think of that might explain a gift. But considering the shock she'd already received, she could imagine several other horrible possibilities. Had she offered Gervaise a token of some kind? And would he be foolish enough to taunt her with it now?

She tore cautiously at the corner of the paper, trying to pretend that she was not as worried as she felt to be presented with both a shock and a mystery, first thing in the morning.

Then she had a brief glimpse of the items contained within before dropping her napkin over it and slamming her hand over the top in her haste to obscure the view.

Her father and stepmother looked up from their food, surprised. 'Do you mean to explain yourself?' her father said gruffly.

'It is from Reighland,' Priss said, swallowing to ease the sudden dryness in her throat. She had been lucky to make it home on the previous day without inciting comment about what had occurred while she was with the duke. Though in the evening, her maid had noticed the suspicious absence in her wardrobe and made no mention other than a sly smile.

'What did he send you, then?' her father said, without looking up. 'Not much of a romantic if he ships a necklace to you in the morning post. But then I do not expect much of the man.'

Her stepmother was watching her closely, with the avaricious glare of a magpie.

'It is personal,' Priss managed, her hand frozen on the top of the package as though she could squash it into invisibility.

Veronica managed to look both disappointed and curious. 'It is rather large to be a billet-doux.'

Priss seized on the idea and ran with it. 'I believe it is a book of poetry. Possibly of his own making. I will read some to you, if you wish.'

'Thank you, no.' Veronica laughed. 'I expect it is quite awful. What talent could a horse trader possibly have in such things?'

Even if her story had been true, she felt a stab of sympathy for the eagerness with which the others at the table were willing to hold the Duke of Reighland up for sport. She drew herself up to what little height she had and in her most haughty voice announced, 'It would be embarrassing for both him and myself to display such an intimate gift for the amusement of others. In fact, I suspect he thought that I would be alone when I opened this particular package. If you will excuse me, I will take it up to my room.' She stood without removing the napkin, scooped both it and the package up, and clutched them firmly to her bosom, before rising and hurrying from the room.

What had possessed Reighland to do something as foolish as this? Had he not suspected the position he might leave her in, or had he not bothered to think at all? Or had the idea of discovery not bothered him? Suppose someone had seen and enquired?

Life here was miserable enough without bringing down the further scrutiny of her father or his meddling wife. Ronnie would have found a way to turn the whole thing into some sort of inappropriate comment while complimenting her on her ingenuity. And her father would demand an immediate marriage between them.

For the thousandth time she missed her sister. Silly would have disapproved, of course, but she'd have stopped the problem before it started. Had she not, she would have been there to shield her little sister, rather than making her the butt of some cruel joke. She would have sorted out what was to be done about the item in the newspaper. Then, perhaps, she could have helped to explain the mixed feelings in her heart, whenever she thought of the duke.

Yesterday's visit had confused her. When she'd arrived at his house, she'd been frightened and wishing she could forget the invitation he had given. The night before, he had purposely suggested the visit in the presence of Veronica, knowing that the woman would not allow her to refuse. But by the end of it, Priss would have been quite content to remain longer. For ever, perhaps. It had been a struggle to get herself back through her own front door. And it'd had nothing to do with the need to walk slowly so that her bare ankles were not seen.

Now, when she was sure the door to her room was definitely closed and not even her maid was within sight, she ripped the rest of the paper from the package and dropped the wrappings into the grate. The contents had almost slithered from their bindings, draping elegantly over her hand.

Silk stockings. She'd worn them often enough, when dressing for a ball. But nothing as fine as these. These might as well have been knitted by spiders, they were so sheer and soft. They were clocked at the ankle with a delicate trail of hearts and flowers, and tied up with a blue silk ribbon was a note: *To replace that which you lost. Wear them and think of me.*

Of all the audacity. She had a good mind to go to him immediately to explain that it would be improper to think of him in any such way. And even more improper for him to suggest that she do it. But lord knew what might happen if she saw him now.

Yesterday, she had meant to keep him at arm's length, to take a single cup with him and be gone again. And in less than an hour she had been writhing in ecstasy as he nibbled her toes.

It made no sense. Other than that it must indicate a flaw in her character, of course. She was fairly sure that she would do something far worse if he were to come upon her while she was handling the scraps of silk he had just given her.

Think of him, indeed. As though she had been able to think of anything else, for all the time they had been apart. Even now she was imagining him taking hold of her bare leg and talking some nonsense about horses while he pulled the hose up her legs, fingers lingering over the tying of garters as she moaned and climaxed. She had never in her life given herself over so completely into the hands of another, nor been so rewarded for her trust. With a few touches, he had reduced her to putty and watched dispassionately as she'd cried out, shuddered and collapsed. And then, just as he had promised, it had been over. She'd lost nothing more than her stockings and her self-control.

Considering the extent of the pleasure, it had been a small price to pay. She allowed herself one wicked and self-indulgent smile before turning her attention to the gift in her hand. Even holding the things in her hand made her legs tingle as though she were wearing them. And the way he had held her ankles and tugged at the stockings, making them shift on her leg and stroke every inch?

She shivered and then smiled again. For all his rough talk and awkwardness, he was as subtle as a serpent. Did he use such misdirection to get his way in the House of Lords? Or did he save it for getting around the ladies?

That idea bothered her, just a little. While she should probably disapprove of what he was doing with her, she did not want to think that he bought stockings and gloves by the hundredweight to seduce any girl he fancied. She hoped that he meant something special by it.

Which meant that it was impossible to deny how much his good opinion had come to matter. The thought of marrying him still terrified her. But he had revealed his own fears as well. He worried that he might hurt others through carelessness, even as he cared little about their good opinions.

That made it all the more horrifying to think that he might have read the few lines in the paper and thought less of her because of it. Perhaps even now he was coming to understand that the taint of her scandal would be transferred to whichever man married her.

She had grown to like the attention he was giving her and would be sad to lose it. Perhaps it was just that she was the favourite of a duke. Any girl would be pleased to have such a feather in her cap.

But how many had found themselves flushed and trembling on a sofa in broad daylight, as said member of the peerage offered assurance that he sought nothing more than her trust? She remembered the soft kiss on the verandah, the reassuring hand on her elbow and the sharp taste of brandy in her lemonade, the heated kisses he had given her in a darkened room and the speed with which he had retreated when he'd realised she was not ready for them. He had done everything he could to prove that while his words might be blunt, his feelings towards her were tender.

If his object had been casual seduction, he'd have lost interest on the first night or taken what he wanted despite her resistance. But if it was the challenge that drew him, he need not be so plain to all who would listen of his intention to marry her.

She poked at the brown-paper wrapping in the fire and added the scrap of paper in her pocket, watching that burn as well. She would think no more of Gervaise. If she did not seek out the dancing master, than he could do her no further harm.

She had told Reighland everything he needed to know on the subject and he had already forgiven her. The stockings in her hand were proof enough of that. Yesterday, he had been quite open about the bedroom waiting for her in his home. She had nothing to fear.

She placed them in a drawer with the rest of her undergarments. But she held the note in her hand for a moment. It seemed wrong to throw it away. She fingered the paper, scanning the room for a safe place to keep it. Then she went to the jewel box on her dressing table that held a neat pile of letters, tied in a hair ribbon. They were gifts from last Season's suitors and really nothing more than foolishness. To see them now embarrassed her, both for the excessive things the men had said and for her own extreme reaction to them. She had wasted many an afternoon reading them over and over.

Since returning from Scotland, they felt as distant as if they had been written to another person. With no more thought, she scooped them up and tossed them on the fire to burn beside the wrappings. Then she placed the single line that Reighland had penned in place of honour, alone in the satin-lined case, and closed the lid.

Chapter Eleven

When next she saw Reighland, on the other side of the Tremaine ballroom, it was just as she'd feared it would be. Her heart beat faster, her cheeks flushed and it was all she could do to keep from running to his side. There was no point in pretending otherwise. Something had changed within her. Tonight, given the chance, she would make a cake of herself over the duke, acting just as silly as every other girl in London.

She had caught herself preparing for this evening with extra care, choosing a gown of blue muslin trimmed with silver that matched sweetly with her colouring, while sporting a neckline that was near to indecent. With it, she wore the gloves and the stockings. And all the while she dressed, she could think of nothing but Reighland's reaction when he saw her. She had actually caught herself turning in the mirror and practising the cautious display of ankle that might best show the stocking.

Now she was standing at her father's side, barely listening to the greetings of the host and hostess, while scanning the crowd for the only guest that mattered to her. She turned, trying to pretend that she was not looking for him, and glanced in his direction.

He looked back at her and smiled. There was the briefest flick of his eyes towards her ankles, but he made no further effort to look. It was as though he'd ascertained all he needed from the look in her eyes.

Apparently he was not as preoccupied by the silk on her legs as she was. She felt the way her thighs slipped against each other, as her little group worked its way through the crowd. Her limbs felt smooth and wonderful. It was a pity that skirts went all the way to the floor. These stockings were made to be admired.

She glanced across the room at Reighland again and felt heat rising, on her face, in her breasts and lower, between her silk-clad legs.

He would want to look at them, if she allowed it. She imagined raising her petticoats for him as far as her knees, perhaps just enough to reveal the hem of her chemise.

She could imagine the feel of his hand on her calf, the other on the heel of her slipper, pulling it free…

'Priscilla!'

'I beg your pardon…' She had bumped into Ronnie, who had stopped suddenly in front of her.

'If you are not careful, you are going to spill your wine. The glass is tipping. And do stop ogling Reighland. If the match is not fully formed, you are hardly entitled to stare at him in public.'

'Yes, Veronica.'

Across the room, Reighland was chuckling as though he had just heard the most diverting story, even though he had been standing alone.

In response, she touched her skirt and gave it a twitch.

His eyes drooped immediately to the hemline, trying to spy her ankle, and then back to her face. There was a mischievous twinkle in his eye and he raised his glass ever so slightly as though offering a toast in her direction.

For a moment, she felt quite like her old self. Last Season sometimes felt like a hundred years ago. She had flirted and been flirted with, and had a throng of suitors vying for her attention. Tonight the magic had returned. She had captivated a man. And as it should have been, it was the most eligible man in the room.

But, more unusual, he had captivated her. Though she still wished it could have been any other man than the one her father had chosen for her, it did not matter quite so much, as long as it was Reighland. She was not accustomed to feeling any answering tug when making a conquest. His note had suggested she think of him. She was happy to comply.

She turned hurriedly away from him, remembering what Veronica had said. He would think she was agreeing to his offer, if she preened at him in public. And she was not sure she was ready for that.

Would it really be so bad to marry him? It would get her out of her father's house and away from Ronnie's continual meddling. He would make her a duchess. She would have access to all the wealth, power, jewels and houses that she could hope for. If they did not suit, then there would be much space in which to withdraw from each other. Even in isolation, she would live in comfort for the rest of her life.

But she did not want a husband to withdraw from. She wanted a soulmate. And after Gervaise, she doubted that was even possible. The pain had not been the worst of it. It had been the loss of control that had frightened her. The feeling of smothering. The demands upon her body that, once she was married, she would have no right to refuse.

She felt the dizzying panic rising again and looked back over her shoulder in his direction. Even if she wished to, how could she bring herself to submit to him? And then she remembered how easy it had been, when they had been alone together.

He was watching with what appeared to be innocent curiosity until she remembered that he had worn a similar expression on their last meeting. Then she had lost her precious control;

it had been so wonderful that she would happily do it again for him, if he wished.

She covered her own face with her fan, fluttering it hurriedly. Last Season, she'd have flashed him some secret message with it, demonstrating her interest and agreeing to a meeting on a balcony, or in some quiet corner of the room. Tonight, her fingers felt numb against the ivory. She had never cared if her signalling to some man or other had been met with a discreet shake of the head. But if Reighland resisted, she did not know what she would do.

It probably did not matter, for it seemed he could not read it in any case. He looked at her and not the fluttering silk, walking across the room slowly until he stood at her side. 'A lovely evening, is it not?'

'Yes.' She looked down at the floor.

'And all the lovelier, now that you are here.'

'Do you seek to flatter me now?'

'As always, I speak the truth. But it seems even that does not please you. You are frowning. Is it that I am calling attention to how desirable you are? Or is it that the comment comes from my lips and not another's?'

'How many times must I tell you, there is no other?' she said, a little too sharply.

'That is not what the paper says.'

He had read it. She saw the darkness in his eyes, just behind the smile, and moved to stand just in front of him, close enough so that her answer could not be overheard. 'So you have seen it, then.' Then she pretended to admire the dancing, as though they were speaking of nothing important.

He nodded. 'I expect half of London has as well. Is there any meaning in it?'

He doubted her. If she asked him, he would swear it wasn't so, but the few lines of text worried him more than he cared to admit. She should not have been surprised. If her father and stepmother did not trust her, then why should this man, a virtual stranger to her, be any different?

It hurt.

She took a breath. 'Of course not. I have not seen him. And if I do, I do not mean to seek him out. But I suppose it is possible that someone saw us in the same place at the same time and assumed the worst. Or it could simply be a lie meant to upset me.' And him as well.

'Very well, then.' She felt a little of the tension go out of him with the breath at her ear. 'If you tell me that it is nothing, we will speak no more about it. I trust you.'

It was an honour to have that trust. But it made her no more comfortable, for it was a great responsibility. 'I fear I will be a disappointment to you,' she said through a bland smile, afraid to turn and look at him. 'I will not be able to control what people say about me. The gossip made mention of you as well.'

He touched her arm. 'While your desire to protect me from my own worst impulses is a noble one, you must let me decide what it is that will make me happy. And I am beginning to suspect that the only thing likely to make me happy is you.'

He said it casually, as he said everything else. And that nonchalance made it seem all the more important. This was not some florid compliment, meant to turn her head. She was the font of someone's future happiness. He truly felt that the room was a more beautiful place for her presence in it. She felt the last resistance in her cracking and breaking from the gentle pressure in a way that a full onslaught would never have achieved.

'Thank you,' she said, with equal neglect, smiling into the room and wishing she could turn and sink into his arms. 'But I would think my family could have told you by now that, for all you might gain by marrying me, I am unlikely to bring you any real joy. They all tell me that I am an endless source of trouble.'

'To them perhaps you are. But I doubt they will understand you as well as I mean to.'

'You offer me understanding?' If he was not careful, he would make her lose her composure and spill the contents of her heart, right here in a crowded ballroom. She wanted to tell him how tired she was of London and of the people in it. And how life only seemed more frightening, the more she learned about it.

Instead, she gave what she hoped was a sophisticated nod. 'An interesting gift. And it has the advantage of being inexpensive as well.'

'Unlike the other presents I've given you, which set me back a pretty penny.' He was leaning forwards just enough so that he could speak into her ear without arousing the attention of the other guests. To them it might look as though he were commenting about the dancing, or the other guests. 'You are wearing them tonight, are you not? I can see the gloves. But I can hardly request that you lift your skirts so that I might examine your legs.'

'I will set your mind at rest, then. The stockings are where you would expect them to be. That was your intention in giving them to me, was it not? That they be worn together.' She smiled, fumbled with her fan for a moment and dropped it upon the floor at her feet. Then said rather loudly, 'How careless of me.'

'Allow me to get that for you.' As he stooped to retrieve the fan, she swayed in time to the music and raised her skirt just enough so that he might see her ankle. Then she let it fall into place again and he rose and handed her the fan.

There was a trace of a sly grin on his face, in place of his usual guarded expression.

'Satisfied?' she asked and smiled back, feeling as wicked as ever she had.

'Not by half. But I hope, soon, to change that.' His voice was a low rumble in her ear that made her nerves dance. And this time it was not with fear, but with the playful excitement that she had felt on the previous day.

'Do not forget where we are,' she said, more to herself than to him. 'This is a rather public place to be having such a discussion.'

'Whatever do you mean?' he countered, all innocence.

'You know perfectly well,' she said.

'Then I suppose you will disapprove when I remind you that the things I have given you be worn next to your skin,' he said, absently. 'Jewellery is far too cold to symbolise what I think, when I look at you.'

It had not occurred to her, before this. She had thought the impropriety came from a lack of manners, but he had known exactly what he was doing from the first moment. Her arms and legs were encased in his gifts to her, a continual and intimate touch. He might be offering marriage, but he was trying to seduce her as well.

'It is not enough that my gifts touch your body,' he said. 'I want each one to be a caress. Perhaps I shall purchase a silk ribbon to wear at your throat. Or a fur muff, to warm your hands in winter. But first, a chemise.'

There was nothing awkward about his suggestions tonight, nor were they meant as jokes. He was speaking truth into her ear. The fact that they were surrounded by people made it all the more erotic. She felt a tingle down the length of her spine, as though he had passed a hand along her skin.

'What do you favour?' he asked. 'Linen? Lawn? Or the smoothest China silk, caressing the most intimate parts of your body.'

Then he laughed to cover the sound she made, which was close to a moan of suppressed desire. She glanced around hurriedly and was relieved to see that the people nearest to them were too caught up in the music to notice her behaviour.

'Perhaps I shall give you all three,' he continued. 'We shall experiment, to see which you prefer.'

'Stop doing this to me.' She could feel the same trembling in her legs that she'd felt in the salon, after he'd stolen her stockings.

'I? I am doing nothing, Lady Priscilla. You said that you were afraid of my touch. And I am barely doing that, you must admit. My hand is on your arm. That is all.' His fingers rested gently on the few inches of bare skin between glove and sleeve. It was hardly intimate.

He must know that she was burning for him. Her knees were weak and her thighs were wet. 'Reighland,' she said in warning, 'I will not even allow you my arm if you do not stop this instant.'

'Very well, then,' he said and his hand dropped to his side. 'Now, back to the subject of your new chemise. I would hope that you select something that is not the least bit practical. I would replace it, of course, if, for some reason, it were to be torn.'

Was he suggesting what she thought he was? It hardly mattered. She could imagine the torment of being rubbed to arousal by silk and picture him putting gentleness aside and ripping some sheer nothing from her body before taking her to bed. She had a brief, fearful memory of what the past had been, then rejected it. Awful though that might have been, right now, every inch of her being ached with the need to be closer to Robert.

'Please.' She turned her head and said it so quietly that no one else but he could hear the need in her voice.

'What, darling?'

'I can no longer fight you. Nor do I wish to. If it is possible to give myself to anyone, then I am yours, body and soul. You may have whatever you want from me. But please, do it quickly, and give me some relief. Do not torment me in public.' Even now, she felt on the verge of the sort of very physical reaction that she had never felt outside her own solitary bed. Never except for her time with the Duke of Reighland.

'Very well, then.' He took her hand and she trembled at the thought of the contact, even through the protection of the delicate leather. 'I doubt that all the guests will be happy with this revelation. But at least we will be sure that the papers will talk of nothing else tomorrow.' As he looked into her eyes, he reached into his pocket and she felt the suddenly increased heaviness of her hand as a ring was slipped on to her finger.

'What is this?' she said, confused.

'The Reighland betrothal ring. You said I could do what I wanted, as long as I did it quickly. And this is it.'

She was shocked and perhaps a little disappointed. When she spoke, her voice was too loud and she could not manage to care if anyone heard. 'I assumed that you meant to pull me into an alcove and ravish me.'

He touched her gloved fingers to his lips. 'First things first. Now that I know I have your co-operation. I wish to formalise our relationship in the eyes of the *ton*.'

'Marriage.'

'Engagement, at least.' He smiled and put a hand on her shoulder. 'It is what couples normally do before attempting congress.'

People who did not include her, she supposed. She hoped that this was not meant as a rebuke to her morals. But it did not seem to be, for he was smiling at her. And he had offered to marry her.

'It is not as if I do not wish to pull you into the musicians' gallery and have my wicked way with you,' he consoled. 'Just not tonight. Mrs Tremaine will be in alt that her ballroom is the location that I make the announcement. It is a social coup. But I doubt her hospitality will extend to allow sporting in dark corners. She was a vicar's daughter, after all. Now, come, let us make the announcement.'

'Announcement?' she said, still trembling from

excitement, but going rapidly numb at the sudden change things that taken.

Robert was leading her towards the front of the room and paused to whisper a few words to Rosalind Tremaine, who clapped her hands together in elation and signalled for the musicians to pause.

All heads turned in their direction. Robert explained, politely, and briefly, that Lady Priscilla had just done him the honour...

She had been trapped, although she was not quite sure how it had happened. He had not showered her with gifts, since two was hardly a shower. Nor had he given her his undivided attention for months on end. Although, in the brief times they had been together, she had felt she had it.

And he had certainly not smothered her with his lovemaking. During the aborted attempt on the floor in his house, she had been quite terrified. But beyond that he had kissed her lips only once. And he'd kissed her ankle, of all places. That was at the same time most improper and hardly improper at all.

And yet she could not help thinking that they

had been together for ages. How else had she become so totally aroused by the thought of the man? Although she had sworn she never would, she was eagerly doing what her father had wanted all along.

It galled her. But it was almost worth it to see the shocked looks on the faces of the other girls. Char Deveril was there in the crowd, looking as though she had just swallowed a toad. Apparently she'd had designs on Reighland, just as everyone else had. But considering the speed with which Char had turned on her last Season, holding her up for ridicule and cutting her when they met on the street, Priss was not the least bit sorry for her.

Her feelings were much more confused when she saw her father. Benbridge looked as she remembered him from before Ronnie, and even before her elopement. For the first time in ages, he was truly smiling at her. He was accepting the congratulations of other guests as though the good fortune was entirely his. Veronica was a portrait of icy triumph, ready to use this new connection to cement her place in society. And when her father looked at her, it was with all the pride and approval he had used so many months ago, when she had still been his favourite.

For a moment, Priss was almost happy. That time had been easier, for her at least. Her sister had suffered, but she had been happy, in her own selfish fashion. She had not realised how quickly favour might be lost.

'Dance with me,' Reighland demanded. The suggestion was ordinary and, as usual, ever so slightly rude. He should have said 'please'. But it pulled her out of her reverie and back to his side. His words were full of invitation and hidden meaning, just as they always seemed to be. Out loud he had demanded a waltz. But in her mind, he had suggested something quite different. *Love me. Make love to me and with me. Let me please you.*

She sensed no conditions upon them. Reighland was as unchangeable as a mountain. He would be her rock. As he led her out on to the dance floor, she leaned upon his arm and smiled.

He leaned forwards to speak into her ear. 'It is not so bad, is it? Marrying me, that is.'

'I am getting used to it,' she admitted, a little breathlessly, squeezing his shoulder where her hand rested and feeling the ring tighten against her fingers.

'Good. Very good. I will still ravish you, of course. You need have no fear that I am uninterested on that front.'

'Oh.' What had she agreed to? The waves of passion that had caused her to agree to him were subsiding, as were the feelings of comfort. And like any ebbing tide, they were likely to uncover things she did not particularly want to think about.

'Tomorrow, perhaps?' he murmured. 'I will be visiting one of my properties not far from London, not even a day's ride. It is in the country, of course. Perhaps it is more rustic than you wish. Not one of Reighland's fine houses, but a place I bought some years back. Still, it will be your home as well, once we are married. But it needs a lady's touch. I would like to know what you think of it. We will be back by evening. Perhaps I can persuade your stepmother to allow an unchaperond trip, now that I have publicly declared my intentions.'

Even with the engagement, she should definitely refuse him. It was quite risky enough to have the little meetings they'd had. If she was gone from home the whole of the day, travelling in a closed carriage with him, anything might happen.

But what might happen would not matter to her father, any more than her indiscretions had mattered before Dru left. They had been hidden and that had been enough to please him. Now, she had accepted an offer of marriage from a duke. And to Benbridge, she might as well have been washed in snow. As long as the end result was her becoming Duchess of Reighland, her father would not give a fig for maintaining appearances. Her stepmother would not love her in any case. Priss sighed. 'I will tell Ronnie that you wish me to have the house measured for furniture and new hangings. She will approve of my spending your money, I am sure.'

'I will arrange it, then,' Reighland said. 'But do not tell her that we will be doing the bedrooms first.' He smiled at her in a way that made her heart flutter, but whether it was excitement or fear she felt, she was not sure.

Chapter Twelve

Priscilla held her breath as the carriage drove round the bend and she caught her first sight of their destination. For all his talk of being a humble farmer, Robert Magson must have done quite well for himself, even before gaining the title. The simple country home that Reighland had described was larger than Benbridge Manor, with acres of parkland, riding trails, a grand house and many outbuildings. She could see the beginnings of gardens that would supply this house and the London property with fresh vegetables and herbs, and orchards blossoming that would be heavy with fruit come late summer and autumn.

But this bounty was not the pride of the property. The fields surrounding the gardens were carefully fenced and the enclosed fields were dotted with horses: glossy blacks, chestnuts, dapple greys and rowans grazing peacefully, some of them great with foal.

As they rode up the curved drive, she could see behind the house that construction of a larger stable was in progress. 'I have only a small portion of the breeding stock here,' Reighland said, glancing out into the field. 'Most are still in the north. But it was too great a sacrifice to take on this supposed honour as Reighland and part myself from everything that gave me pleasure.'

He was smiling down at the barns in a way that he never did while in town. Not even at her, she reminded herself. Most of their interactions seemed controlled and distant, compared to the man she saw today, who laughed more easily as he allowed himself to relax in her presence. He seemed larger as well, as though being in the city was a continual restraint on his character. Perhaps that was why he had been drawn to horses. They were large animals that did not require unusual tenderness on his part. He could be himself around them.

The idea no longer bothered her. When the

time came, she was sure he would take care with her. But it seemed that time had not yet arrived. If she'd expected the whole trip would be spent in amorous play, so far she'd been sorely mistaken. The two-hour journey had been quietly accomplished and their conversation a polite and rather banal rehashing of the previous evening's events. A careful reading of the morning's paper revealed no further gossip about a return of Gervaise. But Reighland had passed her a page with their engagement prominently displayed and assured her that it would settle much speculation and put an end to the rumours about her. 'Do not let them see that you were bothered by the first notice,' he said firmly. 'I was not.'

But he had asked her about it. If it had meant nothing to him, then why did he refer to it now? 'Of course, Reighland,' she said and willed herself to question him no further on the subject and trust that it was closed. Now that they were no longer sparring with each other, it was possible to view the sudden silence that fell between them as a comfortable thing. She need have no fear of what he might think during it.

And it did seem that, if he thought of anything,

it was of horses. The lulls in their conversation were filled with unusually detailed descriptions of his animals, their bloodlines and the sires of their expected offspring.

Then he broke off suddenly and cast an apologetic look in her direction. 'I am sorry if I am boring you more than I usually do. But I do tend to lose track of time when I am talking of cattle.'

She laughed, relaxing a little. 'Some wives might worry about their husbands squandering time at gaming hells, or running up endless tailor bills. But if I need to find you, I shall check Tattersalls.' Of course, some women would assume that their husbands passed the days with a mistress. She would not deny him, if he found her unsatisfactory in that respect. But she did not wish to think of that today. She much preferred to think of him sneaking off to a horse auction rather than leaving her alone.

And riding was a pastime that they might share, if he was not overly protective of his privacy. If the day went well, perhaps she would ask him about purchasing a team and carriage for her use.

Then she reminded herself of the true reason

for their visit and fiddled nervously with her reticule. She had come prepared to spend the better part of the day in a bedroom somewhere in the house, not discussing bloodstock in the barn. She had lain awake most of the night, her mind in turmoil. The sudden alteration of plans left her both confused and disappointed.

But Reighland did not seem to notice her mood. When the carriage drew to a stop, he bounded from it in his eagerness to see the progress made at the stables. He smiled back at her. 'I must speak to the builders, if you can spare me for a time. You needn't bother yourself with coming after me, if you do not wish to be around the animals. I will be done quickly, then we will pass the rest of the day together.'

He appeared to be dismissing her. She had to remind herself that it was quite reasonable of him to put business before pleasure. The animals had been more than a hobby to him for some time and he was concerned for their care and welfare. It would be childish of her to stamp her foot and demand to be entertained every minute of the day. 'Of course,' she said with more grace than she felt. 'I will acquaint myself with the house and the grounds.'

He smiled in relief. 'I have warned the servants to expect you and that they must attend to your every wish. Treat the property as your own. That is what it shall be, in a few short weeks.'

It was a generous sentiment, but not totally accurate. If this land was not part of the entail, it belonged to Robert more than Reighland Court did. But that did not make it hers.

'Perhaps, later, we shall have a picnic,' he said, as though he sensed her pique. But as he did so, he was staring past her shoulder, probably at a horse.

'That would be nice,' she said quietly.

'Very good.' He gave her a short and familiar kiss upon the cheek, then hurried off, leaving her alone.

She looked after him with disgust. It was no less than she should have expected from him, really. He could have at least assembled the servants and introduced her properly, at the house, before running off to inspect the new buildings.

But she could not say she was surprised. It was what she had expected her married life to be like.

She just had not expected it from Reighland, nor had she expected it so soon. But there would be time enough for formalities, once they married. For measuring the bedrooms as well. And at least in some small way, all this would be hers. She would be mistress of both of them and other homes besides—but only because she was marrying their master.

She pushed her bitterness aside. She was to be a duchess. That would be consolation enough. It was a role she had been trained to take, almost from the first moment she could remember. She had always assumed that she would be a wife to some lord or other, managing households and servants, arranging for social gatherings, bearing and rearing children. But she had been imagining something along the scale of her father's wealth. Clearly, this was much different. Everything would be done on a grander scale and with a larger budget.

She smiled to herself as a streak of pure avarice appeared to counter any remaining resistance to the match. She would have to tell Robert of it, when she could find him. It would probably amuse him.

At least her husband would have a sense of humour, she reminded herself. Robert was really quite funny. Understanding, as well. He cared for her and had proven it on several occasions. And now she was standing on as pretty a piece of property as she had ever seen, free to do as she liked.

Freedom.

That was what she had wanted, all along, but she had never believed it would come to her. Now it was finally here. The thought left her trembling with excitement. It was as though she had all the energy in the world and no idea how to expend it. Robert had said she could do as she liked. And he truly meant it.

She walked towards the house, then turned away. It would not be that much different from other houses she had seen. Any tour of it was likely to turn into a list of duties for her: hangings to change, furniture to purchase and a critique of the menus and the servants. It would be much nicer to see the grounds, where there was much to be pleased with and no responsibilities.

In the rose bower, a gardener presented her with a flower. She tasted strawberries behind the glasshouse and found them delicious. She followed a path from there down to the old stables, which were well kept and held an assortment of snorting, stamping beasts. 'Excuse me?' She looked to the first groom she could find, who gave her a quick bow. 'I think I should like to ride for a while to look at the rest of the grounds. Can you direct me to a suitable animal?'

He walked her down the row of stalls to a mare that looked not merely docile, but half-asleep. She touched the animal on the flank with a gloved hand and it barely raised the energy to switch its tail.

She turned back to the groom. 'Is there something with a bit more spirit? A jumper, perhaps?'

'Are you sure, your ladyship?' The groom looked back at her doubtfully. 'The duke'll have my head if I put you up on a hunter and see you tossed into a hedge.'

'You have nothing to fear there.' She pointed to a brute of a horse several stalls down that was stomping at the straw, clearly eager to be ridden. 'How about this fellow? He looks to be needing some exercise.'

The man seemed even more surprised by this.

'We was told that the new lady was not much for horses.'

'Where did you get that idea?' she said, surprised.

'From his Grace. He is off at the other end of the building right now, instructing the others not to frighten you by exercising the stallions.'

'Is he, now?' Then she laughed, remembering the outrageous lies she'd told on the first night. 'The duke was mistaken. I assure you, I am a competent horsewoman. There will be no trouble.' She glanced down at her dress. 'This is not a habit, of course. But I do not care if it is ruined. And I doubt Robert will mind if I do not look my London best while visiting a farm.'

She negotiated with the stable boys for a time and they settled on a chestnut gelding, a bit smaller than her first choice, that danced a little as the side saddle was thrown on his back.

She patted his neck and talked softly to him, leaning her cheek against his mane. She could have a horse of her own. Several, she was sure. And although he had never spoken of them, she suspected Reighland had carriages as well and would not mind her having a curricle and team.

But for now, she would ride. She set out on the path that the groom had recommended, which was sedate at first, but angled downhill, further away from the house, towards a little stream and a cluster of oaks. *Freedom.* The word seemed to echo in the beat of the horse's hooves. The wind was rushing through her hair and she urged him to a gallop, hanging on to the pommel between her legs for dear life. Her sister would have told her to use sense, frightened her by talking of falls and reminded her firmly that ladies did not jump.

But her sister was not here. And Robert need not know as long as she was careful. She pushed the horse towards the fallen log at the end of the field, sure that they could clear it together, and willed her mount to leap. They sailed up, over and down to earth again, in a perfect thump-thump-thump of hooves. She reined in; as she did so, she heard the sound of pursuit and a man's angry shout.

Robert. He had said she might treat the property as her own. But they had not discussed her sneaking down to his stables, or taking any of the horses. While he might be all right with her re-arranging the furniture, he might think something else entirely of her meddling with his livelihood.

It had been a shame, because she had been so happy. She turned her horse and waited for the scolding.

'Priscilla. What the devil?' He was beside her now, reaching for the reins, staring at her crooked bonnet, her windblown hair and her flushed face. 'You ride?'

'Well…' She wondered if an apology for the deception was necessary and then decided to brazen it out. 'Yes, I ride. Does that displease you?'

'You scared the devil out of me.' He pointed to the gelding. 'I thought he had got away from you. When you took the jump, my heart was in my throat.'

'It was very foolish of me,' she admitted. 'It has been some time. And I am not properly attired. But the groom said this was a familiar path and the horse did not seem to mind.' She offered the reins to him, preparing to be led like a child back to the stables.

'You ride' he said it again, dumbfounded, and

pushed the leather back into her hands. Then he pointed. 'There. Take the path that leads into the copse of trees. Canter. Stop when you reach the glade and wait for me. I wish to watch your seat.'

She shrugged and turned the chestnut, kicking it up to the gait he requested. It rode like a dream and she remembered, if he was not too angry at her for this deception, that she might ride often, with the duke for a husband. By the time she reached the break in the trees, she could hear him, galloping to catch up. He swung out of the saddle easily and held out his arms to her, demanding that she dismount as well.

'You ride.' He was breathless, shaking his head in amazement.

'I lied when I said I was afraid of horses,' she admitted. 'In truth, I quite like them.'

He groaned and pulled her against him, all pretence of gentleness forgotten, burying his face in her throat. 'You are perfect, you know that? The sight of you, on a spirited horse...' He groaned again and pushed her to the ground.

'You are not angry?'

He fell on top of her, his mouth on hers, his hands on her waist, kissing her as though it were the only way he could tell her his mind. It was rough with happiness and surprise, and as exhilarating as the ride had been. His tongue thrust into her mouth and she submitted weakly, moulding herself to his body, absorbing the solid strength of him.

When he withdrew, he pushed himself up on an elbow to smile down at her. 'I am overcome.'

He was more than that. She could feel him large and hard through the fabric of her skirt. She felt her mouth go dry and reached up to finger the cloth of his shirt. 'I know that I might have been hurt. But it had been so long… And you said I must treat the place as my own.'

'That horse is the very devil. But you handled him well.' He pushed open the spencer she wore and rested his hand on her heart. 'And there is barely a quiver here. You fearless creature.' He gave a low dark smile and let his hand slip to the side to cover a breast, massaging. 'Let us see if I can raise your pulse for you.'

'Your Grace…' She grabbed at his wrist, but it was too late to hide her reaction. Her nipples had pebbled at his first touch.

He paused. 'Can you not call me Robert? And

as you do it, remember that I have promised not to hurt you.'

'Robert.' She sighed, remembering that she sometimes thought of him as her Robert. She had nothing to be afraid of. With a little effort, she might lose herself in the moment, for what he was doing felt quite nice. He was right. It made her heart skip and her breath catch in her throat to feel his hand resting against her breast.

'My dear?' He was asking for permission to continue.

She released his hand and tugged at the ribbon that gathered the neck of her gown, loosening it for him. Then she closed her eyes. She felt her clothing pushed down and out of the way, then the rasp of his gloved finger against her nipples. It was the barest touch, like his first kisses had been, maddening in its subtlety.

She arched her back and pressed upwards against his hand, only to have him draw further away and continue the gentle torture of it until she whispered, 'More, please.'

'As you command.' He murmured the words into her skin, replacing the dry touch of leather with the wetness of his tongue, circling, laving, teeth nipping, mouth sucking, his hair brushing gently against her chin and his whiskers scratching against the fabric of clothing that had fallen about her waist. He was slow and methodical with his kisses, not sparing an inch of her, even though she had buried her fingers in his hair to urge him on.

And just as she felt the first flutter of orgasm, he pulled away. 'Robert,' she said, more urgently, opening her eyes.

He was reaching for her skirt, tugging it up to free her legs of the excess cloth. 'It is time that our lessons progressed beyond a walk. After what I have just seen, I am sure you are ready for a gallop.' He drew a finger up the inside of her leg and she felt a little frightened, until she reminded herself that he was only touching stocking. They were not even the flimsy nothings he had bought for her in London, but sensible wool hose to protect her legs.

Still, the pressure of his hand against them burned her skin. The leather of his glove was on her bare leg and now it was resting on the place where her legs met. She gasped as he wagged his finger from side to side against her body just as he had done on her breasts. 'Did you lie to me when you said you were afraid of this?'

'Yes. I mean… No.' She had been afraid of something very different than what she was feeling now. This felt more like a reward than a punishment. A flood of sensations was building in her and she fisted her hands in the grass at her sides.

He paused, pressing lightly down upon her. 'I was able to be patient with you, to wait unfulfilled, because I had doubts that we would suit. You did not ride. How could I marry a woman that could not share my one joy with me?'

'You could keep me at home and pay your mistress in matched bays and silver fittings for her saddle.' She was gasping as she said it, but the image in her mind of Robert rolling in the sheets with another was unpleasant. She worked to focus on the feeling the tip of his gloved finger was creating, which was most extraordinary. She circled her hips against it, trying to push herself over the last boundaries of satisfaction.

'Or I could take you in a field of wild flowers, as I mean to do now.' He took his hand away for a moment and ripped a handful of bluebells and showered them upon her face.

'And how do you know I will allow it?' But the thought did not frighten her nearly as much as it once had.

'I can give you no choice,' he said. 'After the sight of your sweet bottom in a saddle, I am hard as stone and desperate for relief. I cannot ride in this condition, my love. And you have led me miles from the house. I doubt I could walk, if I tried.'

'Then it would be churlish of me to refuse you,' she said. Especially as he had been so patient with her. And he had called her his love, just now. Had he ever done it before? She could not remember.

Perhaps he had felt that same rush of emotion, just as she had on realising that her one true dream was realised. 'I seem to be in some distress as well,' she admitted. 'I expect it is what you are doing with your fingers.'

'Bothers you, does it?' His finger returned and he drew another slow circle against her. 'Do you wish me to stop? Or does it leave you wanting more?' He stroked relentlessly against her, making her body feel like a hot, wet void.

'More,' she whispered. 'Perhaps, if you were to use your hand, inside of me...'

'No,' he said, with a small smile. 'If I am without release, you can hardly expect me to oblige you. But if you need filling, I have just the thing for you.' With a last flick of his finger, he did something. She was not sure what, but it was as if her body was a hand that had given a single great grasp, only to come away empty.

He rolled off her on to his back and undid the front of his trousers. Then he turned his head to her, where she lay at his side. 'If you wish further satisfaction, I would be happy to help. Do as you will with me.'

She rolled towards him and leaned on her elbow to look, preparing to be frightened. But her body was telling her otherwise. If there was a problem in the previous experience, she was sure it must have been that Gervaise was inadequate, and surprisingly graceless, for a dancer. Robert was—dear God—Robert was just what she needed. She pulled off her gloves and reached to circle him with her fingers.

His member twitched against her hand and he sucked in a breath. She felt an answering twitch inside of herself, just as the moisture of her body was echoed with a single drop from him. She rose to her knees and touched him more boldly, taking him in her palm and stroking him, watching his fingers spread wide, digging into the earth to keep from grabbing her. 'I am not hurting you, am I?' Although how she could be, with such gentle petting, she was not sure.

'Of course you are, darling,' he said, through clenched teeth. He searched for her with his hand again, brushing against the same tender spot. 'You must be familiar with the agony of knowing that pleasure is so close.' He gave a tortured laugh as she ran a finger over the tip of him.

He responded with a touch that made her gasp. He was right. It did almost hurt to know that something wonderful was so very close. She was nearly as distressed as he was and definitely feeling incomplete.

So she sat up, took a breath to steady her nerves, then spread her legs and straddled him, letting her skirts form a curtain and then reaching beneath them. If she could not see, it might be easier. Or perhaps more difficult. For if he did not mean to help her, how would she know what to do? But when she touched him to her body, she was suddenly quite sure what she wished to do. She wanted to use him shamelessly, to sooth the place that he had touched with his finger. It was what he was made for, surely. Silky flesh, slipping against her own, sending spirals of pleasure through her body, raising the heat inside.

Inside. Perhaps, just a little. But a little was so good, she was sure that a lot would be even better. And before she knew it, she had pulled herself forwards, up and on to him. She felt a moment's difficulty, a stretching of her body and a fullness that seemed to go on and on to the very centre of her being. She squeezed his hips with her thighs, riding him, feeling the slip and pull of their bodies and pressing her palms flat against his chest to hold him still so she could do what she wanted, moving harder and faster, falling forwards on to his mouth, tongue to tongue in time to the rise and fall of her hips. She found she could tighten her muscles and control his response, making him groan under her. And then he clutched her hips and thrust upwards, hard, and something broke inside her until she was shaking as violently as he was, inside and out. Slowly, the insanity that had gripped her subsided and she relaxed and lay still on top of him, feeling his arms stealing around her to hold her close.

He sighed, smiling and untying the ribbon of her bonnet that had slipped uselessly down her back. 'I do not know why men are so enamoured of virgins. Sometimes, a small amount of experience…'

'For their heirs, silly,' she whispered in his ear. Perhaps he had forgotten that fact. When she raised her head to look at him, he was staring up at the sky as though he was not quite sure what had happened to him. 'They fear a woman who has strayed once will make a habit of it.'

'Or they fear they will suffer from comparison,' he admitted, with unusual candour.

'That need not be your fear,' she said, blushing. 'If what has just happened is any indication, you will be first and only in all ways that matter to me. You are magnificent, Reighland.'

He stroked her back. 'And I will not be searching for a mistress to share my rides. I am imaging some long and very interesting picnics taken at various places about my properties.'

'That sounds pleasant,' she said. 'You did promise me a picnic, you know. And riding makes me hungry.' She gave an experimental flex of her muscles.

'Apparently, riding makes you insatiable.'

'It makes you peckish as well.' She could feel him rousing within her.

He was laughing now, kissing her, pressing his face into her neck. 'Never mind your father, and the *ton* and titles and propriety. Marry me, Priscilla. Do it because you want to.'

'Yes,' she said with a smile. 'I think I should like it very much.' He was moving under her in a way that made her forget that she had ever been frightened of him. He was large, but he was gentle when he needed to be. And she was having the most unusual and inappropriate thoughts about the anatomy of a man who would be her husband, and was already a peer of the realm. It felt deliciously wicked, in a way that she had not felt since she was young and foolish, daring and unafraid of being hurt. No matter what might happen, she was quite sure that Robert would not harm her.

'What is it, wench?' he growled. 'Are you laughing at me?'

'Not at you, precisely, your Grace.' But she was laughing, thinking of all the shocking things they were likely to do together.

'Then stop it immediately. The succession is very serious business.' He reached under her skirt and gave her a playful swat upon the bottom, then surged up into her again with a groan of pleasure.

'We cannot be seeing to that, now,' she murmured against his lips. 'You have not married me yet. Perhaps we should stop this, lest we create a by-blow and not a little duke.'

'Stop?' He rolled with her until her body was trapped beneath his, then redoubled his thrusts. 'In a while, perhaps. Long enough to get a special licence and drag you before a vicar.'

'A bishop,' she said breathlessly. 'You are a duke, after all. I want a bishop at St George's.'

'I will marry you before a druid in the woods, if that is what you wish,' he grunted. 'After that, I will lock our bedroom door and you will not wear a thing more than my ring for at least a week. Perhaps two. Dear God, you are sweet. I am undone when I am with you.' To prove the fact, he spilled into her with a sigh and a shudder of pleasure.

'And suppose that is not to my liking?' she whispered.

'Then I will give you what you want. Whatever you want, to make you happy. To make you love me.' He kissed her, fervently, ardently, with all the desperation of a lovesick youth. 'No more games, Priss. Say you'll have me. You'll not regret it, I swear.' His voice was soft, urgent and totally sincere.

She pushed a hand between them and ran a finger down his chest, worming it through gaps in waistcoat and shirt until she could touch the hair on his chest. 'I want a horse.'

'Done.'

'Two, then. A curricle and team of matched Yorkshire Trotters. And a high-perch phaeton to drive in Hyde Park.'

'Yours. All yours.'

She smiled up at him. 'And I would trade them all to hear you say that you love me.'

'I think that I do.' He seemed as surprised as she was. 'I am sure of it, as a matter of fact. I love you, Lady Priscilla.'

It was the strangest feeling, being close to him like this, smelling flowers and hearing his breathing in her ear and the soft sounds of nature, all around them. She was happy and at peace as well. 'And I love you, Robert.' She smiled and said it again. 'I love you.' She raised her head and kissed him again. They belonged together. He had been right all along. And of all the mistakes she had made in her short life, being wrong about Reighland was the one that she was most glad of.

Chapter Thirteen

The time was passing in a whirl and yet it seemed to drag on without end. The banns had been read twice. The church had been reserved, the flowers ordered and a menu chosen for the wedding breakfast.

The only thing Priss had not managed to achieve was an invitation for her sister. Her father would not permit it and crossed the Hendricks name off the guest list when she'd tried to add it. When Veronica had found her handwritten offer she had removed it from the outbound post and reminded Priss of her duty to uphold the family honour.

She would have to go to Reighland with it, she suspected. She was sure he saw the Folbrokes regularly. He must see Mr Hendricks, and perhaps Dru as well. It would annoy Father to no end, but he would submit to rank and let the duke have his way.

That would be the best thing about marriage, she was sure. A rich and powerful man was offering it to her with a twinkle in his eye, daring her to take advantage of his good nature and make him wield his power for her. Robert seemed like a most reasonable man, and she would have the latitude to visit where she wished and to avoid whom she pleased, even if it was her own father. The Duchess of Reighland could see Dru whenever she wanted.

Well, perhaps that would be the second-best thing about marriage.

Priss stared at her smiling reflection in the mirror, as the modiste crouched at her feet, setting pins in her wedding gown. But she could not help but smile when thinking about all the pleasant things she might do with her soon-to-be husband to reward him for his efforts on her part.

Robert had been very proper with her, since that day they had lain together in the flowers. They had not been alone at all in weeks. But when he looked at her, there was something smouldering, deep behind his eyes, that gave the lie to the propriety of his speech and actions. It said that the title and lands were as nothing compared to the winning of her. He was as eager for this marriage as she had become. Even if he'd been a boot boy, the look would still have been in his eye and he'd still have made her feel like a duchess.

Yesterday, she had received a carefully wrapped package from him containing a large and boring book, and a chemise so fine that it could be slipped unnoticed between the pages. There was another note that duplicated the last. 'Wear this, and think of me.'

And as before she could think of nothing else. She had been a fool to have worried about Robert's dark looks and considerable size. She still thought of him as rugged rather than handsome and his manner was sometimes blunt to the point of embarrassment. But she had learned from Gervaise what a pleasant face and pretty manners were worth, once the doors were closed and friends and family far from earshot.

Now that she had joined with him, the thing

that had once frightened her had become the focus of many pleasant thoughts. She wanted it. She needed it. She wore his gifts whenever she was able, even though they were exquisitely arousing. And she had taken to touching herself at night, to gain some relief. While she did it, she thought of how much better it might be, if it could be his hands moving on her body. He must know what she was doing, she was sure. It explained the note.

When they were alone again, she would tell him how she felt. Because of him, she was young and alive, for the first time in months.

One more reason she needed to talk to Dru. She was happy and in love, and longed for a confidant to share the news. She doubted that Veronica would care one way or the other. Perhaps she would not even understand the words. There was no question that Ronnie had married Benbridge for social status, power and wealth, but there was no sign that she had looked further than that.

Priss would have all those advantages with Robert as well, but it was better that there was a deeper fondness. She was eager to see him again, if only to hear his voice and to laugh at his jokes, which were never quite jokes. She wanted him to stand a little too close to her and say the wrong thing, even if he knew the right thing, just to annoy and amuse her.

They would go back to his house in the country and the horses that he was so proud of, which were better than the boring beasts her father allowed her in the city. There were miles of unexplored land to gallop over, and logs and fences in need of jumping. He would not be bothered to lecture her about the need of maintaining a safe and sedate pace so that she might display herself in the right light without mussing clothes or hair. In fact, he would make sure that she never returned from a ride in the proper condition she'd set off in.

The modiste helped her off with the nearly completed gown. And when she had been dressed again she met Ronnie in the front room of the shop, where she had been paging through *La Belle Assemblée* and sipping chocolate. They arranged for the delivery of wedding clothes and exited the shop, walking up Bond Street toward the printers, where invitations awaited her approval.

In the past, shopping with Ronnie had been an endless tedium. But today, each new errand increased Priss's happiness. Even conversation with her father's wife was enjoyable. Clearly, love was utter madness. But it was also quite delightful. Priss wondered why she had resisted it for so long.

And then she glanced up the street and saw him.

Gervaise lounged against the side of a building, watching her as she made her way towards him. Veronica was oblivious, of course. She had never met him and would not see the obvious risk. She would lead Priss right past the man and think nothing of it. An explanation would mean stopping dead in her tracks for a series of questions and answers. It would call even more attention to the possible meeting.

She could tug on her stepmother's arm and demand to be taken across the street. But she suspected that, if Gervaise meant to make mischief, he would follow them. Far better to brazen it out and act as if he meant nothing at all to her. But as they came closer, each step was an agony. An agony that she dare not reveal.

Priss schooled herself, looking ahead and not to the side, focusing on her destination some streets ahead. It was like being trapped in one of her nightmares. The weight of a man's body seemed to press down on her chest, cutting off her breath. As they passed him, she answered some foolish question of Veronica's and heard the thinness of her own voice, as though it came from a great distance. Ronnie was too preoccupied with her shopping to notice the difference.

There. It had been hell. But they were past him and she had managed the cut indirect. Unlike Robert, Gervaise should understand the significance and leave her alone. He was making no move to follow her now.

From behind her, she heard a laugh.

Chapter Fourteen

'Of course, rebellion in the north must be put down with all due haste. There is far too much latitude given to the working classes. And the troops in York…'

Robert did his best to ignore the long-winded rant of his future father-in-law. It would not do to provoke the man in the middle of his own house, especially not when it might further upset his fiancée at her engagement ball. But the earl was trailing him from card room to dance floor and back, and would not leave him alone.

It had not been Robert's intention to spend the whole of the night in male company. He had not seen Priss as often as he'd liked in the last weeks. Now that he could spend time with her, it was clear that the girl was suffering from wedding nerves. She looked tired and worried. But she was as beautiful as ever in a gown made of something gold and shiny, which went well with her hair. He had told her she looked like an angel, for the ribbon in her hair did rather remind him of a halo.

He had expected some sort of thanks in response. Or at least a blush. But instead she'd looked at him as though he were mad and said that all of London knew there was nothing the least bit angelic about her.

He suspected it was the nonsense that had been appearing in the papers that was bothering her. If he were to believe it—which of course he did not—his future duchess was being seen all over town in the company of her old lover. Things would settle down, once they were married and the rumour spreader realised that they had done no good with them.

There was no point in letting the words of meddling fools cause pain. The taunting would only increase, if one responded to it. Such pettiness could be endured and ignored. Soon they would be married, Parliament would be out of session and they could go back to the country and the horses, which were simpler.

Of course, horses could be false jades as well. But when he was with them, there was never a question in Robert's mind as to who was to ride and who was to be ridden.

When they were alone, he would remind Priss that peace was almost within reach, but for now he had managed to calm her as they had waltzed together, making her laugh and pulling her too close until she had slapped his arm with her fan and scolded him for being impertinent.

'I cannot help myself,' he'd whispered. 'It has been weeks since I've had you. And two weeks more to wait until I will have you again. A man has needs, you know.'

That should have resulted in a glib comment or perhaps another scold. But instead she'd looked even more worried and echoed, 'Two weeks. How will I bear it?' as though she were speaking some thought that she'd meant to keep hidden. Then her grip had tightened on his arm and she'd said, urgently, 'Let us not wait. You have the licence. We could run away tonight, if we wished, and be married first thing in the morning. It would be done then and you could have me all to yourself, as often as you liked. Please, Robert? Could we elope?'

It had been quite flattering to see her so eager for him. And strange that he had been the one to remind her of the need for pomp and circumstance, now that the invitations were on their way. She had looked so disappointed that he had suggested that perhaps a clandestine meeting might be arranged.

But she had shaken her head, refusing to leave her house, even to come to his. He must speak to Benbridge about it, if the man would ever leave off talking politics. 'Who is that man that Priscilla has been talking with?' he interrupted, finally out of patience.

'What?' Benbridge was clearly annoyed to be bothered with anything so mundane as his own guests.

'I saw a tall slender man with pale hair offering her a glass of punch just now.'

Benbridge turned his head. 'I see no such person.'

Nor did Robert, at the moment. But the man had been there earlier. He was certain of it. 'He stood up with her earlier, a while after I did. He seemed a bit of a fop.' And an excellent dancer.

Benbridge gave another cursory scan of the crowd. 'He is not here now, at any rate. But if it is a concern to you, you had best ask Priscilla to introduce you to him.'

'Perhaps I shall do that,' Robert said. Although at the moment, he could not manage to find Priss amongst the dancers either. 'If you will excuse me, I think it is time for me to speak with her.' Perhaps it was past time.

'Why are you here?' Priss demanded. It had not been bad enough that Gervaise had appeared at her engagement ball, making her worry which of the guests knew him, and which did not. That had made her nearly dizzy with panic, just as she felt each time she saw him on the street.

Now, when she had gone to search for Robert, trying to find him before the gossips did, Gervaise had been the one to follow her into the hall.

'I am here because you invited me, Priscilla, *ma chérie.*'

'Leave off with that immediately, you horri-

ble man. I am not your *chérie*, and never was.'
She glanced around her, relieved that they were
alone. The solitude would not last for long; she
must get him out of the house before they were
discovered in a tête-à-tête. 'Do you not notice
that I cut you each time you accost me? Why
do you continue to follow me? It should have
been clear after the first day that I do not wish
to renew our acquaintance. And I certainly did
not invite you to my home.'

'Of course you did.' He removed an invitation
from his pocket and flashed it to her so fast that
she could not see if it was an outright forgery or
a genuine card that had been addressed to another and altered. Again, she felt as though she
was trapped in some bad dream, one where she
had been foolish enough to send a card to him,
creating the problem, just as she had by eloping.

He was smiling at her, unctuous and knowing.
'Surely, we need not stand on ceremony. As I
remember it, we were very close friends indeed
on the road to Scotland.'

'Perhaps you do not remember how that
ended,' she said with satisfaction. 'I applauded
from the window of an inn while Mr Hendricks

beat you into the dust. Then he put you into a coach and sent you away.' Gervaise was a man, not a nightmare. And a weak man, at that. He could be beaten.

'But when I heard of your impending nuptials, I returned to wish you well.'

'More likely your money ran out,' she said, buying none of it. 'How much did he give you to stay away? And how much more must I pay to see the last of you?'

'Not a *sou*,' Gervaise insisted. 'I merely seek an opportunity to meet the groom and congratulate him. Perhaps it is up to me to give the bride away, since we are nearly married already.'

'Do not dignify what we shared as a marriage, in body or in spirit,' she snapped. 'And do not think you will be attending my wedding, invited or not. If you are seen anywhere near the church, I swear…'

'You threaten me?' He laughed. 'Surely that is not wise. Perhaps you should show me more courtesy, lest I make your new love aware of your past.'

'Robert already knows.' Priss watched the triumphant smile fade from his face. She had done the right thing in admitting the truth, for what could he threaten her with, if not revelation?

'He cannot know all of it,' Gervaise insisted, refusing to believe.

'You should ask him yourself,' she encouraged, praying that he did not. 'I will introduce you. Of course, he is very large and intimidating. Powerful as well. I do not know if he will welcome an acquaintance with you.'

Gervaise was weakening, she could tell. And with his weakness she felt her own strength growing. If she could manage to frighten him away, the notices in the paper would stop and she would never have to experience the embarrassment of a meeting between Reighland and this unworthy nothing. No matter how many times Robert might forgive her, she would never forgive herself.

She renewed her attack. 'I could introduce you. Since Robert is much larger than Mr Hendricks, I expect, when he strikes you, it will hurt much more.' Of course Robert would not strike him. And if he did not want to resort to violence, then she would not be the one to push him to it. But it was probably better that Gervaise did not realise the fact. So she smiled at her former lover with what she hoped was evil glee from imagining his beating. 'If I were you, Gervaise, I would go back to wherever it is that I had come from. You do not want to interfere with this, Gerard. You really do not.'

'I will leave, then,' he said with a bow. 'After a goodbye kiss.'

'Certainly not.' He leaned forwards and she swatted him smartly across the cheek with her fan.

'You wilful baggage,' he snarled, with no trace of a French accent. 'I did not ask for your permission. I am taking what is my due. A kiss should be nothing to you. You allowed me far more than that, as we both know.' He lashed out quickly, seizing her arm and pulling her against him.

And she froze. It was like it had been in the inn, when things had gone so quickly and terribly wrong. He was holding her and she could not fight him. Her mouth was pinned against his and his tongue was inside her mouth. She did not even think of it as a kiss. For she had learned from Robert that kisses were sweet things to be anticipated and cherished.

This was an invasion and she could find no way to stop it. *Struggle*, she cried out to herself. *Prove that you do not want him.* But the part of her that had been so willing to fight, just a few moments ago, had withered like a plant in the desert, becoming small and dry, twisted and useless.

And then, suddenly, she was free of him. Feeling returned slowly to her body and she was aware of fingers wrapped around her gloved arm, and the warning word 'Priscilla?' spoken clearly into her ear.

'Robert.' She should have collapsed into his arms, sobbing. It would have been a clear demonstration of her true feelings. But like so many other emotions, the relief could not seem to come to her.

'May I have an introduction to your friend, please?'

Was he being ironic? She could not tell. But surely he could see the truth of this without her having to create the scene that would draw the rest of the party goers into the room. 'Gerard Gervaise, may I present the duke of Reighland.'

'Your Grace.' Gervaise was demonstrating the shock that should have been hers. He was white and trembling, obviously terrified of the Duke's reaction.

'I see.' As usual, she could not immediately read the expression on the face of her beloved. 'Good evening, Mr Gervaise, and goodnight.' He grabbed the dancing master by the scruff of the neck and marched him down the hall past several alarmed guests, called to a footman to open the door and shoved Gervaise through it and out into the street.

Robert had never been so angry in his life. Reminding himself that there was probably an innocent explanation for this scene did nothing to calm him. The most logical one was that his fiancée had played him false. Until recently, he'd have sworn she was honesty in all things.

But tonight there had seemed something odd about her behaviour. And she had lied about her love of horses as well. At the time, he had thought it a white lie and a delightful surprise.

But now it seemed nothing more than an untruth about the only things he held dear in the world.

'Priscilla, come with me.' As he walked back down the hall he caught her by the hand and pulled her into an empty receiving room, shutting the door in the face of a surprised matron.

'Robert, you should not have done that. The fact we are alone…'

'Cannot be any worse than the fact that you were seen kissing your lover at our engagement ball,' he responded.

'I did not kiss him,' she insisted. 'He kissed me. And it was horrible.' She threw herself into his arms. Almost without meaning to, he held her, stroking her hair as she muttered into his coat. 'He inserted himself into our ball with a false invitation. I did not try to be alone with him. Truly. He followed me into the hallway.'

'You had but to tell me and I'd have put a stop to it,' he said more gently.

'But you were with Father. And I did not want him to know what happened.'

The girl had a very good reason not to reveal the man in front of her volatile father. If Robert felt angry and betrayed by this embarrassing interloper, Benbridge's reaction might have been far worse. 'Very well, then. It was an unfortunate incident, but it is over now. And as long as it does not happen again.'

And how many times would he have to repeat those words to her, in the course of their marriage? He had told her his reasons for avoiding a fight and she had seemed to understand. But perhaps she saw it as a sign of weakness and meant to use it to her own advantage. She was just like so many others in his life, pretending friendship only to laugh at him later.

He felt her shoulders sag. Though she must know he waited for the immediate assurance that this was an isolated incident, she remained silent.

He pushed her away from him then, holding her at arm's length so that he might look in her eyes. 'You are hiding something from me, aren't you? You told me, when last I asked, that there was nothing to the gossip in the paper.'

'And at the time, there was not,' she insisted. 'But since then...'

'You have seen him?' His voice was louder than he'd meant it to be and he felt her cringe.

'He follows me everywhere,' she whispered. 'I cannot leave the house, even for a moment, without him turning up in the street. I ignore him. I avoid him. But it does no good. I do not know what to do.'

'You could have come to me.' He was almost shouting in frustration. He'd have told her to do just as she had, of course. But at least it would not have been a secret. They could have taken some solace in shared misery.

Rather than snapping back at him, the woman he had thought would be his guide through the confusing waters of society was melting under the burden of her own past.

'And what would you have done?' she whispered. 'Would you have challenged him?'

'Of course I would have,' he said. 'I should have done it tonight.' But that was as great a lie as any she'd told him. He'd purposely let the man escape. Because he'd learned, if he waited long enough, that such problems would go away.

'It is good that you did not,' she said, not bothered by his cowardice. 'I doubt that would have made the scandal less. He might have died for something I instigated.'

'Then what would you have me do?' he demanded. Because any answer would be better than the course he'd chosen. 'Am I to stand meekly by, as your old lover trails after you like a school boy?' *The bone is snapped clean through*, a voice whispered. *We'll have to call for a surgeon. Be more careful, Bobby. Next time, you must be careful.*

'I expect you to cast me off,' she said.

She was right. It was the quickest way to end the scandal, but it was more despicable than inaction. Even he was not so big a coward as to give up the woman he loved. 'Perhaps you should allow me to decide what is in my best interests,' he said, pulling her into him again.

'After what has been written about me, everyone knows that you are marrying a silly trollop.'

'After tonight, perhaps,' he said. And how long would it take before some wag from his school days remarked that it was just like Magson to end up in such a position? 'If you'd had the strength to come to me a week ago, we could have avoided this scene.'

'But I did not,' she said. 'After what you know of me, why does it surprise you?'

'I am not surprised. But I am disappointed. I need a woman who can rise above such things. Are you strong enough, I wonder, for the responsibilities you will face as my wife? How will you help me if you cannot help yourself?' But that was not right. He should be the strong one. He had failed to protect her. And now he was blaming her for that failure.

And she pulled away from him so suddenly that the lace of her gown ripped in his clumsy hands. 'I make mistakes, Reighland. I have told you so, from the first moment we met. And so do you. If you had listened to me then, all this could have been avoided.' Then she turned and raced from the room.

'Priscilla, come back here this instant!' He ran after her, into the hall, but she was already halfway up the stairs, trailing tears, in no condition to come down and face the guests. Was he expected to follow?

Instincts said yes, but manners clearly said no. If being alone with her in a sitting room was shocking, then leaving a party to climb the stairs and pound on her bedroom floor would be a disaster. Damn Benbridge for not allowing the Hendrickses in his house. The girl needed her sister. He must find Lady Benbridge to help her, but that harpy would be a poor substitute.

He turned back toward the ballroom and nearly ran into the Deveril girl, who dropped into a curtsy, blocking his way. 'Your Grace.'

'Please excuse me, Miss Deveril, I did not see you there.'

'It has been far too long since you have seen me at all.' She was pouting, as though he were flirting with her and not stating the obvious.

'Well, yes,' he admitted. Was he expected to apologise to every silly girl in the room for preferring another?

'It is no wonder if you hide yourself in the hall. Come, let us go back to the dancing.'

The ballroom was the first place he would have to search for Lady Benbridge. He could think of no good way to shake off this little parasite, if they needed to go in the same direction. And so, with a frustrated glance back at the stairs, he allowed himself to be led away.

Chapter Fifteen

'Priscilla, come back here this instant!'

Robert was shouting at her from the hall below. And if she could hear him, then half the party must know that they had argued. It would only take one person telling tales of Gervaise to guess the reason for it. By tomorrow, it would be all over London, magnified to be a thousand times worse than it was. The gossips would have her sporting with Gervaise under the very nose of her father and Reighland.

Poor Robert. He had been right to be angry. She had humiliated him in front of the guests. She should have come to him after that first day in Bond Street and explained everything. But she had not imagined that Gervaise would have been so brazen as to come back to the house.

She wiped a tear away with the back of her hand. She could hear running footsteps on the stairs and in the hall, and hurried to the door to turn the key in the lock.

'Priscilla! Come out of your room this instant. We have a house full of guests.' Ronnie's voice had begun as a shout, but ended in an angry whisper just loud enough to carry through the locked bedroom door.

'I have a megrim,' she called back. And a ruined dress. And a ruined reputation. 'Give them my apologies.'

'You little liar. You are hiding again, plain and simple. Your father will be furious. What am I tell Reighland?'

'Reighland knows,' she replied, trying not to cry.

'That he is marrying the most cloth-headed girl in all of London? I suspect he does. I will go back to the ball and see what can be salvaged of the mess you have made. But only because, in two weeks, I shall be rid of you. After that, it will be Reighland's job to deal with your tantrums and foolishness.'

Priss could hear Ronnie retreating with an

angry rustle of taffeta, leaving her alone again. Apparently, she was still ignorant of the extent of the disgrace. Reighland would set her straight on that, soon enough. And tomorrow she could explain that Ronnie and Father would have her on their hands for much longer than a fortnight.

It was not as if she hadn't warned Robert, from the very first. But he'd almost convinced her that she might manage to escape the past. And then, in a few minutes, it had all been ruined. She could not risk Gervaise showing up again at the wedding, or the christening of her first child. And she could not survive the angry scenes that were likely to occur each time and the fresh gossip in the papers.

And what if he caught her alone, as he had tonight? At the memory of the kiss he had forced upon her in the hall, a new wave of shame and revulsion all but overcame her and she had to sit for a moment, eyes closed and breathing slowly to keep from being sick. If she could not manage to control herself around a worthless dancing master, then how could she be a duchess?

She did not want to let Robert go. Even as she gathered pen and ink, her soul wept at the unfairness of it. She wished that he had never shown an interest, or that he had listened any of the many times she had tried to explain the problems there might be.

He had no right, now that he had made her love him, to notice that her past was a difficulty. And to tell her that she must learn to manage it, as though it was a simple thing? As though there was some way to erase what she had done?

The tip of the pen snapped as she touched it to paper, requiring her to sharpen it again before proceeding. As she did, she thought of the words she would choose. Was there any point to call him her darling Robert, when she knew how the letter must end? She would always think of him as such. But for the purposes of a final farewell, he had best be 'His Grace the Duke'.

She added a paragraph about esteeming his acquaintance. It was by far the most inadequate thing she had ever written. But her true feelings for him frightened her too much to put them to paper. How could she admit that he had offered her a miracle, but that that in light of recent events she had decided to refuse it? She settled for a few non-committal words.

After reflecting on our most recent conversation, I find myself unable to continue our association. You must agree that the situation between us has grown impossible. Since I mean you no harm, I cannot hold you to your generous offer of marriage.
I wish you all the best…

In truth, she would rather die than see him happily married to another. Since he so prized her honesty, it went against the grain to lie to him now. But the truth would have him back at her door, arguing that all was forgiven. And she simply could not bear another round of hope followed by inevitable disappointment.

…in finding a woman worthy to be your duchess. But I fear I can never be that woman. And so, farewell.

She slipped off the betrothal ring, folded it up inside the paper and sealed it quickly. Then, before she could change her mind, she called a footman to carry it downstairs for her.

Chapter Sixteen

Priss passed a quiet night, with surprisingly dreamless sleep. It proved that admitting defeat was the quickest way to gain a peaceful soul. And a few hours of rest made the longing for Robert less painful. She had heard the faint sounds of the ball continuing until the wee hours, proving that there was no problem, not even the disappearance of another daughter, that Father could not manage to pave over.

Had Reighland left after reading her letter? She rather hoped so. The thought of him continuing to drink and dance without her, in her own house, was particularly painful. But it had been her decision to break with him in the middle of a ball. She had no right to dictate his actions after.

More worrying was the unearthly silence that had fallen over the house, afterwards. It was normal that the family would sleep late after so hectic a night. But it was well past luncheon before Veronica knocked on the bedroom door. 'You are wanted immediately in your father's study.' When Priss opened for her, Veronica was white faced, her lips set in a tight angry line, and yet she smiled.

Clearly, an understanding had been reached. She had been tried *in absentia* and now there would be hell to pay. But as yet Priss was unsure which action on her part had been the one to do the job. In the strange state of detachment that had arisen since last night's fiasco, she found that she no longer cared. Robert was lost. Father was angry. Beyond that, there was nothing more to say.

She rose without a word and walked through her door, down the stairs, down the hall, relieved that she no longer felt fear, or even the anger at injustice that had so often led her to rebel. There would be shouting, then it would be over and she could go back to her room.

She went to stand at the place before her father's desk, wondering that there was not a worn spot in the carpet from all the lectures she and her sister before her had received here. This would likely be the last of them, for she doubted she would be living much longer in this house. At least in Scotland, or wherever he was likely to send her, she would no longer be able to hear him shout.

Without preamble, her father slammed his newspaper down on the desk between them and stabbed a finger at an article.

She leaned closer to read.

It was widely suspected that a certain Lady P. took a surprise trip to Scotland last Season with her dancing master. Last night, she was caught at her own engagement ball seeking private lessons from him. R. is discovering that London thoroughbreds are hard to train.

'Explain this,' her father said, as though he did not understand exactly what it meant.

'I think it is quite obvious what is intended,' she replied. It is about me. And Gervaise. The R. is Reighland, of course.'

Her father's eyes narrowed. 'And how did this come to pass?'

'I cannot say,' she admitted. 'Gervaise was at the ball, but I did not invite him. Robert found us together.' She would not repeat the particulars of the conversation that followed. They were no one's business but her own, though she suspected that Father had heard them already, if he'd talked to Robert.

But now he was shaking his head in disgust. 'I have allowed you much freedom of late, assuming that Reighland had you well in hand. But I should have known that you would abuse it and seek out your lover.'

'I did not seek out the company of Gervaise,' she said. 'Though we quarrelled—even Robert would tell you that. Anyone who says otherwise is lying.'

'You should know how to recognise a lie, Priscilla. You have told enough of them over the years. You have wrapped me round your finger and given me nothing but grief.' Benbridge smiled. 'But that is at an end. I had hoped, with your marriage to Reighland, that at the very least you would be his problem and not mine. If you have jeopardised that, do not come weeping to me for another chance.'

He did not know? That made no sense. Robert must have chosen to conceal the contents of her letter for a day or two, to keep the evening from becoming even more newsworthy.

But there would be no better time to speak the truth to her father. It was likely to gain her what she had wanted all along. It would save her a second scolding when the story of the break appeared in the papers.

But why, now that the moment was upon her, did she want nothing more than to run to Robert, to climb into his lap and be held by him, burying her face in his shoulder and hiding from the embarrassment of this latest disgrace? She imagined him whispering soothing words in her hair, offering her his flask, making some quiet dry joke about her popularity with the press, then easing her back on to a bed and chasing the memory out of her mind.

But that Robert was gone, as much a fantasy as her fears of him had been. She was alone and it was time to prove to her father that she was quite capable of truth when it suited her.

'I know better than to expect another chance, Father. And I understand that Reighland was the best match you would ever make for me. But after the embarrassment I put him through last night, I could not justify holding him to our agreement. Therefore I have released him from our engagement and returned his ring.'

'You did what?' It was not the shout she had expected. Really, it was little more than a whisper. But she had no trouble hearing it—she could swear that the whole house went as silent as air before a storm.

'I ended the engagement,' she repeated, resisting the urge to brace herself against an impending gale. 'I cannot put him through the shame of seeing his wife as a topic for gossip, of the *ton* questioning the paternity of his children. When I was forthcoming about my past, Reighland graciously agreed to overlook it. I hoped to live honourably with him and to overcome any scandal. But it seems that there will be no escaping from what I've already done. Nearly a year has passed and people talk more about it than they did right after it happened.'

'He knows?' Her father's eyes were bright with

malice. 'And why, pray tell, does he know any-thing about your past?'

'I told him all,' she admitted. 'From the very first. It was only right that he know the truth.'

'Only right,' mocked her father in a high-pitched voice. 'I will tell you what is right. And that is keeping those in the dark who deserve to remain so.'

'He said it did not matter,' she argued.

'Then he is a bigger dolt than I thought. Now you are the subject of *ton* tattle, no other man in London will have you.'

She lifted her head. The worst would be over, soon enough. She would put forth her proposal and he would put her on the first coach out of London. She need never think of any of it again. At the very least, she would not have to deal with the immediate repercussions of her refusal. 'If Gervaise means to reappear each time I re-enter society, then perhaps it is best if I make a permanent withdrawal to the country, for your sake as well as mine.'

'You stupid, stupid girl. What this Gervaise fellow does means nothing. If you could not manage to keep away from the worthless lout who soiled you, than the least you could have done was refused to give Reighland his walking papers. You had a duke well and truly on the hook. And you let him go over something so foolish as your honour.'

'And his,' she insisted faintly.

Her father laughed. 'Do not try to make me believe that this was over anything more than your desire to spite me. For twenty years, you have cared for nothing more than your own wants and needs. You have used whatever tools that came to hand to make yourself tiresome and difficult until you got your way. This is no different than that.'

But it was. Still, she could not fault his argument. Nor was it difficult to see why he might doubt a change in her character. 'I cannot marry him,' she said, hoping that a repetition would be enough.

'And I cannot do better for you. Nor do I wish to see my own character dragged through the mud with my efforts to give you a place.'

She breathed a small sigh of relief. He finally meant to send her from town. He would deliver sentence, sounding no different than he did at Benbridge when acting as magistrate over his tenants.

Now her father stood and came around the desk to stand at her side. She had not thought of him as tall until this moment. He was several inches shorter than Robert, but today he towered over her, so large was the anger he carried with him. Then he took her by the elbow and walked her out of the study and into the hall. 'I suppose you are now thinking that I will foist you off on to some other poor relative, in another failed attempt to expunge the stain on your character with time and distance.' He sounded gentle, almost sympathetic. It was her first warning that something was terribly wrong. 'It is hardly necessary, you know. I have a new wife now. And Veronica has more sense than your faithless mother ever had. I will have a new family. In a few months, there might be a son who will cause less trouble in my life than two daughters ever did. In this last act as your father, I will not be manipulated into giving you exactly what you want.'

Last act? Did he mean to kill her? 'Father...I do not understand.'

'Understand this.' He hurried her the last few steps through the hall and opened the front door; they stood on the threshold together, looking out into a steady drizzle. 'I no longer need you. Since you seem so set upon making your own decisions without consulting me, I free you from any obligation to listen to me at all. And by doing so, I free myself. Let us see how you like it, you wilful strumpet.' Then he pushed her through the doorway and closed the door behind her.

She stood for a moment, trying to process the meaning of this. She was still in a day gown, had no bonnet, gloves or shawl and had been left standing on her own front step in the rain. She grabbed the knocker and let it fall. 'Father? I am sorry I've upset you. But if you would give me a moment to explain.' He would see that this action was not wilfulness on her part, but a carefully considered decision.

There was no response, so she knocked again. Twice. And louder. 'Father!' Perhaps she had been wrong to be so sudden. She could send another letter to Robert and he could be the one to explain the situation to Benbridge. Surely fading quietly from memory was better than another scandalous and sudden parting from a daughter.

'Father!' She pounded on the door until her hand hurt, knowing all the while that it would do no good. Even if the servants wanted to, they would not open. She was sure that Benbridge stood just on the other side to prevent it. He meant to teach her a lesson, leaving her to soak to the skin before he considered allowing her back into the house. If then. It was possible she would spend the night, pacing the street in front of her own home.

Unless he truly meant to send her away for good.

She had imagined a hurried carriage ride from London and a forced visit to some aunt or other. Eventually, she would be forgotten and that would be that.

But if he locked the doors and refused her entrance, where was she to go? She had no reticule, no money to buy a ticket on the coach, no letter of explanation or introduction. She did not even have a cloak to keep off the rain. And it was growing dark.

She knew the direction to Reighland's house,

of course, but she could hardly appeal to him for aid. With her ruined reputation and their broken engagement, there could be only one type of help he could offer.

For a moment, she considered it. She could be his mistress, if he was willing. He still wanted her body, she was sure. His anger on seeing Gervaise had been quite beyond what she would have considered appropriate for damaged pride. He was jealous. And she could use that to her advantage.

If she could stand to part with him again... which she could not. It had been quite hard enough, setting him free. But to be taken into his protection, only to watch him tire of her and release her again?

She shuddered from the cold and the rain and the misery of it, then began to walk.

Chapter Seventeen

The trip had been awful. It could have been worse, she supposed, if the neighbourhood she sought had not been a proper one. Even so, on the way to it she had been forced to endure the offers of help from several 'gentlemen' who were not gentlemen at all. What could she expect, really, wandering the streets dressed as she was, with a muslin gown soaking to transparency? They had thought her a soiled dove, with her wet skirts clinging to her legs and no sign of escort.

She had sent them away with fleas in their ears, using her best drawing-room glare. But there was little consolation in having pride when one was footsore and drenched to the skin. It encouraged the fear that when she reached the end of this evening's long journey, she would find that door barred to her as well.

She stood on the front step, letting the rain drip from her gown, and waited. A housekeeper opened the door and said, 'Oh, dearie', before catching herself in a familiarity and dropping a curtsy. Then she ushered her in properly, calling for a footman to find the mistress.

It was a small house, Priss noted, but it was nicely kept. Warm and comfortable. And just the sort of place she suspected would have a warm drink for a stranger, even if she was arriving unexpectedly, and possibly unwelcome. If they would let her stay the night, perhaps tomorrow she would have some idea of what to do.

'Priss!' Without warning, she was crushed in a hug.

'I know it is past time to be calling. And certainly, I have no invitation…' she muttered into Drusilla's sleeve. It was a more fashionable sleeve than she was used to seeing on her sister's arm. And the familiar smell of her sister's Castile soap was overlaid by unfamiliar cologne. But the feeling of loving arms was just as she remembered it.

'You are talking nonsense, Priss.' At least Dru still sounded like Dru. 'What are you doing washed up on my doorstep like a drowned rat? You poor thing.'

'Father,' she managed, weak with relief at the feeling of being taken in hand by her much stronger, older sister.

'Not another word,' said her sister. 'Not until we have you warm and dry again.' Her arm around Priss's shoulders, she led her towards a sitting room, calling for a toddy and a wrapper.

'I will wet it clean through...' Priss sniffled at the water dripping down her nose from her hair '—and your upholstery and rugs as well.'

'Never mind them. Come up to my room instead; we will get you into a hot bath and one of my nightgowns. And as we do, you will tell me all about it.'

It felt wonderful to be held close and to not have to think any more. Dru had always been so good about organising things, knowing what was needed and procuring it without fuss. Now she was leading Priss up a flight of stairs to a large and comfortable bedroom on the first floor. Priss glanced around her as the footman brought the tub and the maid and housekeeper began filling it with steaming water.

There were men's things in the room. Apparently, Mr Hendricks shared the space with his wife. The cramped quarters did not seem to bother Dru in the slightest, but it reminded Priss that there was another who might have objections to seeing his house turned into a refuge. 'Are you sure that it is all right? Will Mr Hendricks mind?'

'That I have taken in my own sister?' Dru laughed. 'I will see to it that he does not.' There was something about the merry smile that hinted at secrets she would not have expected Dru to have. Priss remembered the perfume scenting her sister's sleeve. She'd have described it as lush and seductive, had she smelled it on another. Apparently, the time away from home had changed Dru more than she'd realised.

'Tell your husband I am sorry.' Priss sniffled again, then sneezed. 'But I could think of nowhere else to go. Father put me out. I never thought he would, but he was angry. Now that he has married Veronica, he says there will be a son. He doesn't need me any more, nor does he wish to give another thought to his troublesome daughters.'

'And we will not think of him, either,' Dru assured her. 'Now that you are engaged, you needn't ever go back. We will take you in until after the wedding.'

'No,' Priss said in a whisper, suddenly afraid that the sniffling might be the beginnings of tears and not illness. 'There will be no wedding. Ever. Gervaise has returned. There have been items in the paper. They did not use my name, but it was obvious. Everyone knows.' The tears began to fall again and she wiped them away with her damp sleeve. 'And it is all my fault. I could not put Robert through that. People will think he is marrying a common whore.'

She waited for the stern lecture that she knew was coming. Silly had been after her for years to mind her reputation and to mind society, begging her to just once exercise some care before acting. She had not listened. Now she was in the soup for certain.

Instead her sister pulled her down on to a couch by the window and stroked her hair, offering her a handkerchief.

Priss took it and blew her nose. 'I have caused

so much trouble for everyone. Now I must pay the price for it.'

'You tried to do what was right,' Dru assured her. 'And Father was horrible to you. Reighland is horrible as well, if he will not stand by you in a time of crisis.'

'It is not his fault at all,' Priss argued. 'I could not force Robert into the shame of marrying me, so I released him from his obligation.'

There was a hesitation, then Dru's grip on her tightened. 'That was very noble of you.'

'Father does not think so. He says I am a stupid girl: Reighland was trapped and rightly so, and that all I had to do was keep my mouth shut and go to the altar. Father says he will never unload me now, so he will have no more of me.'

'You are not stupid. You are right not to want a husband who feels he has been trapped. I do not think it would make for a very happy marriage. But if there has been some event that compromised you...' Dru proceeded hesitantly. 'I can still send John to the duke and insist that he have you. It is wrong of him to turn his back on you, just when you need him. And even worse to leave you at the mercy of the gossips, in part because of his behaviour.'

Priss gave a wet laugh. 'I never expected to have a happy marriage until just recently. Now that I have ruined my chances for one, I do not think I could abide another kind. It was stupid of me to run away with Gervaise. Thank heaven you caught me before Gretna Green, or I would be legshackled to him.'

Surprisingly, Dru had found tact. A year ago, she would have agreed and ended with some pious platitude. But now, though she did not rush to her sister's defence, she allowed, 'You had your reasons for leaving our home. They led you to do things that were unwise. I think you were smarter than you let on when you told me, all those months ago, that you had no freedom.'

'I found, once I was with him, that I could not stand the thought of marriage to him, either. He was horrible to me.' That was as close as she could come to admitting the truth to her sister. 'But I thought if I were ruined, then maybe Father would leave me alone. And we could be spinsters together.'

'I…I didn't think you wished my company.' Dru seemed surprised.

'Of course I did. You are my sister. Why would I not wish to be with you? But I did not think you would ever marry. Even if you were often cross with me, I did not want you to be alone with Father.'

'And I spoiled your plans and ran off myself,' Dru said. 'I left you alone instead.'

'It almost didn't matter. I'd have been gone, soon enough, if I'd married. But it has been awful, having to listen to him and not being able to see you, even at parties. You looked happy. You are, are you not?' she clutched eagerly at her sister's hand and felt an answering grasp.

'Very much so.' Dru almost grinned. 'I have a husband who adores me. And friends. And now I have you again. If worse comes to worst, you shall stay here, in my household, as a doting aunt.'

'You are increasing?'

Dru smiled. 'I think I might be. It is about time, is it not? I wanted so much to see you the other night. But I could not manage to keep my dinner down. The thought of prawns and champagne…' She gave a shudder of revulsion. 'I was likely to shame myself in the middle of the dance floor, before I even got to say hello to you.'

Priss gave a relieved sigh and turned to hug her sister again. 'Then it shall be my turn to take care of you. Burnt toast and tea, until you are feeling yourself again.'

'Dru…' Mr Hendricks had stopped in the doorway and was staring at her where she sat on the couch. A look passed between husband and wife. Suddenly Priss was quite sure that, while Silly might extend the invitation of shelter, her husband would not be completely pleased by it.

'Father has turned her out. The engagement is off. And Gervaise is back.'

Mr Hendricks seemed to grow larger at the mention of the name. 'I told him what would happen if he returned. I will take care of it.' He turned to go.

'No!' Priss took a deep breath, then said in a softer, calmer voice, 'I do not wish you to risk harm on my account. If anything happened to you, even a scratch…and it was because of my foolishness… I could not do that to my sister.'

Mr Hendricks seemed surprised by this and

shot his wife a quick glance before saying, 'Reighland, then. I will call on him and explain the situation. He shall take care of it.'

'Even worse,' Priss moaned, for that brought forth another picture of Mr Hendricks, who knew most of the story, speaking with the only man that knew the rest.

Another quick look passed between the couple. Then Mr Hendricks said, 'Very well. For the moment, I will do nothing, as long as you promise to get hold of yourself. Because if you are distressed by this man, I will be forced to take action. For now, I will send Folbroke to Benbridge and he will see what is to be done to mend this breach. But do not fear, Lady Priscilla, you are safe and welcome for as long as you need a home.'

'Thank you, Mr Hendricks.' She remembered when she'd first met him, barking his name and ordering him about. And God forbid, she had kissed him to make her sister jealous. She looked at him, praying that he did not remember any of it, but sure that he did. Then she said, 'I am sorry. For everything. And especially for involving you in yet another of my many embarrassments.'

Her apology seemed to surprise him, but he smiled. 'That is all right. If not for you, I would never have met my darling Drusilla.'

Mr Hendricks departed and Dru put Priss into the tub, then washed her, dried her and dressed her in one of her own nightgowns. The fabric pooled at her feet, as did the silk of the wrapper, making Priss feel even more like a coddled child. Then Dru combed out her hair and tied the curls out of the way so she could sleep. It felt wonderful, as it had after Mama had died and her big sister had played mother to her, stepping into the role as if she'd been born to it and easing some of the loneliness.

After all was done, Dru offered her a hot drink and led her to the guest bedroom, assuring that she could stay as long as she liked.

Although how she would live here without so much as a petticoat to call her own, Priss was not sure.

The letter she sent to Veronica the next morning, requesting the right to remove some of her possessions from the house, was summarily ignored. Dru's offer to purchase a wardrobe for her was embarrassing, but she could think of no other way to go on but to accept it with promises of repayment when she found her feet again.

Priss was in no rush to do so, for that would admit what a mess she had made of things. So she had. Priss had allowed herself to succumb to the cold that had resulted from walking the London streets in a rainstorm and spent the better part of a week with her stuffed head buried in the pillows, unwilling and unable to rise and take meals with the family. When she recovered sufficiently to rouse herself, she restated her thanks and apologies to Mr Hendricks.

He gave her an arch look from the end of the table, where she had interrupted his reading of the morning's *Times*. 'Please, Priscilla, do not trouble yourself further on the subject. It is quite apparent that you are considerably altered since we first met. While I welcome the improvement in your character, I am sorry that it was a result of the cold manners of your father and stepmother. Let us hear no more of you begging your way back into the house. I could not in good conscience let you go.'

'But whatever will I do to repay you?'

'For a beginning, you can promise not to kiss me, as you did the first time I rescued you.'

'Certainly not, Mr Hendricks.' The awful memory was being casually thrown back in her face and she took a deep breath to prepare further denials as she would have, had she been talking to her father.

Then she noticed that both he and her sister were smiling at her. 'Very well, then,' she said, with more composure. 'I will try to restrain myself.'

'Then you must allow me to tell Reighland of your whereabouts.'

'I will not see him,' she said, firmly.

'He was likely concerned by your letter, followed by your sudden disappearance. Even if you do not see him, I could seek a short interview with him and make your explanations for you.' As always, Hendricks was the soul of diplomacy. Priss suspected that it was something he wished to do, but he would not proceed without her consent.

'Very well, then,' she said. 'You are bound to see him at some point or other, although I should be able to avoid him.' It was just what she planned to do, unless there was some result from the time they had spent together at the farm. But three days with Gervaise had amounted to nothing. She must pray that she was lucky again. 'Send my apologies for wasting his time, and for embarrassing him with my behaviour. If he is angry, then I can certainly understand it. But I do not think that I can bear another scold on the subject.'

Even the thought of their last meeting made the tears well up in her eyes again. She filled the awkward silence with enthusiastic application of marmalade to toast, hoping that her host and hostess did not notice.

'As you wish,' said Hendricks, pretending to go back to his reading. 'I shall take care of it for you. Do not trouble yourself further.'

She felt none of the relief she'd hoped she would, after his assurance. It only reminded her of the times that Robert had wondered whether she was strong enough to be his duchess. If nothing else did, this would prove to him that the answer was a resounding 'no'.

Chapter Eighteen

Robert reached into his pocket and crumpled the paper it held, which was still twisted around his ring. When he'd first read it, he'd almost shouted to all the people in the room that they must go home immediately. There was no cause for celebration. He had been jilted in front of the cream of society and they could all laugh as he knew they wished to.

But then he had remembered that this was not his house, nor were these his guests. A revelation of the note would mean alerting Benbridge to some of the more sordid details of the last few minutes.

It had been difficult enough holding up his head while people around him whispered that his fiancée had run crying to her room, and

that he had been seen forcibly ejecting someone from the house. Benbridge would want to
know the man's name, the reason that Priss had
been alone with him, and why she was protecting the bounder when he clearly needed a sound
beating for taking liberties with another man's
betrothed.

Then there was the matter of the letter. And
the ring. And the fact that, if the girl did not
want him, did he have any more say in the matter? Did he even have the right to be here? A decent father would take one look at the letter and
put him out of the house as well.

But he was dealing with Benbridge. If he
pressed the issue, Priss would be hauled bodily
down the stairs and forced to dance with tears
still wet on her cheeks.

So he had said nothing to anyone, folded the
paper up again, stuffed it into his pocket and
danced and made merry as if his life depended
upon it, leaving the house at dawn just as he
had planned to, and telling host and hostess that
he hoped Lady Priscilla would be feeling better
after a good night's rest.

Almost a week had passed since the receipt of

the damned letter; he had received no further word and no apologies for her hasty actions at the party or her silence afterwards. The silly girl seemed to think that she could hand the Duke of Reighland his walking papers and disappear into the night, like some sort of Bedouin.

This farce had gone on long enough. She would not be permitted to upend his life and turn what should have been a simple business arrangement into a Cheltenham tragedy. He had never intended a love match. But for a moment, he thought he'd found one, only to see it evaporate in the heat of the first argument. It was not to be tolerated.

Since she had not come to him, as he had expected her to, he must seek her out. But it was proving difficult. Benbridge had compounded her insult with his unwillingness to give a straight answer on the subject of the girl's whereabouts. When he'd called, the earl was unavailable, as was the countess. The butler had been unable to give him more information on the subject, other than that Lady Priscilla no longer resided in the house and would not be returning. When he had at last cornered the earl and demanded to know Priscilla's whereabouts, the man had looked through him and announced, 'I have no daughter' in sonorous tones, as though he could erase members of his family by sheer force of will.

The whole lot of them were clearly mad.

If she was not at home, he could think of only one other place in London she might have gone. Two other places, actually. There was always the chance that his worst fear was true: he had totally misjudged her and she had run off with the dancing master again. Although he had reminded himself repeatedly that he had no logical reason to wish marriage with someone who preferred another, the idea made him wish to tear down the roads to Scotland, locate the couple and shake Gervaise until his dancing pumps fell off.

But it was far more likely that she had gone to her sister. At the very least, the woman should know of all the properties Benbridge might have secluded her in. He would come away with a list and visit each of them until he found her.

So Robert had come to beard Hendricks in his den. He ignored the protestations of the housekeeper that the master was not at home and pushed his way past her into the man's study. To be turned away repeatedly at the door of an earl was an insult. He would not stand it from Hendricks.

'I was just about to write to you,' Hendricks said, as though there was nothing unusual about being discovered at his desk when the prospective guest had just been informed that 'the master was out'.

'Really? You could have simply spoken to me at the club, at dinner, or anywhere else in London. I see you often enough. In truth, you have been constantly underfoot, trying to win my approval. Until this week, of course.' Robert gave the man a dark glare that did credit to previous iterations of Reighland. 'Suddenly you are as elusive as Benbridge. I demand an explanation.'

'I have been unexpectedly busy,' Hendricks admitted, without turning a hair. The man's calm was maddening.

'Would this increased activity have anything to do with the sudden disappearance of my fiancée?'

'I was given to understand that the engagement was at an end,' Hendricks replied.

'Not from me you weren't,' Robert replied. 'The engagement will be over when I post an announcement in *The Times* and not before.'

'Normally, it is the young lady involved who makes such a decision,' Hendricks informed him placidly.

'This young lady should not be allowed to make decisions, since she clearly lacks the sense to know what is good for her. She will not wish to end the engagement once I have talked to her again. And I will do it over the dead body of her precious dancing master, if that is necessary. I assume that Benbridge has packed her off to the country, just as she always wanted. Or is she hiding here?' Reighland squared his shoulders and gave Hendricks a look that should have sent the man scurrying to fetch her, while the Robert Magson that still quavered inside him crossed his fingers that the answer would bring him closer to the truth.

'She does not wish to see you.' It was not the same thing as affirmation, but he suspected that

Hendricks would have told him flat out if he did not know the girl's location.

'I wish to see her,' he said firmly. 'She sent me this. Now she must explain it.' He pulled the letter from his pocket, embarrassed that it showed obvious signs of agitated and frequent reading.

Hendricks ignored the crumples in the paper and gave it a cursory examination. 'It seems plain enough to me. She has cast you off.'

'But I never meant for that,' Robert argued.

'Did you do something that might lead her to write this?'

'I lost my temper with her,' he admitted, thinking of the stricken look on her face as he had scolded her.

'And both the girls have seen enough of that to last a lifetime.'

As if that had not been plain to him already. The annoying prickling of guilt that he'd felt after parting with her had grown into a continual chafing, as though his heart was full of sand. 'She does not complain of it here,' He rattled the paper of the letter, trying to shift the blame and feeling all the worse for it. 'The letter is full of nonsense about protecting me from the shame of association with her.'

Hendricks nodded. 'She would not blame you for your arrogance, of course. Benbridge may not have trained his daughters well, but he has done it thoroughly. Dru was told, practically from birth, that all problems were her own fault. I suspect, once she left, that the role of family scapegoat fell to her sister. Circumspection and humility have come late to Priss. In the past she'd got her way in all things. It has not been a kindness to her character.'

'There is nothing all that wrong with her character,' Robert snapped back, 'other than that it is damned hard to read.' Not that he had ever been good at understanding other humans. 'I thought she had more spirit in her,' he admitted. 'She did nothing but fight me for the first weeks of our acquaintance. And just when I thought matters between us had been settled, she changed.' He stared at the letter in his hand. 'I was not particularly surprised at her threatening to break the engagement, but I did not expect she would actually do it. And in such a weak and spineless way as this.'

'And do you think this speaks her true feelings?' Hendricks prompted.

'Yes,' Robert admitted glumly. 'If she has decided she is not worthy, then it is what she truly feels. But she cannot be further than the truth. It is I who am unworthy.' It was only when he saw the surprise on Hendricks's face that he remembered that Reighland would not think thus.

'She has told me she does not want to see you,' Hendricks said, watching him closely. 'She insists it is for your own good. I will not force her to, for there has been too much of that used already.'

Robert debated for a moment, applying the weight of his forgotten title to the situation. Hendricks talked as if the girl was hiding above stairs. If Reighland had pushed his way this far into the house, what was a few more feet? But Robert Magson shrank from a confrontation that might display his inadequacies before the girl's family. If she could not be persuaded to come back, it would gain him nothing.

'Going to let her go, are you?' Hendricks gave him a curiously neutral look.

'She wishes it,' he said, despising himself for

having no better answer. 'She has sent back the ring as well. It might be over, but for the announcement. But if I end it, what is likely to become of her? Will her father find her another match?'

'He has put her out of the house and cut her from the family, just as he did her sister,' Hendricks said. 'In the rain,' he added.

'The bastard!'

'Indeed,' Hendricks agreed. 'She came here with the clothes on her back and nothing more. We cannot get so much as a hair ribbon out of him. She can stay here as long as she needs to, though I will admit that our funds are limited. It will not be what she is accustomed to.'

'She can hardly marry Gervaise in my stead.'

Hendricks was still watching him closely. 'It should be no business of yours whether she does or not.'

'It is my business because...I have feelings for her,' he said, not wanting to sound as miserable as he felt at the idea of her returning to the dancing master. 'Gervaise used her abominably during their supposed elopement and has been dogging her every step for weeks, trying to make mischief between us. He deserves horse whipping, at the very least. But she did not wish me to challenge him,' he added, feeling all the worse that he had not done it before now, despite his reservations.

'She does not wish me to act, either,' Hendricks said, with an ironic smile. 'She was uncharacteristically sure of that fact. It surprised me. Six months ago, I swear she'd have wanted the two of us brawling in the street for her amusement. It seems our Priscilla has developed a heart—due to her association with you, perhaps. But the real question still remains: why Gervaise has returned, after all this time, and why is he eager to renew the acquaintance? The man should not be here. I threatened his life.' Hendricks sighed. 'If I find him, I shall have to call in that particular marker, no matter what Priscilla wishes.'

One such as Hendricks did not say to a duke, 'Stand up for your woman and your honour, or I shall have to do it for you.' But there it was. Robert transferred the onus back to the other man. 'Your threat must not have been very convincing, if he was willing to disregard it and come back to London.'

'Very effective at the time, I assure you,' Hendricks said, indignantly. 'I punched him repeatedly on the nose. And I told him there would be no money, which was the only thing he truly cared about. I suspect that someone else has tracked him down and offered a sum that outweighed the risk.'

'And who might do that?' Robert said, with a half-smile.

'The same sort of person that would share his presence with the papers to destroy a lady's chances with a powerful peer.'

'I could think of several that might consider it.' Three, actually. Of the young ladies he had given his specific attentions to before he had met Priscilla, one had already announced an engagement. The second did not seem mean spirited enough, nor fixed in her affections upon him. 'My money would be on Char Deveril's family.'

Hendricks gave a laugh of surprise. 'You would win the bet, I am sure. Some day, when I am in my cups, I must tell you the connection I have with Miss Deveril. If she knows the full story, she has more than one reason to thwart the future of Lady Priscilla. But freeing up a fat pigeon such as yourself would be more than enough.' Hendricks thought for a moment, and added, 'Your Grace.'

Robert waved it off. 'The title hardly fits. There is nothing graceful about the way I handled this. My only excuse is that my blood was up, at the thought of her with that…' He still could not think clearly on the subject. 'I am not usually so passionate about such things. I certainly had not meant to be. A decision about who to take to wife should not be based on such strong emotions.'

'There are many who would tell you just the opposite.'

'Then they would be blockheads. I acted no better than she did when I saw her with Gervaise. I hurt her. This letter is because she thought I wished to cast her off. She was saving herself some pride by taking the lead, and, strangely enough, it has rebounded upon me. She's admitted her lack of virtue and proven that she is unable to behave properly or manage the scandal attached to her name. She has given me a perfectly legitimate way to avoid an inappropriate match, yet I feel even worse than I did before.'

Hendricks nodded. 'Perhaps you were right about a surfeit of emotion. It would be very difficult for her to be married to a man who so dwelt upon her past mistakes that he was willing to throw them unexpectedly back in her face and doubt her after she had pledged herself to him.'

Damn the man for agreeing with him. He'd found a way to turn subservience into a knife in the back and to twist the blade in the wound. 'But I would not be that man,' he insisted. 'I know well enough how hard it is to live down one's past. I was thought to be a bit of a blockhead in school; boys being what they are, the fellows around me used every chance to remind me of it. When I came of age, I was only too happy to walk away from the lot of them. But now?' Now he was back in the thick of his old enemies and would have to be so for the rest of his life. And much as he might try to pretend it didn't matter, each session of Parliament would bring back all the old memories even if he did prove that he was no longer a weeping schoolboy.

None of which he needed to share with Hendricks. He froze those thoughts in their place, pushing them back, out of the way. 'Let us just say that I understand Priscilla better than most. I would tell her so.' He gave Hendricks a piercing Reighland look. 'If only I knew of some way to contact her.'

Hendricks frowned. 'She will not see you, nor anyone else. I have her permission to offer all explanations that needed making, or I would not have spoken as much as I have. If you wish to send a message, I will attempt to relay it. But I will not guarantee that she will listen. Nor I will not let you speak directly with her. I suspect that pretty words would merely upset her and I will not have that.' Hendricks was looking at him now, with none of the subtlety he usually saved for his betters. It was a clear challenge to someone he deemed a threat to his wife's family.

'Perhaps you are thinking of another man, Hendricks. I have never been known to have a surfeit of pretty speeches.' But much as he had always relied upon them, silence and denial had proven worthless. 'In a case like this, actions are necessary. But she will not know of them, if she thinks to hide in her room.' He thought for a moment, then said, 'If you could persuade her to attend the gathering at the Deverils' house, as she planned to before this hubbub, I will see to it that it is a most diverting evening.'

Chapter Nineteen

'Get up off that bed this instant, Priscilla, and stop being ridiculous. It is nothing more than a little party. And in the home of one of your oldest friends.' It was strange that several weeks had changed little more than the person standing in the doorway to scold her. Comparing the two, Priss much preferred Dru to Ronnie. There was an undercurrent of love in her sister's commands that had been absent from her stepmother's.

Priscilla stared at the ceiling of her borrowed bedroom without moving. 'Charlotte Deveril is no friend of mine.' She was almost sure of the fact. 'Char was watching in the hall when I ran from Reighland. What better reason for that than that she orchestrated the whole thing?'

'But why would she want to do anything so

terrible?' Dru asked, proving that marriage had left her surprisingly naïve to the ways of society.

'Because she wished to discredit me with Reighland. The moment I gave it back, she was probably searching his pockets for my betrothal ring.' She should have not used a possessive, when speaking of it. It did not even truly belong to Robert. But for the two weeks she had worn it, she had never owned a piece of jewellery that felt so rightly hers. 'If Char still wishes me to come to her house, it is merely to gloat over the fact that she has snared him and to laugh when I embarrass myself again.'

Dru nodded. 'It is good to see that you have become wiser in the months that we have been apart. Char was never a friend to you and tonight she will most assuredly make mischief.'

Priss tossed on the bed, flopping on to her stomach like a rag doll, and moaned into the pillow. 'Then you can see why I do not wish to go.'

'On the contrary, that is exactly why you must go. How else will you prove to her that she cannot affect you? You are worth two of her and are the daughter of an earl as well.' Drusilla sounded quite like the martinet she used to be.

Then Dru paused and bit her lip. 'And if she is angry at you? There is a chance that I had something to do with it. Mr Hendricks and I met her on the road to Scotland. It is rather a long story, but it ended with her kissing Mr Hendricks and me stealing her purse.'

'You did not,' Priss said, eyes wide with surprise.

'I am sorry if I created a problem for you,' Dru said. 'But please do not tell me that you mean to let that horrible girl get the better of us. Now get up off your bed and finish dressing. I will give you no choice in the matter.'

'Do you mean to sit in the corner, as you always used to, to make sure that I do not spoil the evening?' When they had gone about together before she married, Dru had been a steadfast but disapproving companion. However, to be honest, Priss had given her many reasons to disapprove.

Today, when she smiled, the old Silly was gone, replaced by the fashionable Mrs Hendricks. 'Of course not. I mean to dance and leave you to settle your own affairs. Like it or not, Priss, you are a woman now and must learn to find your own way. If you cannot have Reighland, then you must at least see that she does not. The Benbridge family honour is at stake.'

'But mightn't my appearance there cause trouble for Mr Hendricks? I have become a public joke, Dru. I will be an embarrassment for him.'

'Whether you come with us or not, people will ask after you. And I do not mean to hide in my house on a night when my stomach is settled enough to go out. You were merely silly when you were younger,' Dru reminded her. 'Now?' She shrugged. 'You are a notorious fallen woman.'

Priss thought for a moment, then said, 'I believe you are right. I have taken a lover, jilted a duke and been disowned by my father. Short of becoming an opera dancer, there is not much lower to fall.'

'And to my knowledge, Char has not rescinded your invitation to this ball, nor have you sent regrets. It might be quite embarrassing for her to see you.'

'Embarrassing for her?' Priss gave a laugh that was more confident than she felt. 'She is nothing more than a common gossip. And have you ever seen her ride? Reighland could never marry her. He would be miserable.'

'Then you had best go to the Deverils' to tell him so,' Dru agreed. 'At the very least, we shall laugh at his impending misfortune. Now come to my wardrobe and let us choose a gown.' Dru searched through her gowns and held out a pale-rose cambric. 'This has never flattered me, but will do for you if we pin up the hem.'

Priss pushed it out of the way and pointed. 'Let us try that one instead. Crimson satin and far too old for me.'

Dru smiled in approval. 'It is scandalously low as well. And here is proof of what a horrible chaperon I was, for I think it will suit you perfectly.'

'I agree. If I am destined to be notorious, It is high time that I started looking the part.'

Priss entered the ballroom a few polite steps behind her sister and Mr Hendricks, to receive the cool welcome of Mrs Deveril and her aunt, who was a dowager countess. The sweeping glance she received through the elderly lady's lorgnette said it all. She was not so much a guest here as a curiosity to be gawked at.

She responded with the chilly smile her father would have used on such an occasion and turned away to survey the crowd. She saw Reighland across the room, surrounded as he always had been with eager mamas and pretty young ladies forced into introductions. He stood a head taller than anyone in his crowd, looking as always like some great bull mastiff surrounded by a tumble of puppies.

He was magnificent. How could she not have noticed it from the first? She still could not lie to herself enough to call him handsome. But he was powerful: socially, politically and, Lord help her, physically. She could still remember the way it had felt to have him inside of her.

Even now, she could feel the vitality of him calling to her. It gave her a strange ache that was both sweet and sad, when she thought of him. It was like grieving. But while the loss might be irrevocable, she could not imagine trading the brief and intense pleasure of their acquaintance for an end to her current pain.

I will always love you, Robert. The thought

came to her, pure and simple like a single monument in a barren field. No matter what might become of her, no matter what great destiny awaited him, she could look back on their few weeks together as a bright, shining moment in her past, where her life had seemed truly right and proper.

Judging by his sudden start and hurried attention to anywhere but the door of the ballroom, he had seen her as well. He might pretend not to notice, but he was aware of her presence, she was sure. She wondered if he felt the same, or if he was already tucking away the memories of her, like toys that had lost their glitter.

She turned away, vowing that she would not go to him, though she wanted to stumble across the room like a lovesick girl and take her place in the mob that pressed in upon him. Her recent actions had permanently closed the doors of the marriage mart for her. She was infamous. And while many opinions might be formed about her, no one would think of her as an innocent, or a girl.

Then she watched the crowd part around her. Though the crush was quite overwhelming, it seemed that she was to be allowed space, as though the other ladies were afraid of coming too close. She was tempted to announce that, despite what they might think, dishonour was not a contagious condition, but then she saw the reason for it. Although it would have been nearly impossible to force her way across the room to Robert, there was an open corridor in the crowd that, if she followed it, would lead straight to Gerard Gervaise.

The usual wave of nervous nausea she felt when she looked at him was replaced with righteous anger. It did not particularly surprise her that Char Deveril would drag her own honour through the mud by inviting him here, if it meant there would be another chance to laugh at Priss's expense. But it was unfair to involve Robert in it. She was meant to be trotted out like a puppet and forced into Gervaise's company, while the *ton* reminded the Duke of Reighland of the dangers of choosing an unsuitable wife who would shame him at any opportunity.

But she had nothing left to lose and did not need to play those games any longer. She would not stand by and let Robert be hurt by this scene.

Not tonight. Not ever. She turned without a word and went down the hall to the retiring rooms. That way would lead to the library, and the door opposite would take her to the front hall and out the door. She would find the Hendricks carriage, if she could, and sit in it until her sister was ready to depart. And if not? She would walk the distance to their house. She had done it once and would do it again, even if it was a hundred miles.

Her exit would be as grand as her entrance had been. She gave a single look of disgust in the direction of her old dancing master, turned with a swish of skirts and marched from the ballroom. She did not hurry. Hurrying was unseemly, at least until she was sure that no one would see it. Then she would be gone from this place, back to her bedroom where she could cry in peace.

'Running?'

'Robert!' He moved quietly for one so large. She had not heard him approach. But he must have moved with some speed to be able to cross the room and be ahead of her already. If her exit had gone unnoticed, his most surely had caused a scene. He stepped in front of her, ending all hopes of escape.

'Your Grace,' she corrected, giving him the respect due a peer. The days of thinking of him as her darling Robert were firmly at an end. She could not allow his sudden appearance to fluster her into rudeness.

He bowed in response, just as formal, while swallowing the hitch in his breath from what must have been a full-speed tilt across a crowded room. 'Lady Priscilla.' But he made no move to step out of her way, seeming to block the whole of the corridor between her and the front door.

Now that she was facing him, she could not find a single word to say. What thought could she express that would not result in immediate and very public tears? She stood there, open mouthed, staring beyond him at the sliver of view still left.

'I asked if you were running away,' he said again. His voice was pitched low, yet it still seemed unusually loud.

'Just seeking air,' she said, staring at his feet. 'I feel…unwell.' That was perfectly true, at least. 'And now, if you will excuse me…' She made to go past him.

'No, I will not.' His fingers closed on her

gloved wrist. He glanced down at the hand, rubbing his thumb gently against the inside of her arm. 'You are not wearing the gloves that I sent you.'

'They are in my father's house,' she said, 'and therefore lost to me. I expect he has burned them by now, along with the rest of my clothes. I proved a great disappointment to him.'

'I will buy you another pair.'

'And I will not accept them. It would not be proper.' *Buy them for Char, you idiot*, she wanted to scream, *but leave off tormenting me.*

'Then I will not.' He smiled. 'As you know, I would not wish to do anything improper. But neither will I allow you to leave.'

'Do you wish me to stay and be tortured for your amusement? I have let you go. Isn't that enough?'

'No. I find that it is not.' He looked sad and his grasp slipped down her hand until they were touching only fingertip to fingertip. 'Have you thought, even for a moment, that perhaps I am torturing myself? It is quite a blow to my pride to see the two of you together. He is a most insubstantial fellow.'

'Do you not understand the embarrassment that awaits us both if I stay? Please allow me to leave so that you do not have to witness a meeting I did not arrange.'

'But that will spoil your fun,' he said, stubbornly.

'There is nothing enjoyable about this, because there is nothing between Gervaise and myself,' she said firmly. 'You wanted me to manage the scandal when last we talked. And I am avoiding his company, just as a lady ought. You can hardly expect me to be responsible for wounds to your pride.'

'This has nothing to do with your responsibility for my feelings. I simply wished you to know of them.' He stepped closer to her, until she was convinced that she could feel the heat of his body. 'But I want you to know that the sight of you in the same room with him drives me mad with jealousy.' He put his hand upon her shoulder; she felt the palm burning hot against her skin.

'You have no reason to be,' she said, trying not to look into his eyes.

'It would be so with any man,' he said. 'Whenever you dance with another, I want to snatch you out of the arms of your partner, spirit you away and keep you for myself.' His tone was different, not the ironic detached man she was accustomed to, but that of a passionate lover. At one time, she'd have enjoyed toying with him, trying to inflame him to more and more ludicrous declarations of devotion, but now she laid a comforting hand against his cheek.

'But Gervaise is the worst,' he admitted, cradling the hand she offered, stroking it and whispering the words into her palm. 'That he ever touched you? I ache with the thought. And that he hurt you?' The hand on her shoulder tightened ever so slightly to draw her even nearer. 'It would be easier if he had made you happy. But tonight, I would die if I could erase the hurt from your mind. Or he should. I would gladly kill him.'

'You do not fight. You said so yourself.'

'But I will if you wish me to.'

'Do not.' She wrapped her other arm around one of his and buried her face against the lapel of his coat, not caring who might see them.

'Because you care for him?'

'I care for you. For your safety. And for your reputation. I beg you again, do not take that risk on my account.'

He dipped his head. 'Very well, then. As you command.'

'And that is why I will not marry you, you know.' She gave a small bitter laugh and pulled away from him as he kissed the top of her head. 'Because I care for you. You do not need to be saddled with my disgrace.'

'It is no burden,' he said.

'You say that now, but admit the truth to me. When you saw me with Gervaise, you doubted. And that was just the first time. Now that she has found him, I expect Char Deveril to keep trotting out Gervaise for the express purpose of embarrassing me. In the future, your doubts and embarrassment are likely to grow. It is better to end this now, I think, while we can still remember the happiness.'

'I doubted,' he said grudgingly, 'but I did not ask for my freedom. I needed time.'

'Says the man who must rush through everything,' she said with a laugh.

'Just as you will run away at the first sign of

trouble,' he accused. 'I could have accepted it, if you'd told me to go hang for my lack of faith in you. I certainly deserved it. I was despicable. Instead, you sent me that mewling note, full of self-pity and cowardice. You took all the blame for what has happened upon yourself.'

'Because it is all my fault,' she argued.

'It is not,' he said firmly. 'But it appears so, because you keep apologising.'

'I'm sorry,' she said, then hurriedly snapped her mouth shut, surprised at how quickly she had affirmed his argument.

His eyes narrowed, clearly angry. And so close, it was a daunting sight. But she knew no real harm would come to her. It was all frustration, and some of it was for her own benefit. 'Perhaps, in the end, you will run from me. But I will not let you run from this.' He reached out and touched her gently on the arm. She remembered every touch he had ever given her and a sweet, sad longing rose inside her.

'The elopement was a scandal of your own making,' he said softly.

'Because I was young and foolish,' she agreed.

'But you are older and wiser now,' he said

firmly. 'What happened when you were with Gervaise was proof that he was no gentleman. He should have treated you with kindness. He could have cherished you, like the treasure that you are.'

As you have done. She felt a wave of gratitude towards the man who stood before her. What had happened on the road to Scotland could have been wonderful. It could have been a wicked, but cherished memory. It could have been like her stolen moments with Robert.

And it was not. When she thought of Gervaise, she felt nothing but pain and embarrassment and shame. Yet she had performed the same act and more with Robert. And she would gladly do it again, married or not, without a care to who knew of it.

'It will follow you for the rest of your life, if you let it. Or it can end tonight.' As always, his words were seductive.

Her heart was as eager as ever to give in to him. 'And just how do I make it stop?'

'Silence will not be enough and I was wrong to encourage it in you. You must do something to prove that you are not bothered by this. Only then will people stop taking notice.'

She did not want to waste time in the ballroom with Gervaise, or anyone else. She swayed to be closer to him, barely able to concentrate. 'They will cut me from their social circles.'

'They were doing that already. Better to have it based on fact rather than on rumours. Do you prefer to be a disgraced coward, or brave but unwise? Tonight, you must choose.' He let go of her hand. And despicable as he was being, he was right.

She remembered all the times he had wondered about her strength of character. And how, each time he had, she had run. Then, after giving herself to him, and promising him her life, she had run again.

Yet, here he was. Warm. Stable. And offering her yet one more chance, if she were brave enough to take it. 'Will you escort me back into the ballroom, then?'

'With our engagement broken, are you not afraid it will give the wrong impression?' He was not taking her back so easily as that. She did not think she would have to beg for her place at his side. But her heart still cringed a little at the memory of how it had been the last time they'd been together.

'You are probably right.' She glanced down at herself. 'Considering the gown I have chosen, perhaps people will think you are taking a mistress.'

'That is a capital idea. I have been spurned recently. My heart is still tender from it. Perhaps I should take a lover.'

She gave him a sidelong glance, as unsure as ever as to whether he joked or was serious. 'We will discuss it later. But for now, do you still have the flask of brandy in your pocket? If I mean to have courage, I had best get it from somewhere.'

His expression hadn't changed. But she had the impression he was smiling at her as he reached into his pocket and offered her a drink.

She took it, letting it burn into her, and wondering what the world would think if it got close enough to smell spirits on her breath. She handed it back to Robert. 'Very well, then.' She glanced into the mirror on the wall of the hallway, staring down the reflection until the young lady there found her composure. 'Back to the ballroom it is.' She glanced back at the duke, low and through her lashes in a way that she was sure he would like. 'If you are lucky, Robert, perhaps I shall save you a dance.' Then she turned and swept down the hallway, as though she could chase all hindrances away with a flip of her skirt.

Chapter Twenty

Priss re-entered the ballroom, as though nothing had happened. If Reighland had followed, she did not know. Though he had walked arm in arm with her for the first few steps on the return journey, at some point he had released her, like a boy sailing a toy boat out on to a troubled pond. He meant to watch her, she was sure, to see how she might do without him.

He was right. For all her grand thoughts about being a woman and not a girl, she had shown no real courage of her own. While it might be nice to think that a powerful marriage could set everything to rights again, she would need to play some part in the rebuilding of her own reputation. If she wished to be his wife, or any other man's, it would be better if she brought some backbone to the marriage.

As she stepped forwards, once again she felt the other ladies withdraw. Inside her, the girl that she had been recoiled as well.

And once again she remembered her father. His plan in any situation, whether social or political, was to attack first and hit hard. Because of this, society feared him all out of proportion to his actual worth. She thought of the mud in her slippers, the ruined gown and the miserable head cold that had come along with the shame of banishment. She had learned a hard lesson on her worth in the family and the danger of challenging him.

Now she could teach a similar lesson to those who threatened her. She glanced around the room, choosing her targets with care. The brandy warmed her blood, making her reckless. Or perhaps that was the warmth she felt from the eyes of the only man she truly cared about, watching her from somewhere in the room.

No one else matters, she repeated to herself. What could they possibly do that would be worse than losing Robert? Everything that he had said and done from the very beginning proved to her that once she had it, she would not lose his love.

But only if she was brave enough to accept it.

'Lady Priscilla, may I have the next dance?' The Earl of Folbroke was standing just beside her, smiling pleasantly.

'Are you sure you are speaking to the right person, my lord? Your choice in me for a partner does not seem to be a wise one.'

He adjusted his gaze carefully, following the sound of her voice so that he might appear to be looking directly at her. 'If there is some problem with it, I cannot tell what it might be.' Then he pretended to look around the room for the source of her concern. 'I see nothing amiss.'

She could not help it. She giggled. 'Thank you, my lord, for coming to put me in a good humour again. I feel distinctly unwelcome this evening.'

'But you will always have true friends,' he assured her. 'Myself. My wife. And your sister and her husband, of course.'

'I worry that I am a burden upon Mr Hendricks,' she admitted. 'He has ambitions, after all. Such an association might be difficult for him.'

'You will find that his sense of justice far outweighs his aspirations. He will not abandon you. And now, the dance I requested?'

'Of course, my lord.'

He gave her a series of *sotto voce* instructions on how best to help him, so that he might lead her through the set without bumping in to the other dancers. They proceeded, nearly without incident. When his blindness caused a difficulty, he took it in good humour, and made apologies so self-deprecating that the other parties could not possibly be annoyed. As the music ended, she whispered directions to him so that they might end where she most needed to be: in the place where she might do the most damage. And then she thanked him, 'I swear, my lord, you are quite the best partner I have had in some time.'

'Even better than Gerard Gervaise? He is here this evening, you know. Or did you arrive together?' Charlotte Deveril inserted herself into the conversation without invitation, just as Priss had known she would. She was smiling, as though whatever response Priss might give would be a welcome treat.

'Gervaise? Here?' She turned to Char and blinked her eyes in a way that would make them seem larger, bluer and more guileless than she had managed in quite some time. 'For the sake of his future partners, I would hope not. I already know him better than I wish to. And I must say, in all confidence, he is not much of a dancer.'

That had done the trick. She heard a snicker from a nearby widow and felt the mob shift as someone went off to tell someone else of Gervaise's inadequacy. Char's expression turned so bitter that her lips nearly sucked back into her head. 'You are shameless, you know that, don't you? To come into my parents' home and make light of your disgrace.'

'Why, Char, I have no idea what you mean,' she said, still playing the innocent. 'I was invited into your house. Apparently, so was Gervaise. Although I cannot think, for the life of me, why you or your mother would allow such a disreputable fellow to come here. Has he been giving you lessons as well?'

'Certainly not,' Char said, her cheeks reddening more with anger than embarrassment. 'You notice I have invited Reighland as well. After his recent unfortunate mistake, he is once again the most eligible bachelor in London.'

'Is that the meaning of this?' Priss gave a merry laugh. 'I suppose you think, after our recent contretemps, he is fair game. It is too soon to count your chickens, dear Charlotte. There has been no notice in *The Times* to mark the end of our engagement. Until you see one, poor Reighland is quite under my thumb.'

Folbroke let out a laugh, but the noise Char was making reminded Priss of nothing less than a spitting cat. When she could find words again she said under her breath, 'We shall see, at the end of the evening, whether you are so confident of your place in society. Gervaise will dog your every step from here until the last trump. It will be quite embarrassing, should he arrive at the church with an impediment, will it not?'

'And just how did Gervaise find the nerve to come back to London?' Priss said, with a smile. 'Could he have had help?'

There was a slight, nervous flicker in Char's eyes. 'I have no idea what you mean.'

'And I have no idea why I ever called you friend,' Priss said, shaking her head. 'I must apologise to my sister for being such a ninny. It must have pained her greatly to put up with you. But I must put your mind at rest on one thing. Gervaise would have no reason to offer impediment to any marriage. It is not as if he can cry bigamy, for we never managed to cross the border.'

Char was quite without speech now, managing nothing more than an unladylike shriek of fury.

Priss gave a casual brush to her skirts. 'You poor thing. You sound quite undone. Perhaps you should attend to your other guests. I would not want to keep you from them.'

As her hostess stalked off, Folbroke whispered, 'Masterfully done, my dear.'

'Do you really think so?' In truth, the last battle had made her want to sink through the floor and it was just the first of many she would have to fight. 'This was all much easier last Season, when I was merely playing at being wicked. The stakes are much higher now.'

'But, Lady Priscilla, if one has fallen from grace, the *ton* is equally fascinated by one's resurrection.' He looked off into the distance for a moment, then said, 'While I have your most charming attention, there is one other matter with which you might help me.'

'Anything, my lord.'

'I have come into possession of a misplaced

piece of jewellery that must be returned to its rightful owner. I am sure some lady is distraught at the loss of it. Perhaps you can help me reunite the two.' He fished in his pocket for a moment and offered an open palm.

The Reighland betrothal ring.

It might have been possible that Robert had lost it, only to have it found and pocketed by a blind man. But it was far more likely that he had given it to a friend so that it might be returned discreetly, before anyone commented on the absence.

Priss closed her open mouth and favoured Folbroke with a smile that was wasted on him and a coo of delight that was easily overheard by everyone around them. 'Thank you, my lord. It is my ring and a gift from Robert.' She touched his wrist so that he might find her hand and slip it on over her glove. 'It is rather large, you see. And sometimes it falls from its place without my noticing.'

'You had best be more careful with it in the future. Tell Reighland to get it properly sized for you and I will say nothing of how I found it.' For a man who wished to say nothing, he was saying it rather loudly, and a nearby matron was all but taking notes on the story. It was quite likely that tomorrow's paper would have a carefully coded account of a future duchess's lost-and-found jewelry.

'And now,' he said, 'if you might direct me toward my wife, it is almost time to go into dinner.' She gave him a touch on the arm and a gentle direction.

Dinner. How had she not thought of that? She glanced around hurriedly to see if Robert was nearby, that he might escort her into the dining room. But though she was once again wearing his ring, he was standing at the side of Charlotte, in close conversation with her.

Was this some final slight on his part, to pay her back for her carelessness? She held her breath and waited. And watched as he turned rather suddenly and spoke to Char's aunt, offering his arm to the dowager with a courtly bow. Char was left standing alone, clearly piqued. To hide her confusion, she grabbed the arm of a rather confused young man who could not manage to get out of the way quickly enough.

'Eet seems we are thrown together again.

Clearly eet eez a sign that fate favours mee. May I offer you my arm, Priscilla?'

Dear Lord, it was Gervaise again. And if possible, his French accent had grown worse with the passage of time. How was she to get rid of him without being rude? But that had been her problem at the last ball. A desire to avoid a scene had resulted in her going off with a person she loathed and creating an even greater scandal.

Tonight, she turned to him and gave him one final scathing glance. 'No, Gervaise, I think not. That would require me to touch you. And I am recently bathed and have no wish to spoil the feeling of cleanliness with such contact. In fact, on looking at you tonight, I cannot imagine what possessed me to share intimacy with you in the first place.'

'But you must,' he said, looking at her in surprise, then at the dining-room door. 'Azz you can see, there are no other gentlemen willing to have you.'

Looking around, it did appear that the few men she knew who might give her aid had already disappeared from the room. She was left with the choice of Gervaise or nothing.

'Then I shall have to go alone,' she said, and before she lost her nerve she proceeded through the doors of the dining room, unescorted, to search out her seat.

Out of the corner of his eye, Robert saw Priscilla's look of horror at the approach of her old lover and had to force himself not to rush to her rescue. She would never learn to manage if he saved her from every embarrassment. Still, it felt as if he had thrown her into deep water, only to see if she could swim.

And hadn't it been she who was meant to rescue him from drowning? When had things reversed so completely? He held his breath. After what seemed like an eternity, she raised an eyebrow, said something that must have been cutting, judging by the shock that had replaced the smugness on the face of the dancing master. Then she swept past him, and past Robert as well, to find her own way to her seat about halfway down the table.

She had been a pretty girl when he had met her, with a pedigree as fine as he could have hoped for, despite her lack of virtue. But as a woman, she was magnificent. Between the red of her gown and the perfect hauteur, she seemed to glow with a fearless grace that made Charlotte Deveril look like a scheming child in comparison. In response to her entrance men all around the room pricked to awareness like stallions in rut.

And he was one of them. Not just one. He was the strongest, the largest, the most important, the leader of the herd and the only one worthy of such a woman. For the first time in his life he was glad to be Reighland. It would make the winning of her an easy thing.

When he had thought of himself as just plain Robert, he had hoped she would be the making of him, with her family name and her careful breeding. But she was still young, almost painfully so, and barely formed in mind or body. It had been too a heavy burden to place all his hopes on her. But tonight, before his eyes, she was becoming the woman he needed, with grace, power and the quick wit to navigate the deep waters they would inhabit.

He found his seat near the head of the table, as precedence dictated, and stared down the table until he'd caught her eye. She looked startled, as though her nerve was failing. But she was wearing his ring again. He glanced at her hand resting on the stem of a goblet and gave a nod of approval. He wished himself at her side, leaning close to speak to her so that she would know that all the trouble between them was over. Instead, he would spend Lord knew how many courses wedged between the hostess and the dowager in awkward conversation.

But it seemed that dinner would be interesting after all. The dancing master was taking a seat across the table from him. To explain the honour, Mrs Deveril made some excuse about an old French title in the house of Gervaise, but all present knew that it was nothing more than a sick joke to seat them together. Gervaise should not be at the party at all. If he was suffered there, he belonged at the foot of the table, or perhaps in the kitchen with the rest of the help. His presence was yet another attempt to humiliate Priscilla and to make Robert not so subtly aware that the rumours had truth in them. His future wife had been another man's plaything. If he did not wish to acknowledge it, society meant to continually rub it in his face until he was forced to cry off.

Down the table, Priss saw what was happening and poked the meat around her plate, waiting for the inevitable misstep by Gervaise that would raise Robert's temper. She took a bite and chewed methodically, clearly tasting none of the food. She meant to ignore the slight, even if it meant that she choked to death on her dinner.

Which meant that he was expected to make conversation with his neighbours, while the whole table hung on every banal word, hoping for a disaster to enliven the evening. Now, of all times, he should not let his composure slip.

Cold fury flooded through him, the desire to strike out blindly at his enemies. And as always, it was followed by impotent rage and the patient voice of his father reminding him that he must control himself, at all costs. What was the good of being large enough to hurt someone, if one never dared use that strength?

But now he was not simply large—his reach as Reighland was longer than any corporeal arm. The strength of the title was greater than mere muscle. And as he thought about the unfamiliar power that had been given to him, he felt the first real understandings of its use. He had been but playing before, Robert Magson acting as he thought a duke should behave. But the truth was suddenly plain to him.

He was Reighland. He sat in a place of honour at another man's table; the places where he would not be given the best seat numbered on less than two hands. Here, he could and would do just as he wished and the people around him could like it or be damned.

He smiled. It would be a shame to send the crowd home without a show.

Then he applied himself to the plate before him, cutting an oversized chunk of meat and stuffing it into his mouth, taking it down with big gulps of his wine. Let him be every bit the country farmer that people thought him. 'So, Mr Gervaise, what do you do to occupy yourself?' He interrupted the dancing master's conversation with his neighbour and said the question overly loud, pointing his knife in the man's direction.

For a moment, Gervaise remembered their last meeting and his eyes rolled white. Then he wet his lips with a sip of wine. 'Since the fall of *ma belle* France, I have been forced to take employment educating the young ladies in the terpiscorial arts.'

'Terpsicory?' Robert grinned at him, showing his fangs. 'And what is that, then? Some sort of gardening, I'll wager. Cutting the shrubs to look like sheep and what not? I would think they'd have servants for that.'

'No, your Grace,' Gervaise said with a smirk. 'I teach zem to dance.'

'Oh,' Robert said, giving a small laugh at his own expense. 'My mistake. What is it your people say? "Love teaches even asses to dance".'

He'd said it quickly and in what he had been assured was perfectly accented French. Perhaps these nothings assumed that he had spent a lifetime mucking stalls. But before the war, he had managed the Grand Tour, just as the rest of them had. All down the table, people seized their napkins and covered their mouths to hide the laughter. But Gervaise remained totally blank, for he had not understood a word.

Priss shifted nervously in her chair. A few looks in her direction showed that the guests were questioning whether all the barbs in that proverb had been directed at Gervaise alone. They were wondering—did he know about her past? And what did he think of it, if he did?

He would show them soon enough.

'Do not worry about your diminished position,' he said to Gervaise, with a conspiratorial grin. 'Before I began with running the country, I had a farm. And look at me now.' He spread his arms wide to prove that he ruled the world, nearly knocking over his water glass.

'How interesting, your Grace.' Gervaise had the nerve to shoot Priss a sympathetic smile. 'And what did you raise on zees farm of yours?'

'Horses, mostly. But there were the usual number of problems that one might expect on a farm. There was always something breeding. The dogs, for example.' Reighland dropped his voice to a whisper. 'Did you know that some men, when presented with an unwanted litter of pups, will simply bag them up and toss them in the river?'

A few of the ladies at the table gave low gasps of disapproval at his topic of conversation.

'Do not fear,' he said, grinning down the table

at them, wagging his finger. 'I am quite fond of dogs. I would never drown some insolent puppy for being a bother. What can they do, after all, but bark mindlessly and gnaw at my boots with their little milk teeth, trying to annoy?'

Eyes went round all around the table. And Gervaise still appeared to be a step behind.

'But vermin? They are quite another manner.' And this he delivered straight into Gervaise's blank face. 'I do not like vermin. They make no end of destruction. They threaten my comfort, my property and my family,' He lost his smile and all trace of the hearty and genial farmer disappeared. 'Vermin, Mr Gervaise, are not to be tolerated. When I find them, I exterminate them. Utterly. When I am through with them, Mr Gervaise, it is as if they never existed.' He brought his knife down so suddenly on his plate that the whole table jumped and he had to glance himself to make sure he had not damaged the Deveril china. Then he brought the blade forwards in a swift stroke, cutting a particularly bloody bite of roast beef, and chewing slowly as though he could feel the flesh of his enemy between his teeth.

Gervaise had gone as white as a parsnip. Apparently, the message was received and understood.

Robert swallowed and looked down the table at his fellows. 'I should be little better, if I were to find that my neighbours had set the rats in the grain bin to do me mischief. Where there should be brotherhood, it would pain me to find betrayal. And I would treat my enemies much the same as I would the rats they released, grinding them into the dirt and sweeping them from my path.'

He took another bite of meat, chewed, swallowed and made another sweeping gesture with his knife that made the people around him flinch.

'There are so many paths available to me I hardly know which way to choose. Duelling, of course, would be deeply satisfying, should I feel someone was threatening me or mine. But that is a rather antiquated way of solving problems, when there are so many subtle courses open to a man of rank and means.' He looked dreamily off into space for a moment, as though imagining some interesting form of revenge. Then he focused on the crowd again. 'But I should certainly not sit quietly while those around me made sport at my expense. Nor would I wish to see other, more vulnerable creatures so harassed. A lady, for instance. I am sure I would come to the rescue of the woman I love and hold her honour as dear as my own.'

When he looked at Priscilla, her hands were shaking so much that she almost spilled her wine. He willed strength back to her and she stilled, raised her glass and drank, giving him a look that raised the temperature of his blood. He had not told the whole room he loved her, but the lot of them would have to be as blind as Folbroke to have missed the fact.

And then he let his eyes rove around the table, to his host, his hostess and their repellant, conniving daughter. 'But one thing I will not do is waste another moment of my time playing games, held up as a country novelty for the entertainment of the common crowd. I lack the talent to hide my intentions behind false smiles, as some of you do, so allow me to speak plainly. I am young yet, new to London and to my title. But unlike my predecessors, I mean to live a good long time.

'Those who are my friends will see the benefits of my patronage. Those who think to slight me now will have years to suffer the consequences of their mistakes. Now, if you will excuse me, I must take my leave and attend to other matters.' He reached into his lap and dropped his napkin on his plate, then stood and left the room without another word.

He walked towards the front door, in a flurry of servants. But before they could attempt to disentangle his carriage from the host of others waiting outside, he held up a hand to stay them. One of his grooms was summoned and he offered a few hushed instructions before heading off on foot towards his next destination, which was barely a mile away.

The servants of the Benbridge household opened for him, but offered some weak excuse about the master being absent, which was utter nonsense. Where else could he be, other than sulking in his own home?

'Then I shall wait,' he said. 'Direct me to a sitting room and tell Benbridge and his lady of my presence so that they might wait upon me when they return.'

He was left to cool his heels for the better part of an hour, as servants scampered up and down the stairs like mice, relaying his message to the master and mistress, and assuring them of the duke's unwillingness to quit the premises. Then a decision had to be made as to whether it was necessary to dress so as to appear to be returning to maintain the charade.

When at last he saw Benbridge and his loathsome wife, the earl greeted him in normal dinner clothes with a shallow bow and a patently false apology for being away from home.

'You hardly could have been expected to wait upon me tonight. I assume there was some gathering or other that I have missed?' He looked hopefully at Lady Benbridge, who automatically supplied, 'There was a ball held by the Deverils this evening.'

'Really.' He feigned surprise. 'I did not think it likely that you would be there. Both of your daughters attended, and you do not seem inclined to speak to either of them.'

'I have no daughters,' the earl erupted with such heat and force that the words might as well have been lava.

'On the contrary. You have two daughters. I have met them both,' Robert corrected. 'I am going to marry one of them.'

'You still intend, after all the news of her, to wed that little fool?' Benbridge's response was half-surprise and half-hope, as though, at this late date, he could retract his bad behaviour towards his younger child.

'Mind your tongue, old man. You are talking about my future wife,' Robert said, finally out of patience. 'I have had enough with your family intrigues. They end tonight. The wedding will continue, exactly as planned, and you will attend it, as will John and Drusilla Hendricks.'

'I beg your pardon?' Benbridge held a hand to his ear, as though pretending he had not heard.

'Let me speak more clearly,' Robert answered. 'It is one thing to politely avoid the company of a person we do not like. That is what I plan to do with you in the future. But it is quite another to make embarrassing public displays of animosity in some pathetic effort to call attention to your own importance.' He glanced in the general direction of the witch that Benbridge had married. 'Just as it is one thing to refuse an invitation and another to have no invitations to refuse. If you wish to play these silly games, I will play them as well and see to it that you are cut from guest lists all over London. In the end, I will come out on top of any argument we might have.'

'Are you threatening me, sir?' the old earl all but crowed in outrage.

'Yes, I believe I am,' Robert said, with a pleasant smile. 'Either we will manage to maintain a cordial dislike and you will treat both your daughters with civility, if not with warmth, or I will go out of my way to crush your hopes and thwart your goals. Your choice, Benbridge. Entirely your choice. And now, I must go. It has been an interesting evening thus far, but for me, it is far from over. We look forward to seeing you in church.'

When he exited Benbridge's house, the Reighland carriage was waiting in the street, just as he'd assumed it would be. The groom helped him into his seat and he gave a benevolent smile to the man on the opposite bench who was trussed like a Christmas goose.

'Gervaise. So kind of you to join me this evening. I will require just a few moments of your time.' He reached across and removed the gag from the man's mouth. At one time, he might have shouted at the man to ensure his fear, but tonight he needed to be nothing more than icily polite. It was clearly effective for the dancing master looked ready to wet himself.

'I did not join you. I was set upon by ruffians,' he stammered.

'Only because I was too busy to wait for you myself. So I arranged for your kidnapping,' Robert said. 'I did not have to lift a finger.' Which ought to satisfy both Priss and the memory of his father.

'Where are you taking me?' Gervaise's gaze darted towards the covered window.

'To a place where you will never be able to disrespect me or my duchess ever again.'

'You mean to kill me. Exterminate me, as you said at dinner.' Gervaise's voice was shrill and there was no trace left of the false French accent he had attempted.

'You admit you are vermin, then?' Robert gave him an encouraging nod.

'Yes,' Gervaise whined.

'Very good. We are in agreement. But now let us set the matter straight. I do not mean to kill you. I wish to kill you. But those are two quite different things.'

'Please, don't.'

'That should be "please don't, your Grace".'

'Your Grace,' Gervaise sputtered.

'You would do well to remember that. As I said, I am not going to kill you. I made a promise to Lady Priscilla not to hurt you, but my vow can hardly be expected to extend to my servants. It appears that they were overzealous in collecting you. I apologise, of course. But I will admit, it does not bother me over much.'

He leaned across the space between them so that he might speak directly into the man's face. 'You would be wise to thank God for the lady's charity and for my sudden decision to value my word of honour over my personal desire to maim you. After what you have done, you are lucky to be so small and pale and worthless. If I were not so sure that I could snap you in half without exertion, you would die for what you have done.'

'What I have done?' Gervaise squeaked with outrage, making him sound even more like the rat he was.

'My intended has told me how you treated her on your aborted elopement. What she describes was little better than rape.'

'She was willing,' he argued.

'She was alone,' Robert shouted and the man quailed back into the cushions of the seat. 'And you hurt her. More than once.' For a moment, Robert forgot his promise and saw nothing but blood. He regained enough control to limit himself to a single, satisfying slap across Gervaise's face, but it was enough to loosen several teeth and would raise a welt that would be purple for a week. The dancer sagged from the seat in a dazed heap on the floor of the carriage. Then Robert remembered all he had been taught: physical violence was no answer, nor was it necessary. Especially not now that he was Reighland. He took a moment to calm himself and then continued the speech he had planned.

'As I said, you may retain your worthless life

because I would find no sport in ending you. But you will not be given the opportunity to bother Priscilla again.' The carriage has stopped and the door opened. He grabbed the other man by the collar, pulled him forwards and dropped him to the ground. 'I have brought you to the docks because, I think, in the interests of your health, a sea voyage is in order. I do not really care where you go, as long as you do not return.' He grinned down at Gervaise, then scooped the man up, set him on his feet and brushed the dirt from his coat. 'So which is it to be? Australia? The Americas? Or do you favour a career in the Navy? The choice is yours. But think quickly, before I drop you into the river and let you drown with the rest of the rats.'

Gervaise was struggling in his grasp, eager to be on his way. 'Whatever boat is nearest.'

Robert smiled. 'The Navy it is, then. And a word of advice, Gervaise. The thing in front of you is called a ship. Off you go, then. *Bon voyage.*' He directed the driver and groom to see to it that Mr Gervaise found his way to the captain and climbed back into the carriage to wait.

* * *

It was almost dawn before he reached his next destination. He yawned and wondered if he would ever adjust to London hours. It seemed the streets were never empty, no matter when he was on them. In his opinion, decent people should be asleep, rather than just coming home.

Then he smiled. He might be thoroughly done up, but there was at least one who was still awake and hoping that he would visit. While a few hours' sleep might be welcome, he had wasted too much time away from her already.

Chapter Twenty-One

'Did you have a good evening, dear?' Dru yawned as she pulled off her gloves and shrugged her evening cloak into her husband's waiting arms.

Priscilla gave her sister an arch look, then smiled. 'You know I did. I hope that my behaviour was not too trying.'

Drusilla smiled back at her. 'Now that it does not affect my prospects for marriage, I find it most entertaining. Of course, if Father hears of it, he will be furious.'

'We have no father,' Priss said, pulling a face that she hoped was a creditable imitation of Benbridge when he was angry.

'We will see how long that lasts, once you become the notorious Duchess of Reighland.' Dru glanced at her husband. 'John, will you help her Grace with her cloak? We want her to remember her humble family with kindness after her marriage.'

'Do you really think so?' Priss asked hopefully. 'He left before dinner was even completed. And he said hardly a word to me. He did not even ask me to dance.'

'You are wearing his ring again, aren't you?'

'Well, yes…but he did not give it to me. It was passed to me by Folbroke.'

'If Reighland did not wish for you to have it, it would still be in Folbroke's pocket,' Mr Hendricks assured her.

'And the way he behaved at dinner did seem significant, didn't it?' Priss sighed as she thought of her Robert handling the cream of London society as though he was whipping show ponies around a ring. Why had she ever thought him coarse or common?

'Does that mean the next time he calls, you will be at home to him?' Hendricks asked.

'You had better be,' Dru reminded her, returning to her old dictatorial ways. 'After tonight, I will not let you mope in your room another moment. It is clear that those hostesses who slight you will do so at their peril. I expect to see a flood of invitations in tomorrow's post. And if we do not see a renewed offer from Reighland soon, he shall likely have to fight for your hand.'

Priss twirled once, then dropped on to the sitting-room sofa. 'There will be no others, Dru. If I cannot have Reighland, then I shall have no one at all.'

'Do not be foolish, Priss. You cannot discount all of London without a fair hearing. You had other favourites last year. I know for a fact that several of them are still single.'

Priss reached out and caught her sister's hand, looking seriously up at her. 'This is not caprice, Drusilla. I am quite serious. If I cannot have Reighland...I simply do not know what I will do.'

Her sister squeezed her fingers, then patted her firmly on the shoulder. 'You do not need to think of that tonight, my love.'

Hendricks pulled aside the curtain and looked out on to the street. 'It is morning, dearest. And it seems she will have to think of it after all. We have a visitor.'

Before they had even heard a knock on the door, Hendricks was out in the hall and opening with a deferential, 'How may I be of service to you, your Grace?'

'You can leave off with bowing and explain to me how you were waiting at the door to let me in. Your foresight is quite uncanny, Hendricks.'

'A coincidence, your Grace, nothing more.'

'Robert!' She could not help it, but she sprang to her feet and ran to the hall, pelting into him and throwing her arms around his body before he had even managed to remove his coat.

In response she felt his arms tighten around her and his body slump gratefully into hers. 'Hendricks, Mrs Hendricks, might I have permission to speak to my betrothed alone for a time?'

'Is that what she is again?' Hendricks asked. 'The *ton* is buzzing with rumours as to whether you will marry or not. Considering the recent scandal and the incidents of tonight, circumspection might be wise.'

'Oh, John, do not be difficult.' To Priss's surprise, the last came from her sister, who had twined her arms about her husband's neck and was murmuring sleepily into his lapel. 'I swear, I am so exhausted that you must put me to bed.' She looked up long enough to give Reighland a sloe-eyed stare. 'We must trust you to treat my sister properly, your Grace. Perhaps tomorrow a special licence might be procured.'

'Unfortunately, not,' Reighland replied and Priss loosened her grip on him, afraid that she had misunderstood everything that had happened in the last few hours. 'We will be married in St George's on the day we reserved it. There will be a bishop at the altar and the Prince Regent shall sit in the first pew. There will be so much pomp and ceremony that all of London will take notice.' He gave Priss a tired smile. 'I am sure I will find it quite unbearable. But when it is through there will be no question that you are my duchess.'

'Father will want to know of it,' Priss said, trying not to sound disappointed by the fact.

'He has already been informed that his presence is required,' Robert said. 'And I assume you will want your sister and Mr Hendricks to stand witness.'

'I did not think it would be possible,' she whispered.

'If it will make you happy, then I insist upon it,' Robert said, looking and sounding less like an irritable bear and more like a sleepy lion who assumed his wishes would be attended to with no further growling.

'It is clear that my sister is in good hands, Your Grace.' Dru whispered something in her husband's ear and tugged upon his arm, leading him towards the stairs. Then she glanced back over her shoulder. 'When you are finished talking, please let yourself out. Priscilla, we will see you at breakfast.'

Priss burrowed a little further into Reighland's coat and listened to the retreating footsteps, wondering if she had actually heard the irony in her sister's voice at the idea that all they would do was talk. Then she pulled Robert back with her towards the couch in the sitting room. 'We have been left unchaperond again, Reighland,' she said.

'Considering how I feel about you, that is probably unwise,' he rumbled. 'But then, when have either of us ever bowed to convention?'

'True enough.'

'This evening, your behaviour was quite scandalous.' He collapsed on to the seat with her and pulled her close until she was practically sitting in his lap.

'I am sorry I have shamed you.'

'On the contrary. You were most diverting. Is it true that you called Gervaise an inadequate lover?'

'Merely a rumour,' she said.

'Then of course I shall ignore it.'

'But there is some truth in the statement,' she admitted. 'He was most unsatisfactory.' The description made her smile. 'Most unsatisfactory indeed.'

'And he deserved to be punished for it,' Robert agreed. 'I have sent him away again, more permanently this time. I drove him down to the docks and put him on the nearest ship. He will be gone with the morning tide. But now to less insignificant matters. What do the gossips say of your other lovers?'

She smiled. 'That I had one of the most powerful men in England at my feet.'

'And you do again,' he said, sliding off the sofa

and on to his knees before her. 'Of course, in that dress, you could bring any man to his knees. You look positively indecent in it.'

'Do you really think so?' A few weeks ago, the comment would have embarrassed her, but now, coming from Reighland, it seemed the most natural compliment in the world.

'Allow me to show you.' He crooked a finger to coax her closer, as though he were about to whisper a secret. But as she leaned forwards, her bodice gaped and he hooked his finger in it and tugged it down to free her breasts. 'Shocking,' he muttered, then buried his face in them.

'Reighland,' she whispered, tugging at his hair, 'does this mean I am forgiven?'

'There is nothing to forgive,' he muttered. And then he paused and looked up, smiling. 'Unless it is I who need forgiving. I left you alone when you needed me. I did not help you, when you were afraid. And I shouted at you, the night we argued. But I mean to make up for that now.' He reached for her slipper, pulled it off and threw it behind him.

She gasped.

'Am I to be treated to such a reaction each time we remove your shoes?'

'Only because I remember what happened the last time,' she said. 'And you cannot be throwing clothing all over my sister's sitting room. It is not proper.'

'Very well, then. Only the one shoe tonight. I will save your full unveiling until after the wedding.'

'That is good,' she said, a little disappointed that it had been so easy to persuade him to behave.

Then he lowered his mouth to her breasts again, taking a nipple deep into his mouth and pulling upon it until she thought she might scream from the excitement. He sensed her agitation and looked up. 'Do you want me to stop?'

'It is almost dawn,' she said. 'The servants will be up soon.' She thought for a moment of the sorry state she was in and the feeling of his kiss drying on her breast. 'I want you to hurry.'

'But I meant to take my time,' he said, kissing slowly upwards in a trail of nips. 'I would not wish to be thought inadequate. I have a reputation to maintain, after all.' He found her mouth and ravished it, his hand cupping the back of her neck so that she had to struggle to escape him.

'Reighland!' she whispered.

He sighed. 'Very well, then. As my lady wishes, we shall do this quickly.' And he flipped her skirt up and buried his face between her legs.

'What...?' It was the last thought she managed before he found the core of her and sucked it into his mouth, working it mercilessly with his tongue. In seconds she was fully aroused, and in less than a minute she was begging him. By the first shudder he had undone his trousers and yanked her out of her seat, on to her knees and on to him, pinning her against the furniture and taking her in short hard thrusts. She kissed him to stifle his groans and her own, digging her hands into his shoulders and letting go of everything else in the world as he lost himself in a rush that swept her along with him.

He relaxed back on his haunches, holding her to him with one hand and tugging her bodice up with the other. Then he whispered, 'Was that as you wished it?'

'That was amazing,' she replied.

'Six days,' he said, 'until we are married. If I

do not mean to spend it here on the floor with you, I had best be going.'

'On the contrary,' she whispered, 'I think you must stay for breakfast.'

'Think of your reputation,' he said with no real enthusiasm.

'I am,' she said with a smile. 'If I do not do something scandalous at least once a day, whatever shall they write in the papers?'

* * * * *